CLARA WU

AND THE

PORTAL BOOK

BY VINCENT YEE

DEDICATION

To the Asian American teenagers and children, so that they may have a new generation of Asian American heroes.

CHAPTERS

ONE

Clara's grin was unmistakable as she swiftly dodged between the throngs of pedestrians in the heart of New York City's Chinatown. As she crossed the busy street, her knapsack and just-past-shoulder-length hair bounced up and down her back in synch with her steps.

Clara grasped the metal handle to the front door of her building as the door's metal bottom scraped against the metal door frame. Her fingers tapped out the key code that unlocked a second door, and she hurried up the steps to her family's second-floor apartment. She reached into her left jean pocket as her jade bracelet slid down her forearm and pulled out a set of keys. She fumbled with them before unlocking the heavy metal-clad door.

The scent of a deep broth wafted into her nostrils as she entered, and she was certain her mother was cooking something delicious for dinner. She carefully slid out of her shoes and placed them by the shoe rack, exposing her multi-striped socks.

"Mom!" said Clara excitedly.

"Hmmm?" she heard her mother say from the kitchen.

Clara slid off her knapsack and held it by its handle, jaunted into the kitchen, and saw that her mother was busily slicing away at some scallions.

"Mom! Can I go to Melissa's tomorrow for a sleepover?" Clara asked excitedly. Melissa Chin was one of the cool Asian girls at school.

But her mother didn't break her culinary focus as she answered. "No, you cannot. You have Chinese school tomorrow, and you still have lessons to finish up."

Clara looked down at the kitchen table and could see that her calligraphy book was laid out along with her lesson plan.

In a moment of frustration, Clara approached the table and slammed her knapsack down onto the floor. "I hate Chinese school!" she stammered as she picked up her calligraphy book and slammed it onto the table, causing a bowl of soy sauce to spill all over it.

"Clara!" her mother screamed as her daughter turned from her and she stomped down the hallway.

Her mother quickly picked up a washcloth and tossed it onto the calligraphy book. It started to absorb the soy sauce as she turned toward the hallway and hollered, "Clara!"

Without an answer, she rushed down the hallway just as the door to Clara's bedroom slammed shut. Upon reaching the door, she tried the doorknob only to find that it was locked. "Clara!" she said once more to a reply that pierced her heart.

"I hate being Chinese!" said Clara in a resentful tone.

Clara's mother rested her head against the door and closed her eyes as her daughter said one more time, "I hate being Chinese!"

TWO

The doorknob to Clara's bedroom gently jiggled before it stopped. Something could be heard being inserted into the doorknob from the outside, then the knob clicked. Another moment of jostling outside, and the door quietly opened as a man entered the bedroom.

He looked down at Clara, who was asleep on her right side, with her back toward him. He smiled at her and gently sat down on the side of the bed. He quietly called out her name, "Clara."

She murmured, and he said her name once more, ever so slightly louder. Her eyes fluttered and she turned her head to see her father looking down at her. She turned over and uttered, "Hi Baba," as she raised herself into a sitting position.

"How's my little princess?" he asked.

"I'm fine, but I'm not little anymore, I'm 15."

"Oh yes, you're 15, but you'll always be my little princess," said her father, as he wished on the inside that she didn't have to grow up so quickly.

"I smell wontons," said Clara as her nostrils flared slightly.

Her father smiled and carefully produced from behind him a bowl that was covered by a napkin. "Do you want some?"

Clara felt a bit ashamed for wanting them, thinking about how she had stormed out of the kitchen earlier and demurred on the dumplings. "Not really," she said unconvincingly.

Her father removed the napkin. The irregularly shaped white porcelain bowl had two holes on either side where a pair of red chopsticks was threaded through. But in the bowl were beautiful wontons in a spicy chili oil sauce. It was one of her favorite foods. He moved the bowl toward Clara's stuffed panda that was sitting next to the pillow. "Maybe Bo Bo would like some delicious wontons?"

"Stop," said Clara quietly. "He only eats bamboo."

He looked at his daughter and purposefully moved the bowl near her face as wisps of the fragrant spicy chili oil floated beneath her nose as her stomach growled.

Her father looked at her and said, "I don't think Bo Bo growled just now," as he held the bowl of wontons in front of her, which she begrudgingly took into her hands. But secretly, she adored her mother's wontons and other Chinese culinary creations.

"Thanks, Baba," said Clara remorsefully as she patiently held the warm bowl of wontons in her hands.

"Eat that at your desk, not on your bed, okay?" he warned before he continued. "I heard you got into an argument with Mom earlier," to which Clara nodded as she held her head downcast.

"I know you really wanted to go over to Melissa's, but we have to plan these things out, okay?"

"Okay."

"Your little tantrum earlier caused a whole bowl of soy sauce to spill all over your calligraphy book and seep into the pages. Your Mom tried to wipe it off, but it made it worse. Now it's ruined and it smells like soy sauce," said her father.

"But everything is fine with your Mom," he said reassuringly as Clara continued to hold the wontons, which she wanted to devour at that moment. "But you'll still need to apologize to her tomorrow, okay?"

Clara nodded in shame as her father gave an approving look. He reached into his pant pocket and produced a lucky red envelope. Her eyes lit up. It was a magical moment ingrained in Chinese culture, and all Chinese children smile when bestowed a lucky red envelope.

"Here. I'm going to give you this to buy a new Chinese calligraphy book. Buy a nice one so that you'll think twice before ruining it with soy sauce, okay?" he asked.

"Okay," said Clara as she took the lucky red envelope into her fingertips but he teasingly pulled back on it. She peered up as he gingerly said, "Promise?" to which she replied, "I promise."

She placed the red envelope off to her right side as guilt and hunger both gnawed at her. Her father reached over and picked up Bo Bo. He turned the stuffed panda toward Clara and said playfully, "Chinese school is important!"

Clara gave off a smile as her father pulled the small white tag at the bottom of the stuffed panda and gestured toward it, "Look, 'Made in China,'" which made Clara giggle.

"Okay, eat your wontons but at your desk, and tomorrow, go pick up a nice new calligraphy book," said her father.

"Okay," said Clara before she pleaded, "Baba? Could you apologize to Mom for me? Please?"

Her father looked down at her disapprovingly, "Really? I convinced your Mom to let me bring in a bowl of wontons, and I gave you a lucky red envelope, and you want me to apologize to your mother?"

"I guess that's a no?" said Clara sheepishly.

"You got that right," he said with a smile. "Have a good night."

"Thanks Baba," she said as her father closed the door behind him.

Clara sat upright in her bed and looked down at the wontons. She looked at the door from the corner of her eyes and then quickly pulled out the chopsticks, expertly plucked up a wonton and gently tossed it into her mouth. Her hand came to rest on the blanket beside the bowl with the chopsticks angled upward. As she quietly savored the taste of the wonton, she glanced at the lucky red envelope and her stuffed panda.

THREE

The sun was starting to set in the west, casting its iridescent glow across the New York City rooftops. Clara pulled back on the handle to a Chinese gifts and crafts shop that she passed frequently. The bell clanged as she entered the quiet shop, alerting a Chinese woman who turned her head toward Clara.

Clara stepped in and gave the older woman a quick nod before heading toward the back, passing the tables of assorted Chinese trinkets. She climbed a set of stairs as beams of sunlight from the skylight bounced off the tops of books along the shelves. Illuminated dust floated gently through the air. She had been in the shop before and knew where to find the calligraphy books.

She picked off a typical book and flipped through the gridded pages where she could see herself laboriously and repetitively brushing out each character for hours on end. It was a dull book, and she was reminded that her father had said to pick out a nice one. She looked at the price tag on the back: $15.

With the book tucked underneath her arm, she pulled out the lucky red envelope from her jacket pocket. To her surprise, she pulled out a crisp one-hundred-dollar bill. She scanned the bookshelves again and found a packet of five books going for $65, $10 less than if she were to buy five of the dull books. But they weren't nice either. Then her eyes caught a large red hardcover book, which she pulled out. Its pages were thick, and though it would have been suitable for her calligraphy, she was disappointed that it was still kind of uninspiring. But it was nice enough. She had almost made up her mind when she caught a glint of light from the top shelf, where a solitary leathery spine caught her attention. A gleam of light shot down the spine. She glanced at the skylight and surmised that the sunlight had caused the spark of light.

She placed the red hardcover back onto the shelf. On tiptoes, her fingertips were just out of reach of the leathery book on the top shelf. She looked down the aisle, where she spied a step stool. She quietly fetched it and placed it beneath the shelf. With both feet steadily on the stool, she was able to ease out the book before stepping back down.

The brown leather was supple as she glided her fingers over it. As she opened it up, it yielded soft, yet firm, silken-like pages that felt luxurious to the touch. There were hundreds of pages, and she felt the book would meet her father's definition of "nice." She looked for a price tag but could not find one. Still, she knew she wanted to buy it. It wasn't just nice but had a luxuriousness to it.

After putting the step stool away, she bounded down the steps toward the front counter. There stood an older Chinese man with grayish hair and gold-rimmed spectacles. She said "Hello," causing him to look up and offer a smile. He adjusted his glasses as Clara gently placed the book on top of the glass countertop. "How much is this?" she asked.

The man took the book into both hands and looked for a price tag but could not find one. He looked down at her and said, "This is a very expensive book. If I remember, it is $120."

Clara looked down at her lucky red envelope and gently pulled out one end of the $100 bill and said, "I only have $100."

He took note of her disappointed tone and asked, "What are you going to use this book for?"

"It's for my Chinese calligraphy."

He gave an expression of pleasant surprise and slipped the book into a flat brown paper bag. He rung it up in his cash register and said to Clara, "That will be $88."

Clara graciously smiled and handed him the $100 bill, and he made change for her. He extended her $12 in change, and Clara reached out for it with her left hand. That's when he saw her deep green jade bracelet.

"Beautiful jade bracelet," he remarked.

"Thanks, my Mom gave it to me," Clara responded.

He smiled and carefully handed the bagged calligraphy book toward her as he said, "Lucky money for a lucky calligraphy book for a lucky girl."

She smiled as she took the book and thanked him in Cantonese, *"Dò Jeh."* She elatedly left the shop.

* * *

When Clara came to the door of her apartment, she hesitated. She had not apologized to her mother yet, and she could feel the shame weighing on her. She quietly fumbled with her keys and opened the door slowly. Her head poked into the apartment, and she could hear her mother in the kitchen as the smell of something aromatic wafted through her nostrils. She quickly snuck in, closed and locked the door, and slipped out of her shoes. Making sure that her mother was well immersed in her cooking, she scurried like a whisper down the hallway. As she entered her bedroom, she took off her knapsack and jacket.

She excitedly slid out her new calligraphy book and placed it atop her desk. Turning, she walked toward her nightstand and pulled out her phone. She saw it was a bit after 5 PM. She plugged in her charging cable and caught Bo Bo looking up at her. She playfully said to her stuffed panda, "Don't give me that look. I'll say sorry to Mom before dinner."

She settled into her chair, flicked on the desk light, and brushed aside her hair as she opened the silken-like pages. She set aside the lid to the ink stone and dabbed her brush onto it, coating the fine bristles with smooth black ink. She almost didn't want to ruin the beautiful pages, but exhaled and carefully and beautifully brushed her surname, "Wu." She looked down at it and though she had brushed her surname hundreds of times, she still admired how beautiful it was.

She dabbed her brush onto the ink stone, turned to the page, and saw that it was blank. Her dumbfounded expression made her pause as she flipped the page. There was no ink on the underside or on the next page. She touched the page where she thought she had brushed her surname, and it was dry. She was baffled and stared at the page once more, glancing left and right.

Once again, she proceeded to write her surname. She stared at the inked black character, and it just stared back at her. *Very strange*, she thought as she dabbed her brush once more and wrote out the second character of her name. *Perfect*, she thought. As she turned to dab her brush once more with black ink, a glint of light caught her eye, and she looked at the two black characters on the page. She looked left and right, and then her desk light flickered momentarily. *It was the desk light*, she thought.

She carefully brushed out the last character, admiring the beauty of her Chinese name, when suddenly, embers of light started to slither forth from the black characters. Her momentarily surprised expression was suddenly engulfed in a bright glowing warm light, so bright that it reflected in the black plastic eyes of her stuffed panda on the bed.

When the light vanished, her calligraphy book was on top of her desk, the three characters of her Chinese name were aglow, and the brush that Clara had been holding had fallen next to the calligraphy book. Her chair was empty.

FOUR

The warmth on her right cheek started to tickle her as Clara's eyes slowly fluttered open. At first, the sunlight blinded her, and she placed her hand before her eyes as she pushed herself into an upright position. As her eyes adjusted to the sunlight, she saw that she was on a grassy knoll with a few boulders around her. The air was amazingly crisp and clear. The quiet was eerie, like an early morning in Central Park.

"Hello?" she hollered as her voice disappeared into the new surroundings.

"Mom? Baba?" she asked nervously.

Clara stood up, brushed her pants, and gave herself a once-over. Nothing was out of place. The grimace on her face soon gave way to curiosity as she wondered where she was. She saw a somewhat worn path beside a large boulder and decided to follow it as she kept looking about.

With her hands clasped in front of her and looking furtively in every direction, she soon heard something snap from around the boulder in front of her. She stopped in her tracks as her ears perked up. She heard another snap. She inched toward the edge of the boulder and peeked around it as her eyes lit up.

It was a large panda, and it was munching on a bamboo shoot. She pulled back behind the boulder and found her heart racing a bit. She had never seen a live panda before, and seeing one made her giddy. She peeked around the boulder once more and saw that it had just munched off the last two bamboo leaves. She eyed a bundle of bamboo shoots with fresh leaves and took in a deep breath.

She slowly came out from behind the boulder and the panda's eyes suspiciously turned to her. She paused and made eye contact with the panda. It went back to chewing while it kept its eyes on her. She furtively walked over to the bundle of bamboo and gently pulled up one of the longer bamboo shoots. The trembling leaves belied her calmness, but she was also excited by the possibility of feeding a live panda.

She held the bamboo shoot in front of her as she carefully closed the distance. When she felt she was close enough, she extended her hand as far as it could go, with the bamboo shoot mere inches away from the panda.

The panda continued to look at her, and its eyes blinked in the most adorable way. It dropped the leafless bamboo shoot onto the grass and grabbed the bamboo shoot that Clara held out. Clara released it, and with its eyes still on Clara, the panda said, "Thank you."

Clara smiled, then suddenly her eyes grew wide. She let out a surprised scream that caused the panda's ears to perk up and its brown eyes to light up. Clara stumbled backwards and tumbled onto her bottom, which then caused the panda to roll backwards into a mound of white and black fluffy fur.

FIVE

"Each and every time," muttered the panda as it righted itself while brushing its sides.

Clara, still on her bottom, with her legs in front of her and her hands extended backward to support herself uttered, "You… you can talk?"

The panda looked annoyed as he looked back at her with his brown eyes set within the black eye patches and said, "Of course I can talk."

"But you're a panda!"

"Yes, I am, and you're a human girl," replied the panda.

"But pandas don't talk," reasoned Clara.

"Pandas from your world," said the panda matter-of-factly.

"From my world?" asked Clara. "I am no longer in New York City?"

The panda looked at her and simply said, "No longer on Earth."

Silence held Clara's tongue as she tried to process what she just heard. "I'm no longer on Earth? Then where am I?"

"All will be explained soon. But for now, allow me to introduce myself, I'm *Gao Gao*, and you are?"

Clara, still dumbfounded that she was speaking English with a panda, said, "I'm Clara Wu from New York City," as she suddenly questioned in her mind why she said where she was from.

The panda shook his head and said, "No, what is your Chinese name?"

Clara was perplexed and wondered if the panda understood Cantonese or Mandarin. But she reasoned that the panda was of Chinese origin, so he must understand one of the Chinese languages. She slowly uttered, "*Wu Chu Hua.*"

The panda eked out an awkward grin as it nodded, "It's very nice to meet you, *Wu Chu Hua.*"

Gao Gao soon got off his haunches and said, "Why don't you follow me, the others should be joining us shortly."

Clara's curiosity perked up as she followed Gao Gao off to his right, walking a couple steps behind.

"Others? What others?" she asked as she continued to stare incredulously at the large and fluffy white and black panda.

"Others from your world."

Soon their voices trailed away as they crested over a small hill toward wherever the panda was taking Clara.

SIX

"All your questions will be answered shortly," replied Gao Gao.

Clara was still in awe that the panda was speaking to her, and for a bit, her worldly concerns slipped her mind. The boulder-and bamboo-lined path rose gently. As she looked up and far off, her breath left her spellbound.

Over the horizon a large planet was starting to rise. It had purplish, blue, and white gaseous swirls and was encircled with rings. She stopped in her tracks as her mouth fell open. Looking up, she saw a number of moons that she had not noticed before as they peeked through in the early evening sky. "Whoa," was all that escaped from her mouth.

"Follow, *Wu Chu Hua*, we're almost there," said Gao Gao. But Clara was still awestruck by the planet and moons in the sky. "*Wu Chu Hua*," he said more firmly.

Clara snapped out of her momentary distraction, nodded a few times toward the panda, and picked up her pace to catch up to him.

They were walking up a slight hill when they passed a boulder that revealed a stone-covered circle. A series of concentric circles were carved within the stone circle, and along the outermost circle were five stone pedestals set at equal distance from one another. A large circle was carved in the front and the back of each pedestal. Atop of each was a stone slab set at a slight incline facing the middle of the circle. But she recognized the leather-bound calligraphy book atop each slab. Four were open and glowing slightly, and the fifth one was closed.

"Welcome to the Portal Circle, *Wu Chu Hua*," said the panda as he crossed into the stone circle.

Clara stepped onto the stone circle and suddenly realized the reality of her strange environment. Her eyes bounced from one open book to the other. Gao Gao interrupted her momentary distraction and said, "I will be back momentarily, *Wu Chu Hua*."

She nodded at him in wonder. As he was about to turn away, she called out, causing him to look at her. As he blinked at her with his brown eyes within the black eye patches, she asked, "Would it be okay if you call me Clara?"

Gao Gao seemed to snort and nodded as he trudged off. Soon he disappeared beyond the boulder.

Without the presence of the panda, Clara slowly walked into the circle and came upon the closed book, which looked exactly like the calligraphy book that she had just bought. However, no matter how hard she tried, the book would not open, nor could she move it off the pedestal. Feeling denied, she went to the next opened book that was also aglow. That book yielded characters similar to Chinese at first, but she realized that they were Japanese. She moved onto the next book, and recognized the writing on the first page, it was Vietnamese, but she didn't understand it. The next book had Korean writing.

Finally, she came upon the last opened book and her eyes lit up as she saw her Chinese name, brushed onto the bamboo-like page. To her surprise, the brush strokes were hers. She touched her surname, *Wu*, with her fingers as glowing embers suddenly appeared at her fingertips. Instinctively, she pulled them away, and the glowing embers dissipated. As she held her right index finger with her left hand and cautiously looked about, her concerns were replaced with a smile. She cautiously traced out the characters of her Chinese name and let the fiery embers follow her fingertip. Carefully, she flipped the first few pages, and while they were all blank, they were warm to the touch. With each touch of her fingers, the book seemed to glisten, almost enticing her. That's when she noticed the bamboo brush at the top of the book, and she picked it up. It was a beautiful brush, with its light color with fine bristles that swirled up into a point.

"Hello?" asked a voice from behind her, which startled her causing her to drop the brush as she turned suddenly. There was a tall Asian teenaged boy just beyond the circle nervously waving to her. She gasped slightly as she turned and bent down to pick up the brush. She placed it back onto the slab. She turned once more to face the newcomer and said, "Hi."

"Hi," he said sheepishly, and he continued. "I know this is going to sound strange, but do you know where we are?"

Clara clasped her hands behind her and could only respond, "Nope." She suddenly felt a sudden warmth around her neck and wondered why she was acting so awkwardly.

The teenaged boy continued to look at her with a friendly demeanor, then gestured toward himself, "I'm Sung by the way."

"Clara, Clara Wu," she said, and she immediately wondered why she added her last name as if she were James Bond.

"Hi Clara. Okay, so let me tell you the wildest thing. I was at home, at my desk and I was writing my name in this new book…" said Sung before Clara interrupted.

"You bought a new book too?"

"Yes, I just did and…"

"Ah, I see that you two have met," the panda said as he was about to enter the Portal Circle.

Sung took a step back as his eyes widened and he uttered questioningly, "You can talk?"

The panda just looked at him blankly and said, "Each and every time…"

"But how… did you know he could talk?"

Clara couldn't help but giggle and wondered if this was how she was when she realized the panda could talk. "Not at first, and I was surprised too! Isn't he just adorable?"

Sung turned to Clara, then to the panda, and to the large shadowy creature that had suddenly planted itself atop the boulder behind the panda. No words came from Sung's mouth as he pointed to the creature.

But before the panda could turn around, a large white-and-black striped mass of fur lunged from the boulder, landing on the back of the panda. Clara snapped backwards along with Sung as they watched a large white-and-black tiger upon the panda, who snarled back at its attacker. The panda gripped the tiger's right paw and pulled him off with a hip throw. With a feline instinct, it landed on all four paws with its claws at the ready, its torso lowered, and its haunches raised when the panda said annoyingly, "Really?"

The tiger retracted its claws, relaxed and behind its smile, said "You have to admit, I almost had you!" taunted the tiger.

"*Soohorang?*" Sung asked nervously.

The tiger's eyebrow rose curiously and turned its blue gaze toward the teenaged boy and relaxed its posture and asked, "You know of our great *Soohorang?*"

Sung looked at the white tiger with awe and responded, "Yes I do." Then he shook his head and uttered, "You can talk too?"

The white tiger sat on its haunches in an upright position and said, "No, I am not *Soohorang*, though he is a revered Guardian Tiger. My name is *Yonggirang*. And what may I call you?"

Still bewildered that he was talking to a white tiger, Sung looked dumbstruck and could only respond, "*Sung Kim.*"

"Well *Kim Sung…*" the tiger began to respond when he was interrupted from a voice above.

"Hello!"

Everyone looked up upon hearing a girl's voice from above. A massive bird with an awesome wingspan started to glide down into the Portal Circle. It landed firmly on its strong legs as its talons clicked on the stone. Clara and Sung looked up and were confronted by a majestically large white-and-black crane with a splotch of red atop the back of its head. From there were also several magnificent red feathers. Its beady eyes blinked a few times as an Asian girl popped into view from atop the crane and waved to everyone.

She climbed off the crane as it lowered its rear, and when she came around, she waved enthusiastically. "Hi! I'm *Yuka!*"

"This one is very friendly," said the crane to the tiger and the panda.

"What the… you can talk too?!" asked Sung.

"I didn't have a chance to bond with my young one yet, as I was stalking *Gao Gao,*" smirked Yonggirang. "I fear that us talking is something new to him."

Clara was taken in by all the happenings, but she snapped out of it as she smiled at Yuka and said, "I'm Clara. I really like your name, it's so pretty."

"Thank you, I like your name too," said Yuka as she looked at Sung and asked, "And you are?"

Sung was still looking up at the crane when he looked in Yuka's direction and replied, "Sung, were you brought here…"

But before Sung could get his question in, Yuka exclaimed, "My book!" She approached the glowing book without trepidation and looked at it in awe. Clara and Sung walked up and stood behind Yuka. Clara looked up at Sung, noticing his thick bouncy black hair. She looked away when he looked down at her with a smile.

"Is that your name in Japanese?" asked Clara.

"Uh huh, *Satoh Yuka.* That's my name!" she said proudly.

"Go ahead, touch the characters," said Clara encouragingly.

Yuka soon glided her fingertip across her family's surname, and just as Clara had experienced, glowing embers flowed upward from each character. But unlike Clara's startled reaction, Yuka embraced it and was in awe of it.

"Whoa, do I have a book too?" asked Sung, and Clara pointed to the book with the Korean words. He rushed over, followed by the curious girls.

"It's the same book at home!" announced Sung and he quickly did the same gesture with his fingertips. He was entranced to see the Korean letters of his name glowing at his fingertips.

"What does it say?" asked Yuka.

"*Kim Sung,*" he said.

"What about yours, Clara?"

"Oh, come see mine!" Clara said invitingly.

"It's like this each and every time," said the white tiger.

"Yes, each and every time," said the panda.

There was no answer from the crane as it was preening itself, but its attention was piqued when the white tiger emitted a low snarl.

The crane's large beak came around along with its beady eyes and said, "You'll have to excuse me, it was her first time riding me and a few of my feathers are ruffled."

Clara picked up her brush and spun around to face Sung and Yuka when they heard, "People! Finally!" as another teenaged Asian boy ran up to the Portal Circle. "Hey! Do you know where we are?"

But before Clara, Sung, or Yuka could respond, they were taken aback by the large water buffalo that sauntered up behind him. His massive, backwards-curving horns were a stately sight to behold. He crossed into the Portal Circle and approached the three other animals and muttered, "A very impatient one this one is," as it reared its horned head toward the second teenaged boy.

The second teenaged boy approached the three other teens. He was just as tall as Sung with a slender athletic build, barefoot but wearing a t-shirt and blue jeans. Without introduction, he asked again, "Do you know where we are? How did I get to this place?"

"We know just as much as you do," said Clara.

"We were transported here by our books," Yuka offered.

"Transported? What kind of nonsense talk is that?" the teenage boy said condescendingly, which caused Yuka to take a step back.

"Hey! That's not nice!" interjected Sung who took a step toward the teenaged boy.

"Yah? And what are you going to…"

But before the second teenaged boy could finish his sentence, a loud roar thundered about the Portal Circle, reverberating into the soul of each of the teenagers and making the hairs on the back of their necks rise up.

"Silence, please," implored the white tiger as silence befell the teenagers, who stared back in a mixture of awe and fear. "They are yours now," he added, as he nodded toward the panda.

"They can all talk?" whispered the surprised teenaged boy under his breath as Sung looked at him with a smile.

The panda moved into the Portal Circle and asked the teenagers to go to their Portal Books. Clara, Sung, and Yuka quickly moved toward their books, leaving the new teenager looking lost. Yuka caught the lost teenage boy and tilted her head in the direction of the last opened Portal Book, and he quickly made his way over to it. He suddenly saw his Vietnamese name upon the glowing Portal Book and was held spellbound until the loud snort from the buffalo caused him to turn around at attention.

The panda began to speak, "Welcome, young ones. You are probably wondering why you are all here and what this place is. Let me and my fellow guardians welcome you to the Azen realm."

"What? Azen realm? We're not in Houston anymore?" asked the teenaged boy.

Clara emitted a cough, caught his bewildered attention, and pointed behind him. He turned around and suddenly saw for the first time, the purplish and blue planet with white gaseous swirls encircled with rings. He could only let out, "Whoa."

The stiff buffalo's snort caught his attention once more, and he spun around, finally alert.

"As I was saying," said the panda. "You are now on Azen, a realm that is far away from your world. The books that you see before you are the Portal Books of the Portal Circle. Their twins are on your world. It is these Portal Books that brought you to Azen. My name is *Gao Gao* and I am the Guardian Panda. To my left is my stalkerish companion, the Guardian Tiger, *Yonggirang*. To my right is the majestic Guardian Crane, *Tatsuo*, and lastly, my strong companion, the Guardian Buffalo, *Viet Mai*. We are some of the guardians that protect Azen."

There was silence from the four teenagers as they stared at the four guardians as the sunset behind them cast them aglow.

"We welcome you to Azen. We know you have many questions, and they will be answered in short time. But as we are all new, could you re-introduce yourselves in your true name of your heritage?" asked the Guardian Panda as he nodded to Clara.

"Hi, I'm *Wu Chu Hua*, but you can call me Clara."

"Hi, I'm *Kim Sung*."

Hi! I'm *Satoh Yuka*."

The last teenaged boy said self-consciously, "I'm *Danh Nguyen* Parker, but you can call me Daniel."

The panda continued, "Thank you. We are honored to meet you. As you can see, you've all been paired up with a guardian. Before it gets dark, it will be necessary for us to take you back to our kingdoms so that you may rest, as tomorrow will be a busy day."

Sung's raised hand caught the Guardian Panda's attention, "Yes?"

"Um about that, I have this chem test that I need to study for…" stated Sung before the wave of the Guardian Panda's paw silenced him.

The Guardian Panda said curtly, "Your earthly concerns are no longer the concerns here on Azen. All that matters now is here on Azen, and what Azen needs of you. I'm sure you are all tired and hungry."

Yuka nodded and glanced down at everyone's feet, and like herself, noticed that they were without shoes. She felt lucky she didn't need to trek the distance shoeless; she was certain everyone else's feet would be tired.

"Very well then, we must be on our way before it gets too dark, and we'll gather here first thing in the morning. Guardians, please take your young ones."

With that, the Guardian Crane walked into the Portal Circle and crouched down. Yuka quickly climbed onto her back. She found the rope harness underneath its great feathers, and she took off aboard the crane headed southward. "See you all tomorrow!" she exclaimed as her voice trailed as she ascended.

The massive buffalo moved toward Daniel and beckoned with its snout for him to follow. Daniel looked at Clara and Sung and said, "I guess I'll see you two tomorrow." He followed the buffalo out of the Portal Circle in a northerly direction.

"*Kim Sung*, you may follow me," said the Guardian Tiger. Sung nodded, still in awe of the white tiger and looked over at Clara, "See you tomorrow," he said to which Clara responded with an unsure smile, "You too."

As the Guardian Tiger and Sung exited the Portal Circle toward the west, the Guardian Panda looked at Clara and said, "If you will follow me."

As Clara followed him, she asked, "Where are we going?"

He replied, "To my home."

"Is it far?"

"A bit, but your human legs will get you there."

"Will I get shoes when we get there?"

The panda turned and looked down at her sock-covered feet and said, "Yes, you will get shoes."

"Great," she said as she followed the Guardian Panda in an easterly direction.

SEVEN

Clara's feet were getting sore, and she was glad that she at least had socks on as she trekked along the soft dirt path that the Guardian Panda was leading her on. She stopped asking questions as most of them were answered with, "Your question will be answered soon enough."

They must have walked for miles, she thought, and without her phone, she lost all sense of time. But one thing she did notice as they got closer to their destination was the bamboo stalks were getting bigger. They had become so tall and thick that she had to stop and marvel at them, which the Guardian Panda indulged until he nudged her to move along.

As darkness started to descend, the path was soon illuminated by large crystals hanging from the bamboo stalks. They had an iridescent light within that glowed softly.

"What are those lights?" Clara asked.

"Those are the illumination jades. Quite abundant on Azen. They give us light at night," answered the Guardian Panda.

"Whoa, cool! I've never seen clear jade before!" Clara exclaimed.

The Guardian Panda stopped and turned to Clara and asked, "Are you afraid of heights?"

Clara looked up into his brown eyes and said, "I don't think so. I've been in the Freedom Tower and that's really high up."

"Good, then you should have no problem crossing the bridge," said the Guardian Panda as he moved out of the way.

Clara's eyes lit up as she saw a beautiful bridge constructed of large bamboo stalks spanning a rocky crevasse. Two large green bamboo stalks, about fifty feet apart from each other leaned into the crevasse. They were met by two opposing bamboo stalks on the other side, creating a triangular bamboo frame that spanned the crevasse. The floor of the bridge was lined with bamboo planks. At regular intervals, cables were strung upward and attached to the triangular frame of the bridge.

As her eyes travelled beyond the far end of the bridge, her eyes rose up once again toward a massive wall lined with bamboo stalks that dwarfed the already large ones along the path. Larger, brighter illumination jades were carefully placed into alcoves in the bamboo wall itself.

"What in the world?" asked an amazed Clara, her mouth agape.

"Welcome to Bamboo City," said the Guardian Panda proudly.

With her eyes still taking in the view, she answered with, "Wow, this is amazing!"

"Follow me as we shouldn't keep the Panderess waiting," beckoned the Guardian Panda.

"Uh, who?" asked Clara.

"The Panderess, she is ruler of all of Panda Kingdom," he answered.

"Um, okay?" said Clara, unsure what was happening.

As they moved beyond the path, Clara saw that there were other pandas about, but they were dressed in armor and wore the cutest green bamboo helmets. Most were carrying bamboo staffs and soon, one caught sight of the Guardian Panda and came forward.

"Guardian Panda," he said as he gave a curious glance toward Clara. "We have the carriage ready."

"Thank you," said the Guardian Panda as he glanced down at Clara. He pointed her to a covered carriage, and she followed him to it. There were four additional pandas, all standing at attention.

"What's going on?" asked Clara.

"Bear with me, young one, but we need to be discreet about your arrival. Please enter the carriage and we will deliver you to the Panderess," asked the Guardian Panda.

One of the pandas opened the door to the bamboo carriage. Clara climbed the steps that flipped out from the bottom of it and eased herself into it. There were two benches facing each other, each wide enough to hold at least four people or two pandas, she thought. The inside was bright, and the illumination jade gave off a soft glow. The Guardian Panda then said, "Be patient, we'll be there shortly," as he closed the door.

On his command, the carriage suddenly jolted upward, causing her to grab both sides of the soft seat cushion to steady herself. The jolt also shook the window shade on her left, which was one of six, three on each side. Soon the carriage started to move, and as she peeked between the shade and the windowpane, she saw that a panda had hoisted the carriage atop his shoulder and assumed the same was happening at each end of the bamboo stalks that the carriage rested on. They moved in perfect synchronicity as they walked to her destination. Along the way, she peeked through the shade each time it jostled. There were pandas everywhere. They were of all shapes and sizes, and the adorable cuteness of the panda cubs melted her heart.

Soon the carriage stopped and slowly lowered, then the door opened. "Hurry, young one," asked the Guardian Panda as she carefully stepped out and what she saw before her startled her even more. It was one lower section of a green bamboo stalk that was so large, she could not see around it. It was at least twenty feet wide, and an archway was cut neatly through it.

"Welcome to The Ring," said the Guardian Panda. "The panda guards will cover your flank."

"Flank?" asked Clara.

The Guardian Panda winked at her and restated, "They will walk along your left and right side."

"Um, okay," was all Clara could answer with. She shuddered for a moment as the panda guards closed in on her. *They were so soldier-like,* she thought, and soon, they started to walk through the bamboo tunnel. She noticed how smooth the walls were and how large the illumination jades were that were hung high above at regular intervals. As the edge of the tunnel's end gave way, what came into view left her spellbound: About a thousand feet away was a single large green bamboo stalk reaching into the night sky, and surrounding it were other bamboo stalks, smaller in circumference, arranged in neat concentric circles.

They continued their jaunt toward the large middle bamboo stalk, but she could suddenly hear murmurs coming from other pandas as they pointed and whispered at her. She wondered why she was causing so much curiosity, but before she could give it more thought, they arrived at the biggest bamboo stalk she had ever laid her eyes on. As she turned around, she saw hundreds of pandas staring back at her as their eyes blinked every so often. Suddenly, she felt embarrassed and didn't know why.

"Welcome to Bamboo Tower, young one," said the Guardian Panda proudly.

"The bamboo here is so huge!" exclaimed Clara.

"Yes, these are the bamboo of Azen. They are quite remarkable. Follow me as we step into the lift," said the Guardian Panda.

Clara saw before her a dark archway, its entrance flanked on each side by a panda guard and soon, a lighted lift appeared. At the Guardian Panda's gesture, they both stepped into it, and he sighed. The lift was open on two sides, was of meticulous bamboo construction, lit by two illumination jades from above, appointed with two cushioned seats at opposite ends, and a bamboo pole in the middle that they could hold onto. The Guardian Panda's large paw was on the pole, and Clara reached out for the pole with some trepidation. The upward ride was surprisingly smooth, and from where they entered, she could see the smooth inner shell of Bamboo Tower. At regular intervals, the lift would stop, and she could see through a window into Bamboo City. The other side revealed the floors of Bamboo Tower and different scenes of panda life within it.

After about five floors, Clara asked, "How high are we going?" and the Guardian Panda responded, "Close to the top."

"Oh," was all that Clara could say.

Finally, the lift stopped, and the Guardian Panda asked her to step out. As she did, she stepped out into a large, ornate circular room, but she was ushered along the path, covered in a reddish carpet. They passed several pairs of guards and other pandas until she saw a regal panda at the center.

They stopped a short distance away from the regal panda, who was draped in a loose red robe that came just above her knees. Across her chest was a slender chain, gold perhaps, from which dangled a circular bamboo carving. In the center was a large green jade. Atop her head was a simple but regal Chinese headdress made of bamboo strands. She blinked a few times at Clara before the Guardian Panda said, "Panderess, may I present to you, *Wu Chu Hua*, or Clara as she would like to be called."

The Panderess nodded at the Guardian Panda and looked at Clara, "Welcome, Clara. I am the Panderess, ruler of all Panda Kingdom. We have been waiting for you."

"Hi," said Clara nervously as she felt suddenly out of place.

The Panderess motioned her to follow her, "Please follow me, we need to be sure."

Feeling compelled to do her bidding, Clara followed the Panderess with the Guardian Panda in tow. They approached another archway, and soon Clara could see that there was another beautifully constructed bamboo bridge, though slenderer and connected to another bamboo stalk. But as she exited the archway and stepped onto the platform, the wind caught her attention, causing her to look down into a dark abyss.

She gulped for a moment feeling suddenly small and vulnerable in the vastness of the crevasse that she was stepping across. The Panderess turned to her, "Do not worry, this bridge is sturdy and sure. Follow."

There was something soothing and comforting in the Panderess' voice. Clara followed her and stepped onto the bamboo bridge. It was about six feet wide and one hundred feet in length. As she neared the bamboo stalk on the other side, she noticed something odd. The bamboo stalk wasn't growing from the ground but rather from the air!

She marveled at this new sight, which distracted her from the perilous height. As her eyes adjusted into the night sky, she saw that the bamboo stalk was growing from the underside of a rocky ledge.

"Dangling Bamboo, they grow upside down," said the Guardian Panda.

"Whoa!" was all that she managed to utter until finally she stepped into a large circular room of the bamboo stalk. The floors were smooth-hewn bamboo and spaced out at regular intervals along the wall were eight panda guards in more elaborate armor. In the center was an elaborate bamboo stand that held something along its center.

"Follow, Clara, we are almost there," said the Panderess.

A mixture of excitement and nervousness welled up from within Clara as she followed the Panderess, who stopped abruptly. She moved off to the right and turned sideways to Clara, revealing within the elaborate bamboo stand, a bow.

It was a beautiful bow, hewn from a single piece of bamboo. Its middle, forming the grip, was slender, and each side swelled and bent outward before tapering at the end, where the drawstring was attached. Above the grip, at its most bulbous point, was a green jade inset, which glistened ever so slightly.

"Please gently pick up the bow with your left hand and bring it towards you," asked the Panderess as the anxiousness belied her outward calmness.

Clara looked at the Panderess and turned to the Guardian Panda, who encouraged her with the nudge of his nose. She turned toward the bow, stepped up onto the platform and reached out for it. She gripped it firmly, lifted it off the stand, and brought it toward her. Suddenly, she felt a sudden warmth from the grip of the bow as a white light started to spiral out from the center of the green jade. It suddenly flashed and radiated outward.

Clara's mouth flew open, instinctively spun around, wanting to ask what just happened when she saw the Panderess, the Guardian Panda, and each of the panda guards bowing. She could see that each of the jades around the pandas' necks, including that of the Guardian Panda, who had pulled out a jade tied to a string from beneath his fur, was glowing.

The Panderess then announced, "Our new Panda Warrior has arrived. Welcome, Empress Warrior *Wu*."

EIGHT

Riding atop the Guardian Tiger, Sung was in awe of the beast's massive muscles. They were thick, and he could feel every tendril of muscle beneath him. There was no choice but to ride atop the white tiger as the terrain turned from grass to soft dirt, and then finally to rocky terrain. His sock-covered feet were no longer able to endure the pain of pebbles digging into his soles.

They had been traveling for some time, and silence had settled in for the last part of their trek. Sung had stopped asking questions when the Guardian Tiger finally snarled at his incessant questioning. Soon the rocky terrain opened up, and the Guardian Tiger said, "We are almost at the gate."

Sung looked up. Before him was a grayish rocky path that led toward a tall stone wall with a large archway in the middle. Atop of it was a large wooden structure with two swooping ornate roofs.

"Whoa! *Seodaemun*," exclaimed Sung as his eyes widened.

The Guardian Tiger's ears perked up and he responded, "You know of our gates?"

"Yes, my father grilled it into my head. He's a professor of Asian American studies. I know all the gates though I have never seen any of them in person, *Bukdaemun, Dongdaemun, Namdaemun*, and *Seodaemun*. But this one looks like *Seodaemun*."

"A wise father you have. However, this gate is *Seosomun,*" said the Guardian Tiger.

"Can't be. *Seosomun,* the gate of the southwest, was destroyed," said Sung.

"Not here on Azen," the Guardian Tiger replied.

Sung wasn't going to argue with the Guardian Tiger as they approached the archway, where he noticed tiger guards on each side. Each was standing erect, almost like a human, wearing robes that were similar to traditional Korean garb while holding a speared trident in its right paw. As the Guardian Tiger got closer, he stopped and reared his head upward while uttering, "This is where you need to walk the rest of the way. Can you do that?"

"Sure, I think so," said Sung as the Guardian Tiger lowered himself allowing Sung to slide off. The Guardian Tiger winced as Sung accidentally pulled on his fur.

"Sorry," said a startled Sung as he pursed his lips while the Guardian Tiger gave him an annoyed look with his steely blue eyes.

"It'll take more than a tug of my fur to hurt me," said the Guardian Tiger. That's when the Guardian Tiger pulled himself into an upright position and Sung watched in amazement as his joints seemed to realign themselves to allow him to walk like a human.

"Please follow me, young one," said the Guardian Tiger as they approached the archway. This caught the attention of the closest guard, who walked over, trying to sneak a peek at Sung.

The Guardian Tiger muttered something under his whiskers, and the guard nodded his fluffy white-and-black striped head. As the guard headed back, he snarled in the direction of the second guard, who darted into the archway.

By the time the Guardian Tiger and Sung arrived by the archway, the second guard had returned and bowed to the Guardian Tiger, who responded in kind. In the guard's arms was a piece of clothing. The Guardian Tiger unfurled the garment and asked Sung to put it on. It was a hooded cloak, which Sung put on obligingly. But what amazed Sung was how the front edges of the cloak magically came together.

"Magnetism," said the Guardian Tiger before he continued. "The rest of the path is paved with stone, and I believe your feet will be fine the rest of the way. We must keep your identity a secret until I present you to the Tigeress."

"Who's the Tigeress?" asked Sung.

"She is the leader of White Tiger Kingdom, home to the mighty white tigers," said the Guardian Tiger with some reverence.

"Um, okay," said Sung.

"Follow close behind me and don't be alarmed when two additional guards come to each side of you. They are there to shield you. Are we clear?" asked the Guardian Tiger.

Sung nodded, and the Guardian Tiger started to walk ahead of him as Sung followed closely. As they entered the archway, he saw a glowing light from above that seemed to emanate from several evenly spaced-out crystals. As they exited the other end, two guards holding tridents approached him on both sides, and Sung suddenly felt very small. The draft he felt through his socks made him feel very naked, despite being cloaked.

But soon, he marveled at the architecture, and he felt like he was transported to ancient Korea. The wide stone paths were lined with buildings echoing old-style Korean architecture with swooped roofs covered in dark crescent-shaped stone tiles. But what astounded him most were the number of white-and-black striped tigers milling about doing seemingly everyday things, like shopping.

But as Sung looked up from his hooded cloak, he unintentionally made eye contact with some of the white tigers, and they started to point at him. Some tried to come closer to take a look at the human in their midst with the drafty socks.

Sung tried to pull the hood of his cloak closer while looking downward. However, he saw many tigers lining the streets trying to catch a look, and he suddenly felt like he may be their dinner.

"Um, I don't think this is working," said a nervous Sung as he saw tens if not hundreds of larger tigers trying to get a look at him. That's when the Guardian Tiger emitted a low growl that reverberated through the air and suddenly, all the murmuring stopped, and the closest tigers looked down and away.

They finally reached the end of the path, and the two guards turned facing away from him to guard his backside. Sung carefully lowered his hood and stood in awe of a steep mountain. A stone wall had been carved into the mountain. In the middle of the wall was a beautiful archway that opened into a tunnel that seemed to bore through the depths of the mountain. On each side of the archway were stone steps that ended at a platform connected to another set of steps carved into the mountain and leading upward to a place lost in the clouds.

"Welcome to Claw Mountain, home of the white tigers," said the Guardian Tiger proudly.

"Wow!" exclaimed Sung.

"We'll walk up those steps, only 1,000 of them to Claw House," said the Guardian Tiger.

Sung looked displeased as he clenched his sock-covered toes.

The Guardian Tiger smiled and continued. "But luckily for you, we are in a rush to meet the Tigeress, and so we will take a lift," said the Guardian Tiger as he led Sung down the tunnel's path.

"Did you build this?" asked Sung inquisitively.

"Not me personally, but many tigers before us. They were true craftsmen, and the pandas were very helpful. They are true artisans when it comes to bamboo," answered the Guardian Tiger.

"And how is it that you can walk like me?"

"We're not like the tigers of your world. We are more, how would I say, stately?"

Sung was silent as he was still trying to wrap his mind around human-like walking tigers who could speak. The Guardian Tiger soon stopped in front of a cylindrical basket seemingly made from bamboo. Four metal rails extended downward about a foot from the circular opening at the bottom of the shaft. The bamboo basket also had four outer metal rails aligned to the ones that extended from the opening above. Metal wheels and clamps married the aligned rails together.

The Guardian Tiger opened the bamboo basket, and Sung stepped in. The Guardian Tiger followed and closed the basket. He told Sung to hold onto the middle pole and soon, they were whisked upward into the shaft.

A cold draft rushed downward, and it would have been dark if it weren't for the illumination jade fixed into the roof of the bamboo basket. Soon it started to slow and Sung could feel that it was much colder. He realized they had already reached the top of the mountain. The Guardian Tiger opened the basket door and Sung exited, followed by the Guardian Tiger.

"Wow," said Sung as he looked outward over the base of the mountain that was paved with large stones. Far off, he could see the Gate of *Seosomun* and in between, all the structures that he had passed.

"Follow me, young one, the Tigeress awaits," beckoned the Guardian Tiger.

Sung turned around and he caught his first sight of the large gate house with its signature double swooped roofs. Placed at regular intervals were more tiger guards whose robes were replaced with armor. He followed the Guardian Tiger up the wide stone steps and he couldn't but ask, "Did you build this on top of a mountain?"

The Guardian Tiger retorted, "We did. The entire mountain top was flattened out, and Claw House was built on top. It is truly a beautiful piece of work."

Sung continued to look in awe. The Korean-inspired Claw House was more expansive than he could ever have imagined.

The doors to the lower level slid away to allow them to walk through. Sung followed the Guardian Tiger into an ornate hall lined with large columns with partitioned rooms off to the side. Illumination jades glowed from above, warming the ambiance. Tigers were milling about, but their attention turned to

Sung as he followed the Guardian Tiger.

The Guardian Tiger stopped and moved aside. Before Sung was another tiger, slender, dressed in a more ornate robe with her hands folded together. Hanging from her neck was a blue jade set into a metal ornament. The Tigeress looked at Sung and nodded.

Sung responded in kind, and instinctively said in Korean, "*Sungeuni mangeukhaeumnida*," meaning, *your grace is immeasurable*.

The Tigeress' ears perked up, and she looked at the Guardian Tiger, "A respectful one this young one is," she stated before looking back at Sung.

The Guardian Tiger nodded and stated, "Tigeress, may I present to you *Kim Sung*."

The Tigeress beamed down at Sung and offered, "*Kim Sung*, I am the Tigeress, ruler of the White Tiger Kingdom. Welcome to the Claw House. Please follow me."

Sung did as he was told, and she led him not far to another room where there were four tiger guards at each corner. Inset into the stone floor was a circular pattern made up of stone wedges. She looked to a tiger in the corner, who nodded. He tapped the stone floor with his staff and as Sung watched, his attention was stolen when another tiger guard did the same, then the other until some string of mysterious taps echoed through the air. Soon, something mechanical could be heard from below, and the stone wedges fell away, forming a spiral staircase.

"Follow me into the vault," entreated the Tigeress as she started to descend the stone spiral staircase.

When Sung reached the bottom of the staircase, followed by the Guardian Tiger, he could see that each large stone step was held up by a thick metal pole that disappeared into the floor. He looked around and found himself in a circular room carved into the mountain itself. Four additional tiger guards stood equally away from one another around the room, each wearing similar armor as the tigers above. Two archways lead into some unknown rooms, and he wondered if these guards slept in the vault, protecting whatever it was in the lone bamboo case against the wall.

The Tigeress led Sung to the bamboo case. In the middle was a lone staff, seemingly forged of a grayish matte metal. In its middle was an oval opening with a blue jade set into it. Sung stared at it. It was just a bit shorter than he was, but his eyes fixated on the blue jade that seemed to glisten.

"Take hold of the staff, *Kim Sung*," asked the Tigeress.

Sung looked at her and reached out for the grayish matte metallic staff. It was deceptively light but felt solid. As he took it out of the hole that held it, a bead of light spiraled from the blue jade. A bright flash radiated outward and was suddenly gone.

Sung didn't know what happened. When he turned around to ask, he saw that all the tigers in the room were bowing. He could also see that a blue jade on the chest armor of each tiger was also glowing. That's when he saw the blue jade atop the Tigeress's headdress and a blue jade that the Guardian Tiger was holding in its paw were also aglow.

The Tigeress then announced, "You are our Tiger Warrior. Welcome, Emperor Warrior *Kim*."

NINE

The wind swept Yuka's hair back. She was right up against the large neck feathers of the Guardian Crane, held in place by the bamboo rope harness hidden underneath her feathers. Yuka had asked the Guardian Crane to fly fast, and she acquiesced to Yuka's wishes with a smile. Yuka was enjoying with abandon the freedom of soaring through the air. They had left land a while back and were now flying over water.

"We're almost there," said the Guardian Crane as she started to slow and glide toward an island set further out in the dark bluish waters. Yuka looked upward and saw several moons starting to appear in the night sky. She admired them in awe.

The large and sprawling island started to come into view. A stunted mountain rose from the middle of the island, surrounded by thick treetops. Large structures resembling *tō* towers peaked through them. She saw many cranes flying between them. As they flew closer, she could see cranes flying into the structures in an orderly fashion and being greeted by crane attendants. The floors were gently lit, and the cranes were milling about on *tatami* mats.

"Wow! The *tōs* are so large and tall!" exclaimed Yuka.

"I'm glad you think so. These are the primary structures that we use to live and nest in," said the Guardian Crane nonchalantly.

Yuka giggled underneath her breath as the Guardian Crane mentioned, *nest in.*

"Please hang on. We're going to fly up and into the caldera," said the Guardian Crane.

"What's a caldera?" asked Yuka.

"It's the mouth of a dormant volcano that has collapsed in on itself," said the Guardian Crane as Yuka's eyes lit up. "It's where Crane Castle is located."

The Guardian Crane swooped upward, and as it approached the rim of the caldera, Yuka could see two slender *tō* structures rising into view. Several cranes were on each floor, and they exchanged a few guttural squawks with the Guardian Crane. As they passed, Yuka thought she saw a large crossbow on one of the floors. The Guardian Crane straightened out her beak as she crested the rim of the caldera and started her descent.

Yuka's eyes widened as a large and wide *tō* structure came into view. It rose out of the middle of the caldera, set atop a large square stone foundation. It was surrounded by water that glistened from the moonlight above. It was peaceful and tranquil, and Yuka could see that the entire rim of the caldera had several of the slender *tō* structures at regular intervals. They were like watch towers, Yuka thought, protecting the majestically large and wide *tō* structure in the middle.

The Guardian Crane fanned out her large wings to slow her descent. She expertly glided into one of the floors and landed on her feet. Yuka looked up and saw several cranes to her left and right, standing away from the rice paper partitions. The ceiling was high, allowing for what Yuka thought to be short flights through the airy floor. The entire *tō* structure was constructed for the cranes' use.

"Welcome to Crane Castle. You may carefully slide off me now," beckoned the Guardian Crane as Yuka collected herself from her state of wonderment.

"Oh yes," said Yuka as she realized she was still gripping onto the bamboo rope around the Guardian Crane's neck. She carefully slid off the crane, not wanting to ruffle her grand feathers. As she landed on the sturdy straw *tatami* mats with her thin socks, she immediately felt at home and caught the eyes of the other cranes looking at her. She politely looked each in the eye and nodded slightly as the cranes nodded back.

"Follow me," encouraged the Guardian Crane. Yuka followed with giddiness.

They approached a partition wall, which was pulled back from the inside by two cranes. Yuka was astounded to see that the cranes were wearing *kimono*-like robes. They were beautifully embroidered with designs that she herself were familiar with.

"Are they wearing *kimonos*?" Yuka inquired.

"Yes, they are," replied the Guardian Crane. "Do you have one yourself?"

Yuka's eyes lit up as she exclaimed, "Yes! I do."

They passed through another partition then yet another, and Yuka found that she was nodding slightly to each crane who opened the partition doors. Finally, they passed through another partition but this time, there was a regal-looking crane beaming at her and the Guardian Crane. Atop her red crown was a beautiful plume of red feathers.

The Guardian Crane approached, bowed slightly, and said reverently, "Ascendant."

"Guardian Crane," the Ascendant Crane bowed with her beak.

Yuka also bowed while looking up at the Ascendant as her well-groomed feathers seemed to gleam from the spherical illumination jades dangling from the ceiling like a strand of pearls. She wore a silken robe, and around her neck was a round red ornament with a white jade in the middle. When she saw Yuka bowing, she also bowed as the Guardian Crane took notice.

"A very respectful young one this time around," said the Guardian Crane as the Ascendant nodded. "Ascendant, may I present to you, *Satoh Yuka*."

The Ascendant looked down at Yuka's wondrous eyes and said, "Welcome to Crane Castle *Satoh Yuka*. I am the Ascendant, ruler of all Red Crown Crane Kingdom."

"Amazing," said Yuka.

The Ascendant looked at the Guardian Crane and said, "Let's proceed," as she let out two quick squawks as two other cranes gently swooped in from each side. With their beaks, they quickly removed the Ascendant's silken robe and then in unison, flew away across a massive circular opening behind her.

"Climb onto my back and harness yourself in," instructed the Guardian Crane. Yuka eagerly climbed aboard her back. She gently ran her hand along the bamboo rope harness and found the metal clip, slightly protruding from a round metal housing. She pulled out a length of rope that she wrapped and clipped around her waist. Yuka looked up and said, "Ready! Where are we going?"

"Down," was all the Guardian Crane said when suddenly, the Ascendant dove down into the circular opening, and the Guardian Crane followed as Yuka felt her stomach in her chest. She immediately pulled tightly against the Guardian Crane and as they descended, they passed floor after floor of the *tō* structure. As the two cranes dove deeper and faster, they dove toward the floor with an outline of a circle. Before Yuka could scream, curved blades spiraled away revealing a dark hole. In an instant, they passed into the dark abyss.

It was almost pitch black. But about the vast cavern were illumination jades in the walls that exuded a calming light. The two cranes pulled up and flew level. They pulled their wings inward, and Yuka saw that they were headed toward a tunnel of sort. She let out a scream as the two cranes swooshed into the tunnel as silence trailed them.

Yuka held on tight as the Guardian Crane followed the Ascendant, who flew elegantly through the dark tunnel, which was also illuminated at regular intervals by illumination jades. They flew upward and entered a small rocky walled chamber that was lit with several spherical illumination jades dangling from above. They came to rest on a ledge with an alcove that was seemingly carved into the inner wall of the magma pocket.

The Guardian Crane turned away from the ledge and asked Yuka to carefully unclip herself and slide off her back. Yuka's socked feet found sure footing on the rocky ledge that was large enough for perhaps four cranes.

"*Satoh Yuka*, do you see against the wall, the moon star *shuriken*?" asked the Ascendant to which Yuka looked and nodded. "Please approach it and hold it in your hands."

Yuka looked hesitantly at the Guardian Crane, but then nodded. She approached the rocky alcove, then realized that the arch was actually the crest of a crane's beak, which pointed toward the floor. On each side of the arch were two lit illumination jades that resembled the eyes of a crane, and above the arch was a red lacquered flare resembling the red feathers of the Ascendent and the Guardian Crane. Yuka focused on the shiny black metal moon star *shuriken* with a white jade embedded in the middle. She carefully pried it out from the rocky recess that cradled it.

She looked down at it when without warning, a light spiraled out of the white jade and radiated out in a big flash of light.

Yuka was awestruck by the flash. She spun around to see the bowed beaks of the Ascendant and Guardian Crane.

The Ascendant then said, "Our Crane Warrior has arrived. Welcome, Empress Warrior *Satoh*."

TEN

"Are we there yet?" Daniel asked the Guardian Buffalo as they trudged along the path, which had turned from soft dirt to light sand. He had noticed the white sand getting between his bare toes and liked the feel of it. He had always enjoyed the beach and the water ever since growing up as a kid.

"Patience, young one," the Guardian Buffalo said as he shook his head from side-to-side. He continued to trudge up the dune as bamboo stalks poked up from the sand in clumps. He stopped at the ridge of the dune and waited for Daniel.

"Hey, are we like near a beach or something? There's sand everywhere and…" Daniel was left speechless upon reaching the ridge, where the Guardian Buffalo stood. He looked out into the expanse of the wide white coastal bay that lay before him as the navy-blue waters rolled in. His eyes were drawn to the rock formation that ringed the bay, where it broke in the center, allowing water to flow in. The steepness and height of the rock formation was breathtaking.

Within the bay were two limestone outcroppings that were covered with beautiful green plants. A wooden vessel was just gliding past the closest limestone outcropping. It was dropping its sails to pull up alongside a wooden pier that extended all the way onto the beach.

"This is awesome!" exclaimed Daniel.

"Welcome to Horned Bay," said the Guardian Buffalo proudly.

"It's totally dope!" said Daniel.

The Guardian Buffalo looked down and confirmed that his young human was in awe. "Yes, it's… dope."

The Guardian Buffalo allowed a moment of admiration to pass before he encouraged his young human to follow him down the dune toward the ship. The saltwater air hit Daniel's nostrils, and he took it in as the gentle wind played with his dark brown hair. As they got close to the dock, he saw several buffalos working on the wooden ship and the dock. But what caught his curiosity was that the buffalos were standing upright, almost like humans. Standing erect exposed their strong barreled chests and the immense muscles of their hind legs. As he got closer, he noticed that they were looking at him as well.

When they reached the dock, the Guardian Buffalo pushed up and off his front legs. Daniel watched in awe as the Guardian Buffalo's body seemed to transform, putting him into an upright position. He towered over Daniel as he looked down at him.

"We're not like the domesticated buffalos of your world," said the Guardian Buffalo as he pushed out his chest.

"No, definitely not," said Daniel. "Are we going on that?"

"Yes, it is one of the fastest vessels we have, and it will get us to the palace. As long as the limestone towers don't crash into us."

"Don't you mean as long as we don't crash into them?"

The Guardian Buffalo snorted. "You shall see. Please climb aboard. Why don't you take up the aft position?"

Daniel walked up the wooden plank, stopped midway and looked at the Guardian Buffalo and asked, "Um, where is aft?"

* * *

The vessel was indeed fast, and as soon as the sea buffalos unfurled the sail, it was off. Daniel and the Guardian Buffalo were in the back, where Daniel held onto the railing. The Guardian Buffalo lowered himself back onto all fours. He was solid like a rock. The buffalo captain of the vessel steered and hollered out commands to his crew as they reset and unset smaller sails while the vessel raced toward the rock opening.

As the opening came into view, Daniel could see beyond it several limestone outcroppings protruding from the water, which were draped in lush greens as well. He nodded as the Guardian Buffalo told him to hold on, and the wooden vessel swiftly passed through the opening in the rocky formation that ringed Horned Bay.

As he looked out into the bay, he saw a vastness of limestone outcroppings and formations that reminded him of Hạ Long Bay in Vietnam. His mother had spoken of them and couldn't say enough about their natural beauty. Then one limestone tower caught his attention: It was moving.

Daniel's eyes widened. He had to watch again as one of the limestone towers actually moved toward a stationary one. As it approached, it slowed down to within a few feet of the other tower before starting to move away. He couldn't believe that something so massive was moving in the water. Then he realized the vessel was headed right toward it.

He anxiously looked up at the Guardian Buffalo to catch his attention. But the Guardian Buffalo only remarked, "Fascinating, aren't they? It's impressive each and every time we pass by them."

Daniel's eyes shot open and he hollered over the sound of the waves, "We're going to pass in between them?"

The Guardian Buffalo simply nodded his head. "Hold on, young one."

Not in a position to protest, Daniel steadied his feet against the wooden rail and hugged one of the wooden columns in the corner where the railings met.

"Time it perfectly, Captain," the Guardian Buffalo hollered out as his eyes fixed on the gap between the stationary limestone tower and the one that was moving.

The moving limestone tower was making its final approach, and the captain of the vessel commanded his sea buffalos to unfurl the sails. The wind caught them immediately, powering the vessel forward just as the moving limestone tower started to pull away. A depression in the water formed and as water went in to fill it, the pull of the water jolted the vessel forward.

The roar of the water was immense, and as Daniel watched in excitement and fear, he saw that the moving limestone tower was heading back as the wooden vessel sailed right into the gap. But as it did, the crush of water swelled, and the vessel barely crested it. The water bellowing out pulled the vessel forward just as the aft of the vessel cleared the enormous approaching limestone tower.

Daniel looked on in horrified excitement and turned to the Guardian Buffalo, "That was so rad!" he screamed.

Passing through that perilous gap allowed the vessel into a network of limestone outcroppings, including small and moving outcroppings. It wasn't necessary for them to pass through any more gaps, so the buffalo captain smoothly steered them through the limestone formations. There were several other wooden ships navigating the waters as well. As they passed a limestone formation that towered overhead, Daniel craned his neck upward to admire the massive limestone formations.

"How do they move?" asked Daniel as he lowered his head to face the Guardian Buffalo.

"Turtles, very big turtles," replied the Guardian Buffalo.

"Turtles?" asked a confused Daniel.

The Guardian Buffalo looked over at Daniel and spoke, "Legend has it that beneath these waters live massive turtles, and they hold up the moving limestone towers that you saw. So, every time when they move, they move."

Daniel looked at him blankly, "Turtles. Big turtles."

The Guardian Buffalo didn't say a word.

On any other given occasion, Daniel would have doubted that explanation but in the last few hours, he had met a talking panda, a white tiger, a crane, a buffalo and a team of sea buffalos that operated a wooden vessel and successfully guided it through massive moving limestone towers in the sea. He just shook his head and muttered, "Big turtles."

The Guardian Buffalo smiled and looked away.

The wooden vessel soon pulled into a high-walled, crescent-shaped limestone formation. In the middle of the watery crescent, was a massive limestone tower covered in lush greenery. Wooden docks and several wooden vessels could be seen along them. They pulled alongside an empty dock, and as the sea buffalos worked to moor the vessel, the Guardian Buffalo snorted and gestured at Daniel to follow him.

As the Guardian Buffalo and Daniel disembarked from the wooden vessel onto the wooden dock, Daniel couldn't help but notice that several other buffalos were giving him quick glances. He suddenly felt insecure and didn't know why.

"We'll wait here," the Guardian Buffalo said as he looked upward. Daniel looked up as well and saw wooden beams hanging over the edge of the limestone tower. Soon, he saw something being lowered. It was a large wooden platform with wooden sides and an opening on two sides. The Guardian Buffalo stepped onto it, and Daniel followed. When they were in the middle, the platform jolted upward, causing Daniel to rebalance himself.

But the initial jolt soon smoothed itself out as they started to ascend. Suddenly, Daniel could admire the view from a totally different vantage point. He saw the walls of the limestone tower splotched in various shades of gray and white, and wherever lush greenery could attach itself, it gave the limestone formation a splash of life.

He turned around and saw the vastness of the sea before him and the immense network of limestone outcroppings and towers. Atop the larger towers were what looked from afar to be structures, and he could make out hundreds of buffalos moving about them.

"Impressive, is it not?" asked the Guardian Buffalo.

"Totally dope," replied Daniel in awe of what he was witnessing for the first time.

The platform stopped, and the wooden beam acting as a cantilever started to slowly turn toward the edge of the limestone tower until the platform was over it. The Guardian Buffalo hopped off the platform, and the shift in weight momentarily caught Daniel off balance. But he regained his footing, hopped off the platform and onto the stone slab, barefoot.

"Follow me. We are almost there," said the Guardian Buffalo.

"Where's *there?*" asked Daniel.

The Guardian Buffalo pointed down the stone slab pathway. Daniel looked downward when his eyes fell upon a grand building. Its bottom section was an intricate stone formation, and atop it was a foreboding wooden structure with low, sloping reddish roofs. It was surrounded by a moat with a wide stone bridge that spanned it. Along the stone slab path leading up to it were buffalo guards at attention, their massive horns on full display.

"Welcome to the Palace of Divine Horns," said the Guardian Buffalo.

"Wow. Is this where you live?"

The Guardian Buffalo reared his head a bit but answered, "For now I do. Please follow me."

They walked down the stone slab path, and the buffalo guards paid him no attention, standing tall and resolute. They quietly crossed over the stone bridge. Daniel wanted to admire the intricate carvings, but the Guardian Buffalo was bent on getting to his destination, so Daniel kept up with him.

They ascended the stone steps and into a grand hall. Illumination jades lit the space from above, giving off a warm but majestic ambiance. Daniel was finally glad that his bare feet were finally on a plush red carpet as he followed the Guardian Buffalo. At long regular intervals were ornately decorated red columns. Finally in the middle of the hallway was another buffalo, whose presence he could feel. But what caught Daniel's attention was she was wearing a form of an *Ao Dai*, a traditional Vietnamese dress. Across her neck was a chain where a metal casing held a red jade. She looked resplendent as she nodded toward the Guardian Buffalo.

Daniel felt out of place as he pulled his hands together, not knowing where to put them, and being barefoot did not give him any sense of comfort.

"Horn Protectoress, may I present to you, *Danh Nguyen* Parker. Though he seems to prefer to go by Daniel," said the Guardian Buffalo

The Horn Protectoress looked down at Daniel, "Welcome to the Palace of the Divine Horns. I am the Horn Protectoress, Protector of all Buffalo Kingdom."

Daniel stood silently and wasn't sure what to do. He extended his hand to the Horn Protectoress. She looked at him dumbfounded and looked at the Guardian Buffalo.

The Guardian Buffalo looked down at Daniel, who looked up at him then back at his outstretched hand. The Guardian Buffalo quickly waved his hoofed front leg, and Daniel lowered his hand.

"We don't shake hooves, I mean hands here. A respectful bow will suffice," the Guardian Buffalo gently chided.

There was a recognition in Daniel's eyes, and he bowed slightly in the Horn Protectoress' direction.

"Very well, Daniel. Please follow me," she said as she led them both to a well of water that could be accessed via a sloping ramp that was ten feet in length.

"Do you see something in the well?" the Horn Protectoress asked.

Daniel peered into the crystal-clear water of the well, and after a few seconds, he saw a long dark object at the bottom. He looked up and nodded his head.

"Excellent. Please dive in and fetch it," asked the Horn Protectoress.

"You want me to do what?" asked Daniel incredulously.

"If you are who we think you are, you should be able to dive in and hold your breath for at least a minute in order to fetch it," said the Horn Protectoress.

"Why would I do that?" asked Daniel.

"Well, if you can't, you can't then. Just by looking at you, I'd thought you'd be strong as a bull and fetch it with no problem," said the Guardian Buffalo tauntingly.

"I can easily hold my breath for two minutes," Daniel boasted as he pulled off his t-shirt showing off his sleek and pale swimmer's body. He gave both buffalos a look before he pulled down his jeans exposing his boxers. He peered over the well's edge and focused on the dark long object.

"Just fetch it, right?" asked Daniel.

The Guardian Buffalo looked down at Daniel as his dark brown hair fell across his forehead. "Yes. Trust your instinct."

Daniel didn't like to be challenged, especially if the challenge was easy. He inhaled deeply and jumped into the well and once submerged, he maneuvered his body downward and dove deeper into the well.

"There's something different about this one," said the Horned Protectoress.

"Yes," said the Guardian Buffalo. "I could sense it too."

Both buffalos turned their attention back to the well as Daniel dove deeper.

As Daniel looked around, his eyes bulged when suddenly a flare of fire shot past him. He kicked out of the way as his eyes widened and looked about. *Fire? How could fire be in water?* He flapped his arms outward and dove deeper when another flare of fire shot past him. He kicked his feet faster and when it was within reach, he grasped the twisted slender object. As he looked at it, he saw another flare of fire coming at him and turned quickly allowing it to pass him. Without wasting another second, he kicked upward and soared through the water. He exited the well and pushed himself onto the ramp. He walked up along it until he finally broke through the water's surface. He exhaled and inhaled new air while holding a spindled club, adorned with a red jade at the top. As he emerged from the water and onto the ledge, he spun around to confront the two buffalos.

"What was that? Why was there fire in the water?" asked Daniel angrily.

But the buffalos didn't answer as they looked at each other.

"It should have happened by now," said the Horn Protectoress.

A moment passed and the Guardian Buffalo asked Daniel, "Daniel, would you mind touching the red jade on top?"

Daniel looked agitated as water dripped from his dark brown hair.

"Sure," said Daniel begrudgingly. He touched the red jade with his fingers. At first, nothing happened. But a moment later, from the jade itself, a white light came forth and radiated outward and disappeared as quickly as it appeared. Daniel was momentarily blinded by the light but as his eyes readjusted, the Horn Protectoress and the Guardian Buffalo bowed toward him.

With the red jade about the Horn Protectoress' neck glowing and with her head bowed slightly, she announced, "Our Buffalo Warrior has arrived. Welcome Emperor Warrior *Nguyen*."

ELEVEN

The empty bowl once held noodles, the empty plate a few *baos*, and the empty cup, water. Clara was able to satisfy her hunger as she held the warm teacup in her hands with the most fragrant tea she had ever tasted. Her eyes scanned past the opened bamboo shutters as she took in the view of the bamboo stalk dwellings before her. Several of the bamboo shutters were also open, and the illumination jades within showed several pandas moving about. She was also reconciling her thoughts that all the large bamboo stalks she was seeing, were inside one section of bamboo that used to be part of an unfathomably large bamboo, that was now called The Ring.

She was mesmerized by the entire nighttime scene as she brought the teacup to her lips. Her jade bracelet slipped down slightly from her left wrist when a knock came at the door. She looked to her left as the Guardian Panda entered.

He saw that she was leaning against the window, in her changed clothes and wearing socks. *How much more comfortable her feet must be after the long trek*, he thought. Her bamboo bow and quiver were on the bed.

"How are you, Empress Warrior Wu?" he asked.

Clara's eyes lit up as she replied while she headed back to the edge of her bed, "I'm good."

The Guardian Panda closed the door, came to the corner of her bed, and all his white and black fur swayed gently as he plopped down onto the floor. Clara giggled as she still couldn't believe that such a massive panda was next to her and speaking to her.

"How are you enjoying your room in Bamboo Tower?" he asked.

"It's very cool for a room inside a big bamboo," she said with a smile.

"I'm glad to hear that, and if you need anything, just ask your assigned attendant and he will get anything that you need," reassured the Guardian Panda.

"Thank you, but I do have a question. Why am I here?" she asked inquisitively.

"I know you had a long day and I promise, all your questions will be answered in the morning. It's best when all the other warriors hear it at the same time," said the Guardian Panda.

"So, Yuka, Sung, and Daniel, they're all warriors too?"

"Yes, they are," he said as he rose. "Please, get a full night's rest and I will come get you in the morning."

"Okay," said Clara as she said, "Have a good night."

"Rest well, Empress Warrior Wu," he said as he left her quarters.

* * *

Sung admired the faintly glowing blue jade in the middle of the metallic staff. He spun it a few times in his arms to see how it felt as it effortlessly sliced through the air. He showed a certain familiarity with the use of the staff. Then without warning, the partition to his room opened, and he momentarily fumbled it as he saw the steely blue eyes of the Guardian Tiger approach him.

His paws quietly grazed the stone steps as he approached Sung, who first held the staff in both hands in front of him before he shifted quickly and turned it upright in his right hand. Sung still hadn't gotten used to calmly welcoming a large white tiger.

"Good evening, Emperor Warrior Kim. I assume dinner was fulfilling?" he asked.

Sung looked at this empty bowl of noodles along with the *ban chans*, and two empty cups. "Yes," said Sung. "But I probably could eat two bowls of noodles."

"Very well, I will have the cooks make you a double serving next time," said the Guardian Tiger.

"Oh, please don't go through the trouble just for me," said Sung sheepishly.

"It's no trouble at all. It's our duty to keep our emperor warrior well fed."

"Yes, about that. What am I the emperor of?" asked Sung.

"You are the esteemed Emperor Warrior Kim of Claw House," said the Guardian Tiger with a tone of reverence.

"Am I like a ruler?"

"No, the Tigeress is ruler of all White Tiger Kingdom. But you have an important role nonetheless."

"Oh, okay. And what is that role?"

"All your questions will be answered tomorrow morning along with the other three warriors. I imagine you must have had a long day," the Guardian Tiger said.

Sung felt it would be more prudent to be patient and agreed, "Yes, *gam-sa-ham-ni-da*," he responded with *thank you* in Korean.

"Very well then, Emperor Warrior Kim, have a restful night," said the Guardian Tiger as he spun his massive body around and gracefully bounced over the steps and exited.

* * *

Yuka watched in awe from the ledge of her quarters as night descended. Several moons appeared out of the grayish night sky with the behemoth ringed planet behind them. The night was quiet except for the soft swoosh of a large crane taking off from a ledge beneath her before it caught enough wind to glide toward the rim of the caldera.

Soaring through the air while on the back of the massive Guardian Crane earlier gave her a sense of freedom that she hadn't felt in a long time. Her trance was disturbed when the partition slid open, gently scraping the bottom of the door frame.

The imposing Guardian Crane entered, with her wings tucked close to her sides. Yuka turned to meet her. She bowed, and the Guardian Crane blinked and also bowed. Her beak turned toward the bed and spied the moon star on the corner of it. The empty bowls had been neatly stacked, and the cups were moved toward the center of the tray.

"I see you finished your dinner. Was it to your liking?" asked the Guardian Crane.

"Oh, very much so. The noodles were so fresh. *Domo arigato*," said Yuka with a slight bow.

"I'm very happy to hear that," said the Guardian Crane. "Enjoying the night view before a night's sleep?"

Yuka turned toward the night sky and replied, "Yes, it's all so beautiful, amazing and peaceful."

"I'm glad you're settling in," said the Guardian Crane. "Please get a good night's sleep before we begin tomorrow."

"Begin what?" Yuka wondered.

"All will be told tomorrow, Empress Warrior Satoh," said the Guardian Crane as she spun around. "Have a good night."

"Goodnight Guardian Crane," said Yuka gratefully.

* * *

"When can I go home?" demanded Daniel of the Guardian Buffalo.

They were in Daniel's palace quarters, which overlooked the ocean from a high vantage point.

"Young Emperor Warrior Nguyen, I ask you to calm down. All will be explained tomorrow morning," beseeched the Guardian Buffalo.

"Don't get me wrong. I'm really impressed, and this place is amazing, talking animals and all," stammered Daniel. "But I need to get back home to my mother."

"Your mother is fine," said the Guardian Buffalo. "The Portal Books have always seen to that."

Daniel took a couple of steps toward the imposing buffalo before the Guardian Buffalo reared upward and came down on both front hooves, which shook the room. Daniel stopped in his tracks and knew that he had no chance of intimidating the buffalo.

"Emperor Warrior Nguyen!" stammered the Guardian Buffalo as his red eyes beamed at Daniel. "This is enough. I ask you for your patience. Your petulance will do no one any good right now."

Daniel felt a cold shiver shoot down his spine as he suddenly felt inept. He muttered, "I'm just worried about my *me*."

"It's honorable that you would be worried about your mother, but believe me when I tell you, she is fine. There are greater things at stake, and I need you well rested before tomorrow morning when we meet up with the other warriors and guardians."

All of Daniel's pent-up angst left him as his shoulders drooped. He shook his head and was resigned to trusting the buffalo. "Okay, but you promise, all my questions will be answered in the morning?" he asked respectfully.

"Yes, they will be. Also, please eat your dinner, you will need your strength," asked the Guardian Buffalo.

Daniel turned to his tray of food; a bowl of noodles, a cup of water and tea, and another cup brimming with a white liquid.

"Is that milk?" asked Daniel. "Where did the milk come from?"

The Guardian Buffalo stared at Daniel and simply said, "Definitely not from me, I'm a bull."

Daniel stared back at him momentarily and then understood what the Guardian Buffalo meant as a frown appeared on his face.

"Please eat well and sleep well," said the Guardian Buffalo as he started to turn around.

"I didn't mean to sound so disrespectful just now," offered Daniel.

"I understand. Have a good night, Emperor Warrior Nguyen," said the Guardian Buffalo.

"You too, Guardian Buffalo," said Daniel as he walked toward his dinner.

TWELVE

"So, the bamboo here in Azen is almost magical!" exclaimed Clara as she walked alongside the Guardian Panda while holding her bamboo bow.

"Almost, they just have different properties than the ones you're familiar with," he replied as they came upon the Portal Circle.

Clara looked up. She could see that she was the first to arrive. She noticed how picturesque the Portal Circle looked in the morning sun as the open leather-covered Portal Books seemed to bask in the light. There was something powerful about the Portal Circle from her view from the outer rim. She took in the full wonder of the sight that she hadn't had time to appreciate the day before.

"Hey." Clara turned to the voice and saw Sung approaching with his majestic white Guardian Tiger following close behind. They both walked into the Portal Circle while the Guardian Tiger walked toward the Guardian Panda.

"Hi," said Clara with a smile as she admired how the beige double wrap top draped over Sung's slender athletic chest. It fit him perfectly and like her top, she could see that the top edge of the flap was in blue, while hers was green. "Is that your weapon?" she asked.

"Yah, it's some staff made out of a metal that I've never seen before. They call it, Clawdium," said Sung smiling as he noticed the same outfit on Clara. "Is that a bow?"

Clara raised her bow upright in front of her and smiled, "It sure is! This the Bow of Destiny. I guess I'm supposed to be an archer of some sort," she responded as she pointed to the blue edge on Sung's top. On it were embroidered Korean letters along with an icon. "A tiger's head?" she asked.

Sung reached across his chest and ran his fingers across the white embroidery on the blue edging and finally on the icon of a tiger's head. He glanced at it and looked at Clara with a smile, "Yep. It's a tiger's head. Pretty cool, and this is my name in Korean. Is that your name in Chinese?"

Clara glanced down at her green edging, nodded and asked, "What do you think of this top? Does the inside flap hook onto the inside of your outer flap and then it just magnetically snaps into place along the side?"

"So cool, right? The Guardian Tiger told me it's all magnetic. Our tops have Clawdium fibers woven in and the outer edging is magnetic, so it just snaps in place," said Sung excitedly.

A shadow of a bird with an impressive wingspan appeared inside the Portal Circle causing Clara and Sung to look up as they brought their hands up over their eyes.

"Hello!" exclaimed an excited Yuka, as she carefully slid off the Guardian Crane, who had landed softly and was walking into the Portal Circle toward her fellow Guardians. Yuka walked toward Clara and Sung, and she wore a similar double-wrapped top, with the top edging in white and pants made of the same material. But unlike Clara and Sung, her moon star was affixed at the center of her waist.

"Man, you get to fly?" asked Sung.

Yuka grinned as she shrugged her shoulders upward and walked up to her fellow warriors.

"What do you think about us being empress and emperor warriors?" asked Yuka.

"I'm still getting over the fact that we're on another planet with talking animals," responded Clara.

"Totally. I just feel that this has got to be a dream," said Sung.

"Is that your Chinese name on your collar?" asked Yuka as she gently pointed to Clara's green edging of her top.

Clara ran her fingers along the embroidery of her Chinese name, "*Wu Chu Hua.*"

"Yes! I see you have the same but yours is white and the crane icon is so cute!" exclaimed Clara.

"Thank you! I love your panda too!" said Yuka as she gently brushed her fingers on the black embroidery of the crane icon next to her name.

"Mine is a tiger!" said Sung excitedly, not wanting to be left out of the conversation as he pointed to the white embroidered tiger on the blue edging.

"Hi," said Daniel who happened upon the Portal Circle with the lumbering Guardian Buffalo behind him, who snorted as he walked toward the other guardians.

Clara, Sung, and Yuka offered their greetings as Daniel walked up to them with the Club Horn of *Kting voar* slung over his shoulder. That's when Yuka noticed his dark brown hair, and he instinctively responded, "I'm half Vietnamese."

"Oh, I see," said Yuka as her gaze settled onto the red edging of his top that had the embroidery of a bull's head beside his Vietnamese name.

"How was everyone's night?" asked Daniel.

"I don't know about you guys, but I was glad to just get these boots!" Sung said as he lifted one of his feet for all to see. Everyone laughed as they wiggled their feet to show off similar low ankle boots.

"Is that your weapon?" Sung asked Daniel.

Daniel lowered the club horn and brought it down into his other hand and looked at it admiringly. "Yep. It's the actual horn of a mystical creature called the *Kting voar*, and it's got this red jade at the top, see?"

"Way cool," responded Sung.

"What's your weapon Yuka?" asked Clara.

Yuka carefully removed the Moon Star *shuriken* from her waist and carefully spun it in between her two index fingers as it caught the sun's gleam.

"A throwing star! Looks sharp!" said Sung.

"I heard that our clothing and the boots were made of spun silken bamboo threads. And Sung said that woven into the threads were the metal fibers from his kingdom!" said an excited Clara as everyone looked at her. "We are definitely not home."

"Speaking of home, where is everyone from?" asked Daniel.

"I'm from New York City," said Clara.

"I'm from Arizona," said Yuka.

"Houston here," said Daniel.

"Wow, we're from all over. I'm from Los Angeles," said Sung as Yuka added, "Oh, I used to live near there, but I'm in Arizona now."

"Empress and emperor warriors," said the Guardian Panda. "I'm sure you have questions, so please stand by your Portal Book. You may place your weapons into the bamboo stands by each of your books. These were placed there earlier in the morning for you."

With a few furtive glances, the warriors walked up to their Portal Books as the guardians took their positions in front of their warriors on the edge of the Portal Circle.

The panda stepped into the circle, the footsteps of his padded feet were almost silent. The Guardian Panda stood at the center and slowly spun around in a full circle before stopping at Clara.

"Welcome to the realm of Azen. As you have come to realize by now, you are no longer on your planet, which you know as Earth. You have been brought here by the Portal Books because you are the empress and emperor warriors. We need your help to defeat the dreaded demon armies of the Warlock of Nadi."

There was silence until Clara asked, "Warlock?"

The Guardian Panda stretched his arm toward Clara's Portal Book, and with a flick of his paw, summoned it to life. Streams of glowing embers burst forth from the Portal Book and formed a flowing image of a large menacing head sitting atop massive shoulders. In a serious tone, the Guardian Panda said, "The Warlock is he who wants to conquer Earth and all its people."

THIRTEEN

The young warriors were silent as the Guardian Tiger entered and the Guardian Panda exited. He rose onto his hind legs, and his joints realigned to give him a human posture. He was pensive as he crossed one arm and rested his opposite elbow on top of it.

He flung out a fluffy paw, summoning from Sung's Portal Book the same streaming strands, which assembled to show the planet they were on and its orbiting moons. The large sun also appeared. The warriors were awestruck.

"Every few years, four of the moons above you align in a way that creates four consecutive lunar eclipses. Each lunar eclipse allows the Warlock to unleash a spawned army that he can teleport to any of the four cardinal points, north, south, east, and west, in any order that he so chooses," the Guardian Tiger explained.

He continued, "His goal is to seize this Portal Circle on which you are standing and its Portal Books so that he may control the portal back to your Earth."

The strands of fire danced in disarray and reassembled to show a terrain with the Portal Circle at its center, the four kingdoms and the four areas where the battles would take place.

"But each time, the combined kingdom armies fought him off—but only with the help of the emperor and empress warriors whose Qi powers their jade, which then powers the jade embedded in our armor and weapons. When the jade is powered, our armor becomes stronger, and our weapons become more powerful. Without the power of the jade across our soldiers, we would be slaughtered under the relentless onslaught of the Warlock's armies," said the Guardian Tiger gravely. "The Portal Books have chosen you and summoned you here to lead us into battle."

Clara raised her hand, and the Tiger addressed her, "Yes?"

"You want us to fight?" asked Clara nervously.

"Yes, the Portal Books have selected you," said the Guardian Tiger with resolve.

"But... we're only teenagers. I'm 15. I'm not a warrior," stated Clara dumbfoundedly.

"No, you are a warrior. You just don't know it yet," said the Guardian Tiger sternly as he turned and made eye contact with each warrior. "It is in your blood and your unawaken Qi."

Daniel raised his hand and asked politely, "What is Qi?"

The Guardian Crane sauntered in as the Guardian Tiger exited and looked at Daniel.

"Your Qi is your lifeforce," said the Guardian Crane as she wove a flaming stream from Yuka's Portal Book as Daniel's eyes followed. The flaming stream reassembled into a 3D model of the human body. Glowing strands flowed along its spinal column and branched off toward its limbs and head. "This represents your Qi. Here it is normal, but when it is awakened, see how the Qi glows ever so much more," said the Guardian Crane as the Qi glowed brightly.

"Your Qi powers the one singular jade that you possess within your weapon. That is the primary jade, and when it is powered, it invokes any like jade near it. The Panda Warrior powers the green jade. The White Tiger Warrior powers the blue jade. The Buffalo Warrior powers the red jade, and the white jade is powered by the Crane Warrior."

"Way cool," muttered Sung under his breath.

The Guardian Crane continued, "The only jades that are not powered are the illumination jades, which are powered naturally and serves as our light source, which I'm sure you've seen in all of our kingdoms. But some jades have additional power."

The Crane turned to Yuka and smiled at her awestruck face. "Empress Warrior Satoh, please hold out your Moon Star *shuriken*."

Yuka held out her Moon Star and stared at the Guardian Crane's eyes.

"Now, place your other hand over it. Yes, just like that. Now for a moment, clear your mind and swipe down on the white jade," urged the Guardian Crane.

Yuka pursed her lip, let out a sigh and pressed gently on the white jade when she felt something clink in her clasped hands. Her eyes lit up and she looked at the Guardian Crane who motioned her to lift her hand. When she did, in her hand was second moon star, without a white jade.

"Magic!" exclaimed Yuka as she pulled out the second moon star for everyone to see.

"Whoa," said Clara.

The Guardian Crane smiled at Yuka and continued her lesson. "With practice, Empress Warrior Satoh will be able to fashion moon star *shurikens* at will. Once she masters the technique of throwing the moon star *shuriken*, the power of the white jade will endow each throw with accuracy."

The Guardian Crane turned to Daniel and said, "The power of the red jade will deliver twice the force that you wield with the Club Horn of *Kting voar*. Emperor Warrior Kim, your blue jade will resonate to shatter objects your staff comes in contact with. And you, Empress Warrior Wu, your aim with your bow will always be true, that is its destiny."

Clara looked at the Bow of Destiny and admired the glowing green jade before watching the Guardian Crane exit as the Guardian Buffalo entered.

Like the Guardian Tiger, he straightened up onto his hind legs.

"In addition to your jade-powered weapons, we will also put you through training. This will consist of martial arts training from your respective heritage, followed by weapons training and finally, manifesting and invoking your elemental Qi powers."

Sung anxiously raised his hand, and the Guardian Buffalo nodded at him. Sung spoke anxiously, "But I have a chem test next week…"

The Guardian Buffalo stammered, "If we do not defeat the Warlock armies here, there will be no test to return to, let alone your world."

Silence fell onto the Portal Circle as the thought of the Earth's demise suddenly weighed on them.

The Guardian Buffalo walked off the Portal Circle, his posture reverting to the four-hooved stance of a buffalo. The Guardian Panda took to the center once more. His heavyset belly hung low but high enough that it was off the stone circle.

"We have limited time to train you and transform you into warriors…" said the Guardian Panda who saw Clara raising her hand. "Yes, Empress Warrior Wu?"

"What is the fifth book for?"

The Guardian Panda blinked adorably with his eyes, looked toward the closed Portal Book. In a moment of recollection he said, "Oh yes, that Portal Book belongs to the warrior who wields the Wu element, metal."

There was a moment of silence and Clara asked, "Metal?"

The Guardian Panda panned his gaze upon each warrior before returning to Clara. "Oh yes, each of you represent a Wu element."

FOURTEEN

"Each of you represent a Wu element," lectured the Guardian Panda. He turned to Sung. "You, Emperor Warrior Kim are the Wu element, water. You, Empress Warrior Satoh, are the Wu element, air. You, Emperor Warrior Nguyen are fire. And finally, Empress Warrior Wu, you are the Wu element, earth."

"I'm named after a Wu element?" asked a surprised Clara.

"Coincidentally, with your last name Wu, it seems so," answered the Guardian Panda.

"But what about the Wu element metal? Why is there no warrior?" asked Clara.

The Guardian Panda summoned Clara's Portal Book, which cast another streaming image of the planet and its moons, which hovered and glowed in the middle of the Portal Circle.

"A regular alignment cycle usually has four consecutive lunar eclipses where each moon is directly aligned with the planet and the sun. However, on an off-cycle alignment, a fifth moon will also align and create a fifth lunar eclipse. This is an off-cycle lunar event, and the Portal Book will choose another warrior to join the Portal Circle. In this scenario, the Warlock can conjure a fifth army and place it at any of the four cardinal points, but we would have five warriors and five kingdoms to battle the five Warlock armies," lectured the Guardian Panda."

"Guardian Panda?" Daniel asked uncertainly.

The Guardia Panda turned and nodded to Daniel, who continued, "So, are you telling me that I will be able to control fire?"

"Yes, but only after you manifest your Qi elemental power and learn to invoke it properly," answered the Panda.

"Sweet!" said an excited Daniel as everyone looked intrigued. "How do we do that?"

The Guardian Panda instructed each warrior to turn to their Portal Book, and they excitedly did so as their guardians stood off to the side.

"Now, pick up your brushes and open your books to the first blank page," instructed the Guardian Panda.

Clara eagerly and gently flipped to the first empty page. Her fingers quickly ran down the page to flatten it out, and she couldn't help but notice how smooth and warm it felt. She curiously looked about the stone tablet and around the Portal Book as a confused expression appeared. She looked upward to her Guardian Panda and asked, "Where's the ink stone?"

"These are Azen brushes, you won't need ink here," said the Guardian Panda as the other guardians instructed the same to their warrior.

"Really?" said Clara as she stared at her brush. "So what are our brushes made of?"

"Well, yours is bamboo," said the Guardian Panda. "Emperor Warrior Kim's brush is made of Clawdium. Empress Warrior's Satoh's brush is a red feather. And Emperor Warrior Nguyen's brush has been fashioned from a buffalo horn."

"So cool!" said Clara.

"Now, we are going to teach you a word in your respective language, and you will brush it out on the page and practice until it's perfect. Only when it is perfect will the Qi element be manifested. The key here is that you must allow your natural Qi to become part of your brush strokes," the Guardian Panda instructed.

The Guardian Panda then looked down at Clara as she looked up at him with a frown on her face. "What is wrong, Empress Warrior Wu?"

Clara looked down at the empty page, the brush and back up at the Guardian Panda and muttered, "It's like Chinese school!"

FIFTEEN

When the Guardian Panda told Clara that her first Chinese character was *wall*, she was glad she already knew the character. As she looked at the page, a grid suddenly appeared, and she gasped. The Guardian Panda said that the Portal Book can sense the intent and display pages meant for the writing task. But for Clara, the grid brought up tedious memories of Chinese school. She looked at it with annoyance, but she relented.

Her first characters for *wall* were a bit off, since she had to get used to black ink appearing from the bamboo brush when there was none. She had delicately brushed out the character for *wall* for the twentieth time but had nothing to show for it. Confusion settled over her face as she looked up into the brown eyes of the Guardian Panda.

"Am I doing this right?" Clara asked of him.

"You have to feel your Qi and connect your Qi with your brush strokes," he encouraged.

"But I didn't know I had Qi until an hour ago, how do I even know how it feels?"

"Put the brush down on the tablet, Empress Warrior Wu. Now, close your eyes. Yes. I want you to focus on the warmth within your body, a warmth that has always been there, but you may not have consciously thought about it. Now feel that warmth radiating out and extending into your arms and legs. Do you feel it?"

"I think so," said Clara dubiously.

"There can't be any doubt, you must feel it, or you don't. Try again," beseeched the Guardian Panda.

Clara let out a sigh and relaxed her shoulders and eased her hands down to her sides. She inhaled deeply and imagined feeling her Qi in her chest. She believed she felt the warmth of the Qi that the Guardian Panda talked about. She imagined that warmth extending into her arms and legs. She unwound her right hand and focused on the warmth there and for a moment, felt something anew. Her eyes opened as she exhaled slowly and turned toward the Portal Book. She picked up the brush and looked at the page, which became blank as a new grid appeared in place.

She focused on the warmth of her hand and brushed out a perfect Chinese character for *wall*. She watched the black inked character, when suddenly, small fiery embers emanated from the black character and it lifted off the page to her wondrous eyes.

"Whoa, what the…" But before she could finish, the floating fiery character for *wall* floated toward and seeped into her chest. She brought her hands to her chest and looked at the Guardian Panda and exclaimed, "Where did it go?"

"You have successfully manifested your first earth Wu Qi element," said the Guardian Panda.

"Now what?" asked an incredulous Clara.

"Empress and emperor warriors, come over," the Guardian Panda called out and the warriors did as they were asked. "Your fellow empress warrior has just manifested her first Qi element. Each manifested Qi element is then absorbed by your Qi, ready to be invoked upon your command. Empress Warrior Wu, please show your fellow warriors how to manifest the Qi element for the Chinese character *wall*."

Clara looked at the curious faces of her fellow warriors and felt a sense of anxiety. However, she nodded at the Guardian Panda and turned toward the Portal Book. She relaxed, exhaled, and carefully brushed out the Chinese character for *wall*. Once again, fiery embers emanated from the black ink before it lifted off the page and floated toward a fixated Clara. It soon seeped into her chest and disappeared as she turned toward her fellow warriors in awe.

Their eyes were awestruck, and they quickly sprinted back to their Portal Books. When Daniel returned, he looked up at the Guardian Buffalo and said insistently, "Teach me Vietnamese."

The Guardian Crane watched Yuka expertly brush out the Japanese character for *wall*. When the character didn't manifest, she just continued brushing another one until she brushed out her fiftieth attempt. It didn't manifest and she looked down at the page blankly. She was about to turn the page when the Guardian Crane rested the tip of her beak on the page and looked into Yuka's brown eyes.

"Your brush strokes are perfect. You have excellent command of your Japanese written language," said the Guardian Crane.

"I'm fluent in spoken and written Japanese," Yuka exclaimed proudly.

"Yes, you are but you don't need to prove that to anyone here," chided the Guardian Crane. "You are not in class, rather you are manifesting Qi elements."

Yuka looked despondent and asked, "What am I doing wrong?"

The Guardian Crane looked down at her and simply said, "Just brush out the Japanese character for *wall* and feel it."

Yuka nodded and looked down at her Portal Book. She instinctively swiped away her previous attempts and they disappeared as a new grid appeared. She exhaled and brushed out the character for *wall* while imagining a wall. To the delight of her eyes, her black inked Japanese character for *wall* burst into tiny fiery embers as it lifted off the page and seeped into her chest. Her smile was from cheek-to-cheek and she clapped her hands with giddiness. She looked up at the Guardian Crane who smiled and winked at her with one of her beady eyes.

"Whoa! It's lighting up and it's…" said an elated Sung who finished by saying, "And it's in me now. Wow, that was amazing!"

"Excellent, Emperor Warrior Kim, you have successfully manifested your first water Wu Qi element. Now let's do some more," said the Guardian Tiger.

Daniel looked at his three warrior companions and felt frustrated by their success as he struggled. He only had a basic grasp of the Vietnamese alphabet and was just relearning it at home. The Guardian Buffalo was patient and helped him recall the Vietnamese alphabet. He turned back toward the Guardian Buffalo and nodded as he said, "Okay, show me how to write *wall* in Vietnamese again."

As Clara successfully manifested her twentieth Chinese character for wall, she asked, "Why do I have to manifest so many of the same character?"

"You can only invoke the power of the Qi element for each one that you manifested," said the Guardian Panda. "The manifested power is not limitless, but you can build up a number of manifested Qi elements ready to be invoked at will."

"How many manifested Qi elements can my body hold?" asked Sung of the Guardian Tiger as he overheard Clara's question.

"An infinite number," replied the Guardian Tiger.

"What happens if I invoke all my manifested Qi elements?" asked Yuka of the Guardian Crane.

"Once you invoke all your Qi elements, you will not be able to invoke any more, and you will need to manifest more from the Portal Book," answered the Guardian Crane.

"Ugh! I can't do this!" as Daniel's outburst caught the attention of his fellow warriors. He firmly smacked the horned brush onto the tablet above the Portal Book.

The Guardian Buffalo looked at Daniel and stated, "You will have to work twice as hard."

Daniel beamed at the Guardian Buffalo and blurted out, "It's because I'm only half Vietnamese! Is it! I didn't ask to be half Vietnamese. Screw this!" Daniel abruptly walked off the Portal Circle in frustration without looking at his guardian or anyone else.

SIXTEEN

Later that night, Clara was in her own tent that had been set up near the Portal Circle. Separate tent compounds had been set up for each of the warriors and attended to by attendants from their respective kingdoms. Her tent was large, with a bamboo bed frame topped with a firm mattress, blanket, and pillow in the middle. There was a nightstand on either side, each with an illumination jade in a bamboo holder. In the far corner was a large wardrobe filled with training gear. Adjacent to the tent was an opening that led to a spacious bathroom. The outer wall of the tent had a window flap that was pulled back to reveal a mesh-lined window from which she could see the night sky. She had just finished her dinner, a flavorful soup with ingredients similar to a winter melon, mushrooms, and of course, slices of tasty bamboo.

She was brushing the character for *wall* into the air with her right fingertips with delight. Though she had manifested over a hundred Qi elements for *wall*, she was tickled when each one came to fiery life and seeped back into her chest.

The Guardian Panda had told her to go to sleep early, but her mind was racing. She was happy to see that Yuka and Sung were taking delight in mastering their Qi elemental powers, but she felt sorry for Daniel. She assumed that being half Vietnamese, he may not have been exposed to his Vietnamese heritage. She wanted to help him but didn't know how as she didn't know Vietnamese.

Still feeling restless, she sat upright and swung her legs over the edge of the bed. She could hear the cicadas chirping slightly outside of her tent. She stealthily went to the entrance of her tent and slipped into her boots. The tent flap easily gave way, and she peeked outside. There were a few panda attendants walking about but no one was watching as she quietly snuck out.

The path to the Portal Circle was gently lit by the moonlight from above. She passed a boulder and went down her usual path toward the Portal Circle when she heard a noise; A voice, an excited one at that. She slowed her approach, came upon the last boulder before stealthily entering the area right outside the Portal Circle. She saw Daniel at his Portal Book across the way. She watched him brushing into his Portal Book and saw a fiery string lift off the page and seep into this chest. She could see his excitement from his body language, and she smiled.

She heard a low snort and looked to her left. The glowing red eyes of the Guardian Buffalo caught her attention. With the flick of his snout, he silently beckoned her over and she complied. After quietly making her way over without distracting Daniel, she saw that the Guardian Buffalo was lying comfortably down on his belly. But his dual horns were impressive and massive, each ridge gently glistening in the moonlight. He motioned with his hoof to sit down beside him, and she did.

"He returned after you three had left with your guardians. I waited for him, of course, and when he did return, his anger had been replaced with frustration and defeat. But I got him back to his Portal Book. Without the pressure of others, we reviewed the Vietnamese alphabet and worked on the word for wall," the Guardian Buffalo whispered to Clara.

Clara felt something large come up on her left and before she could notice, she was met with the shimmering blue eyes of the Guardian Tiger. He had silently snuck up beside her. His thick white and black striped fur was prominent, even under the moonlight. He smiled at her as she nodded to him. The Guardian Buffalo looked at him and returned his gaze toward Daniel as the Guardian Tiger laid down on his stomach. Even just lying down, the musculature of his body was imposing.

"After about an hour, he manifested his first fire Wu Qi element in Vietnamese, and his face lit up in excitement. When it seeped into his chest, he placed both of his hands on his chest and looked up at me. He was so proud of himself," said the Guardian Buffalo.

"I'm so glad he's happy," said Clara quietly.

"And since then, he's been out here, diligently manifesting," said the Guardian Buffalo.

"He must have a tiger mom," said the Guardian Tiger nonchalantly as his strong tail waved back and forth.

Clara looked at the Guardian Buffalo who turned annoyingly toward the Guardian Tiger's mischievous smile. The Guardian Buffalo snorted in response and turned away.

Clara brought both of her hands to her mouth to stifle a chuckle.

SEVENTEEN

The following morning, Clara walked briskly to where the others had already gathered, around a large rectangular table made of bamboo. There was a spring in her step after a restful sleep, but she was famished and looked forward to breakfast. Discovery of her newfound Qi elemental powers left her titillated, though she didn't yet know how to put them to use.

Panda attendants in aprons were putting out chopsticks and cups at each of the eight seats. Daniel was standing and excitedly gestured into the air to the full attention of Sung and Yuka. The Guardian Buffalo was near the corner seat closest to Daniel as he watched his emperor warrior, while the Guardian Crane and Tiger were conversing near the corner of the table closest to Sung. The Guardian Panda wasn't in sight until Clara turned toward what seemed to be an open kitchen area with a large tent next to it. He was talking to the kitchen staff.

Clara sauntered up and said, "Morning," jovially. Yuka turned with a smile as she waved at Clara while Daniel stopped his oratory and said, "Hi Clara!" Sung got up and as Clara approached, nodded slightly as the front part of his hair dangled down a bit as he said, "Morning Clara."

Clara looked at him coyly and brushed aside her hair and said, "Wow, so formal. Oh, am I supposed to sit here?" she asked as Sung pointed to the empty seat across from him and next to Yuka.

The Guardian Buffalo looked in Clara's direction and uttered, "Good morning to you, Empress Warrior Wu," to which she responded with "Morning," as she smiled sheepishly as she was still getting used to being called by such a title.

"Good morning empress and emperor warriors," came the Guardian Panda's voice. Behind him were several panda servers as they fanned out to place a plate of food at each seat. The Guardian Tiger, Crane, and Buffalo took up the corner seats next to their warriors while the Guardian Panda took his seat last.

As a plate of food was placed in front of each warrior, Sung exclaimed, "Eggs! Man, I wish there was some steak to go with these eggs... ouch!"

He shot a quick stare at Daniel, who had kicked him as he stared at Sung with a shocked look.

"What?" asked Sung annoyingly as Daniel whispered, "Dude," as he gestured with his wide eyes toward the Guardian Buffalo behind him.

"Oh… I mean, I'm good with these eggs. I wonder where these eggs came from, they're huge… ouch!" uttered Sung as he looked in Yuka's direction after she kicked him.

She nudged her chin toward the Guardian Crane who was looking at him with one of her beady eyes. Sung's cheeks flushed deep red at his gaffe and muttered, "Thank you for the breakfast, Guardian Panda," as he bowed his head toward his food.

Clara giggled at poor Sung's embarrassment, and she looked up at her Guardian Panda. "What are these *baos*?"

The Guardian Panda pointed with his big fluffy paw and enumerated the breakfast items, "These are bamboo *baos* with a bamboo paste in the center. Next, we have steamed bamboo and mushroom dumplings. Then a small bowl of rice, and as Emperor Warrior Kim noted, delicious eggs."

"That's a lot of bamboo!" stated Clara.

"Bamboo is life, Empress Warrior Wu," the Guardian Panda said with a wink of his eye. "Please eat up, and we will continue with your training."

"What is the Guardian Crane eating?" asked Clara as she spied her slurping up something into her beak.

"Oh, she is slurping up silken bamboo flat noodles, flavored with scallions and mushrooms," responded the Guardian Panda.

The Guardian Crane slurped one up and shook her beak as the bamboo flat noodle slid down her gullet. She then leveled her head and looked at Clara, "My favorite."

Everyone let out a laugh. As Sung turned back with a smile, he caught Clara looking at him and she quickly glanced toward Daniel. "Hey, Daniel, did you continue with your manifesting yesterday?" asked Clara, not letting on that she had been watching him the previous night along with the Guardian Buffalo and Tiger.

Daniel smiled, "Man, it was so awesome! I came back after and started practicing that one word, and my Vietnamese is like rusty. It's why my mother wanted me to get back into Vietnamese lessons. But it started to come back and when finally, it flared up and the word just floated toward me and disappeared into my chest. It was so cool! I think I must have manifested like one hundred more!" he said proudly.

The Guardian Buffalo looked down at his emperor warrior, "You did well, you didn't give up."

Daniel looked up and humbly nodded. "Thank you, Guardian Buffalo. I never thought learning Vietnamese was important until now."

"Eat well. There are many more words to learn to help you control your Qi elemental powers," said the Guardian Buffalo.

"How about you, Yuka? It looks like you are fluent in Japanese," asked Sung.

Yuka smiled and placed her chopsticks down on the table and nodded slightly, "Yes. I've been learning Japanese ever since I was young, so I'm fluent. How about you?"

"I'm okay. I learned how to read and write *Hangul*, which is what we call our Korean language. My father makes me learn it because he's a professor of Asian American studies but he also teaches Korean language every weekend. But I've been keeping up with my Korean through K-Drama."

Clara's eyes perked up and she interjected, "K-Drama? Which one? I just recently saw an old one, My 'Sassy Girl'…"

"'My Sassy Girl' isn't that old, but I watched that too, did you…" answered an excited Sung before the Guardian Panda let out a cough.

"Empress and emperor warriors, we need to finish up soon so that we may continue our training," requested the Guardian Panda.

The warriors focused on their eating and soon afterward, they were led back to their Portal Books.

Each of the guardians took up position opposite their warrior outside of the Portal Circle. The Guardian Panda nodded at Clara and stepped into the center of the Portal Circle.

"Empress and emperor warriors. Yesterday, you learned a lot. To be sure we are all clear, who can tell me who you are?"

There was as awkward silence as the warriors first looked at each other until Clara raised her hand, "We are warriors for your kingdoms?" she answered tepidly.

"Yes, and who chose you to be our warriors?" continued the Guardian Panda.

"The Portal Books?" answered Daniel cautiously.

"Yes, and what makes you special?" asked the Guardian Panda as he panned the Portal Circle.

Yuka raised her hand, "That we power the primary jade in our weapons?"

"Yes, and what else about the jade?"

Yuka added, "My jade gives me the power to replicate the moon star, and that they will hit their target?"

The Guardian Panda nodded and then looked at Sung.

"My jade gives my staff the power to resonate to shatter things it comes into contact with," said Sung. The Panda nodded and looked to Daniel.

"My jade doubles the force of my strike from my club horn," Daniel said as the Guardian Panda spun around to Clara.

"And my jade will make each of my arrows' aim straight and true," answered Clara confidently as she secretly wanted to try.

"Yes, all of you are correct, but what else does the jade do?" asked the Guardian Panda.

There was a bit of silence and with a smirk, the Guardian Panda reached underneath his fur around his neck and pulled out his slightly glowing green jade.

Clara rushed her hand up, "I know! It powers the armor that the jade is attached to when it is worn by any of the soldiers of Azen."

"Yes, that is right," said the Guardian Panda. "Now what other powers do you have?"

Sung responded, "We have Qi powers?"

"Yes, you have Qi elemental powers," said the Guardian Panda who spun around to Daniel's voice.

"And each Qi elemental power controls a Wu element, like mine is fire," said Daniel excitedly.

"Yes, and what else?" asked the Guardian Panda.

"We build up the Qi elements by manifesting them in our Portal Books," said an excited Yuka.

"Yes and?" queried the Guardian Panda.

"And we can invoke the elemental Qi powers?" Clara said questioningly.

"Yes, and you will learn how to invoke your elemental Qi powers... once you manifest more from your Portal Books. So please begin," entreated the Guardian Panda.

The warriors excitedly turned to their Portal Books, picked up their brushes and started to manifest the character for *wall* in their respective Asian languages.

As late morning neared, Sung manifested possibly his one hundredth Korean word for wall in *Hangul* when he placed the Clawdium brush back down. He rubbed his right fingers with his left hand and peered over to his left at Clara. He saw that she was still manifesting away, not showing a hint of tiredness. He smiled and was about to pick up his Clawdium brush when the Guardian Panda called for everyone's attention.

"Empress and emperor warriors, please put your brushes down and follow me," he said. Each of the warriors did as they were told. They gave each other passing glances as they trekked down a path with the other guardians in tow.

They ended up at a wide grassy passage lined on each side with a stone wall that slanted outward. Along the walls were boulders in varying sizes and entrances. It was probably at least a hundred feet long.

The warriors gathered near a spot with the Guardian Panda in front while the other guardians stood off to the side. He gestured with his fluffy paws and stated, "This is the Gauntlet. You will prove your Qi elemental powers, your martial arts, and your weapons training here. But right now, we are going to show you how to invoke your manifested Qi elements."

A nervous excitement came over the warriors, and when Clara was called up first, she looked surprised but eagerly stepped forward.

The Guardian Panda continued, "Empress Warrior Wu, you control the earth Wu element, so you will invoke your Qi element for wall to create a wall of dirt."

Clara cast a confused look at the Guardian Panda, who continued, "Look down the Gauntlet, know that the earth beneath you is yours to command. Once you focus on that, I want you to call out the word wall…"

"In Cantonese or Mandarin?" asked Clara.

The Guardian Panda looked down at Clara and blinked. In a moment of realization, he answered, "Either. The Qi element is conjured by your verbal command."

Clara nodded in feigned understanding and continued to listen to the Guardian Panda.

"Once you call out your Qi element, you'll need to brush it into the air at the same time to conjure it. It doesn't need to be perfect. Then tighten your fist and cast it out. Understood?"

Clara nodded, and the Guardian Panda stepped aside. She looked over at her fellow warriors, who looked at her with wide eyes and blank expressions.

She reviewed the steps in her head and exhaled. "*Teng-bing,*" she said weakly in Cantonese as she traced out the character when suddenly, the character for *wall* appeared in her hand. It glowed beautifully in a glistening blue hue. She couldn't help but stare at it as it balanced on her fingertips.

"Cast it out, Empress Warrior Wu," urged the Guardian Panda.

Clara came back into focus. She flung out her weakly clenched fist as the glowing character flew outward and dove into the ground. Suddenly, earth from beneath rose up creating a small wall of dirt that was about waist high and six feet in length.

Her eyes widened at what she created as she looked incredulously down at her fingers.

"Excellent first try, Empress Warrior Wu!" proclaimed the Guardian Panda as the warriors looked on with surprise. "You invoked your first Qi element. Now for your next one, make sure you tighten your fist harder as you cast outward. Focus on where the wall will erupt from the earth."

Clara nodded in earnest, pursing her lips. With focus, she called out, "*teng-bing!*" as she traced the character for *wall* into the air, conjuring another bluish glowing Qi element at her fingertips. With a steeled fist, she quickly flung out her arm. The Qi element flew out of her hands and disappeared into the earth. The earth rumbled as a wall ten feet high and twenty-five feet long grew forth like mahjong tiles being stacked.

"Whoa!" exclaimed Clara leaving her mouth gaping at what she had done.

She looked over at the Guardian Panda, who nodded in approval. He gently nudged Clara toward the group as the Guardian Tiger brought Sung over.

The Guardian Tiger looked down at Sung and asked if he remembered the steps that the Guardian Panda had given to Clara. Sung nodded as the Guardian Tiger stepped aside and simply said, "Now try."

Sung took a deep breath, relaxed his shoulders by shaking them and looked down at the dirt wall. He focused and called out, "*dahm*" in Korean for *wall* as he traced into the air and like Clara, he was mesmerized by the bluish glowing word as it balanced on his hand. He looked forward and cast it out with his arm as the Qi element disappeared into the air. But from where it disappeared, a wall of ice formed parallel to the dirt wall and just fell a bit short of its total length.

"Insane!" exclaimed Sung as he looked down at his empty hands.

"Well done, Emperor Warrior Kim!" said the Guardian Tiger. "Now let's let Emperor Warrior Nguyen try."

A visibly excited Daniel came up who was anxious to try. The Guardian Buffalo looked down at him and asked, "Did you hear the steps clearly?"

"Yah, let me try," said Daniel eagerly as the Guardian Buffalo lowered his voice, "Patience, Emperor Warrior Nguyen."

Daniel looked up and for a moment realized his impatience. He stopped his bouncing up and down and offered, "Sorry Guardian Buffalo. I'm just excited."

"It's understandable. Now the fire Wu Qi element will either ignite the air around it or build on an existing fire. Fire is more potent, so for your first try, a light fist is fine," advised the Guardian Buffalo.

Daniel nodded in understanding and looked down the Gauntlet. He exhaled, called out the Vietnamese word for wall, "*the-oung*," while tracing it out, but nothing happened. He looked stupefied and looked at the Guardian Buffalo.

"Your pronunciation, it's '*the-oung*,'" said the Guardian Buffalo in Vietnamese.

Daniel wasn't even fazed that the Guardian Buffalo spoke in Vietnamese. He shook his arms and looked down the Gauntlet and shouted the word, "*the-oung*" in Vietnamese while tracing it out. The glowing bluish word appeared from his hand. He flung it outward with a somewhat tight fist, and a fiery wall formed parallel to the ice wall.

Daniel took a step back seeing his fiery creation and let out an excited holler as his fellow warriors looked on in awe. "Intense!" he said as he clenched his fist toward his chin and pulled it downward in self-promotion.

"Emperor Warrior Nguyen," said the Guardian Buffalo tersely as Daniel looked up at him. "Manners."

Daniel realized his abundance of excitement, relaxed and appeared downcast, "Sorry. I'm just so excited."

The Guardian Buffalo nodded and motioned him back to the warriors as an eager Yuka stepped up with the Guardian Crane.

"You get the benefit of seeing everyone go before you. Are you ready, Empress Warrior Satoh?" asked the Guardian Crane.

"I am!" said Yuka excitedly but she asked, "So I'm going to create a wall of air alongside Daniel's wall of fire?" to which the Guardian Crane nodded with her beak.

Yuka nodded in understanding and looked down the Gauntlet. She could see that the ice wall was starting to melt a bit from being next to the fire wall. She focused down the length of the fire wall and called out *"kabe"* while expertly tracing out the Japanese character, setting the Qi element aglow at her fingertips. She smiled at the Qi element in her hands and flung it down toward the wall of fire. The Qi element disappeared into the air and nothing.

Yuka looked up at the Guardian Crane in disappointment, and she looked back down at Yuka. "What did you expect? That you would see a wall of air?" the Guardian Crane said with a smile. The Guardian Crane nodded at the Guardian Panda, who signaled for a bow and arrow from a nearby panda attendant.

"Like air, you can't see it, but it's there. The Guardian Panda will demonstrate," said the Guardian Crane as she nodded to the Guardian Panda.

The Guardian Panda stepped away from the group of warriors and drew back his bow, releasing a glowing jade-tipped arrow. It flew straight at an angle toward the fire wall but suddenly stopped a few feet from the fire, confirming that the wall of air was there. He let fly a couple of more arrows. Like the first, they seemed to become embedded in midair a few feet away from the fire wall.

"That is amazing!" said Yuka as she looked up at the Guardian Crane.

"Well done. The tighter your fist, the denser the wall will be," said the Guardian Crane. "Also, if you squint your eye a bit, you can see that the wall of air is thicker than the surrounding air. The light will be cast a bit differently through the wall of air."

"Refraction!" Sung yelled out. "Sorry, just learned that in my physics class."

Yuka nodded with a big grin as she looked down the Gauntlet as she let out a gasp, "What's happening to the ice wall?"

Everyone gazed down the Gauntlet as the ice wall started to melt and the fire seemed to become stronger.

The Guardian Crane announced, "Ah, your Qi elements are natural Wu elements and behave similarly. Fire would melt ice and air feeds fire. But over time, the Qi elements that you invoke will dissipate."

"How about my dirt wall?" asked Clara.

The Guardian Panda turned to her and retorted, "Your dirt walls are permanent until they are broken down by another force."

"Oh…" said Clara, and the Guardian Panda added with a chuckle, "Which is why, your next Qi element will be 'flatten.'"

"Ha! I get it," said Clara.

The Guardian Panda looked at the other warriors and told them that they would manifest the reversal words, evaporate for water, extinguish for fire, and evacuate for air for their next lessons before conjuring up more Qi elements.

EIGHTEEN

The moons were becoming bright in the night sky. But the serenity of the blinking constellation was interrupted by small fireballs being thrown into the air, only to be pierced by icicles and then blown asunder by a gust of wind.

Daniel was playfully trying out his new Qi element, the fireball. He was keen on learning to control its size, intensity, and launch direction. Sung invoked icicles of all shapes and sizes and launched them at the airborne fireballs. Yuka sent up gusts of wind whose intensity she could control. She also discovered that she could envelop her fellow warrior's Qi elemental creations. Clara could only watch her fellow warriors as her new Qi element, splitting the earth, didn't have the playful possibilities of the other Qi elements.

Clara sighed, a bit envious at the fun that her fellow warriors were having. She had a mischievous thought of splitting the earth beneath them to swallow them up. A grin appeared before she cast away that mischievous thought, relieved that dinner was being served.

The warriors took the center seats while their guardians took the corner seats once again. Before them was an assortment of *ban chans*, small and varied Korean dishes, and Sung's eyes opened wide with excitement.

"Yo, are we having Korean BBQ? What I wouldn't do right now for *galbi*, ouch!" stammered Sung as he shot a look at Daniel who was gritting his teeth as the Guardian Buffalo looked down at him. Sung's eyes rolled as he realized his gaffe once more and bowed his head toward the food as the varied *ban chans* were being laid out by tiger attendants.

"I'd like to remind our warriors," started the Guardian Tiger. "That here on Azen, we do not eat our friends from other Azen kingdoms."

Everyone nodded and Sung was downcast as he gingerly picked at the *ban chans* but was pleasantly surprised at how fresh and delicious the *kimchi* was. Thoughts of home cooked meals with his family suddenly raced into his mind and whetted his appetite.

"This *kimchi* is amazing!" blurted out Sung.

The Guardian Tiger offered, "You must try the *kimchi* bamboo. Here, allow me." The Guardian Tiger expertly picked up a piece of the *kimchi* bamboo with his chopsticks and topped it off onto Sung's rice bowl that he held in his left hand.

Sung froze for a moment and looked down at his metal rice bowl and Clara giggled. "What? Never had a tiger place food on top of your rice with chopsticks?"

Sung looked up at Clara's wondrous eyes that he only noticed that night and let out a laugh, "There's a first time for everything!"

The warriors laughed as the guardians looked at one another, not understanding the sudden shared laugh.

"Did I miss something, Emperor Warrior Kim?" asked the Guardian Tiger with his steely blue eyes.

Sung smiled, picked up the *kimchi* bamboo with his chopsticks and turned upward toward the Guardian Tiger. He imitated a bow with the *kimchi* bamboo in his chopsticks and replied with a *thank you* in Korean, "No, it's all good Guardian Tiger. *Gam-sa-ham-ni-da!*" that garnered a nod from the Guardian Tiger.

"Do you miss the food at home?" Clara asked Sung.

Sung looked up, swallowed and said, "Sure do, my mom loves to cook and my dad…" Sung paused as he realized he was about to mention grilling meat and continued, "Let's just stick with my mom's cooking. We'd get all these *ban chans* like these, and she makes a tofu *chigae,* and her *kimchi* pancakes are amazing!"

At that moment, the tiger attendants plopped down large *kimchi* pancakes in the center of the table, along with rice cakes slathered in sweet Korean pepper sauce and a bowl of boiling tofu *chigae* for each person. Sung's mouth dropped, and the other warrior's eyes brightened up in surprise. Sung looked up at the Guardian Tiger, who responded, "I like my Korean food as well, Emperor Warrior Kim. Eat well."

"I will! Oh my god, this all smells so good!" as he and the other warriors dug in.

"My mom does most of the cooking. She loves to cook, usually Chinese food. My dad and I are spoiled by her. She makes the most amazing dumplings, I tell you!" said Clara as everyone listened while they ate.

"Is it just you and your parents?" asked Sung as he slurped on the tofu *chigae.*

Clara nodded and Sung turned to Yuka, "And how about you?"

Yuka looked up as she dabbed her napkin to her lips. "Oh me? My mom loves to cook too, she spoils us. My dad is a fisher…" her voice trailed as she looked awkwardly at the guardians and she quickly pivoted, "Sushi, we eat a lot of vegetable *makimono* rolls, like with cucumber, and… *tamago*! Lots of *tamago nigiri*," said Yuka with a sigh of relief.

Yuka quickly turned to Daniel and asked gently, "And how about you Daniel?"

Daniel looked up as he took a bite from a piece of the *kimchi* pancake, "Oh me? Nothing special, my mother does cook a lot of Vietnamese dishes, which I really like. Who doesn't like a bowl of *Pho*…" said Daniel who also had to pause when he realized he enjoyed the beef brisket and flank steak in his *Pho*. "Mac & cheese, my mom cooks that too."

Clara looked at Daniel, "And your dad?"

Daniel turned to Clara and looked down, "Oh, it's just me and my *mẹ*, that's what I call my mother in Vietnamese."

Clara suddenly felt embarrassed and quickly offered, "Oh, I didn't mean to…"

Daniel waved his hand, "Oh it's okay. My father left me when I was young. All for the best, he wasn't a good guy, as my mom realized too late."

A silence fell over the table until Daniel said what everyone else was thinking, "I wonder what our families are doing right now?" he asked.

Clara put down her bowl of rice as her thoughts went to her mother and how she regretted leaving things so badly with her. She felt a knot form at her throat when the Guardian Panda spoke.

"Empress and emperor warriors. I know it's difficult to have left your families, but I assure you, your families are fine. Whether or not you know it yet, what you will be doing will save your families. You are destined to save their lives."

Yuka looked up at her fellow warriors, whose expressions bore the unknown weight of responsibility that was suddenly thrust upon them. She then looked down at her bowl of rice and began picking at it with her chopsticks in silence.

NINETEEN

The sun cast a beautiful morning glow upon the Portal Circle, and the air was fresh and soothing. Each of the warriors stood with their backs to their Portal Books as their guardians stood behind them. Their hands were relaxed at their sides.

The Guardian Panda walked into the Portal Circle and announced, "Empress and emperor warriors. You have started to understand your Qi elemental powers, and over the course of your training, you'll harness their full potential. But your Qi elemental powers will not be enough to complete your training as a true warrior of Azen. In addition to harnessing your Qi elemental powers, you will be taught the martial arts of your heritage and after that, how to wield your weapon."

"Way cool," muttered Daniel under his breath.

The Guardian Panda faced Daniel and stated, "You, Emperor Warrior Nguyen, will learn Vovinam." He turned to Yuka and stated, "You, Empress Warrior Satoh, will learn Karate," to which she smiled. Looking at Sung, "You, Emperor Warrior Kim, will learn Tae Kwan Do," to which Sung nodded. Lastly, the Guardian Panda turned to Clara, "And you will learn…"

There was a pause as the Guardian Panda looked at her. He lowered himself into a horse stance, curved his left arm and hand inward and out before coming back across his chest where he threw a punch with his right hand. "You will learn Kung Fu, Empress Warrior Wu."

Clara's eyes squinted as she let out a soft giggle and the Guardian Panda asked gently, "What amuses you?"

Clara smiled and let out joyfully, "Kung Fu Panda."

The Guardian Panda had walked back to the Portal Book and stood in front of Clara as the other warriors turned to their guardian.

"Empress Warrior Wu, you are going to learn Kung Fu not from me, but from the Portal Book," he stated.

Clara's blank expression as she looked down at the blank page of the Portal Book was telling as she looked back up at the Guardian Panda. "How?" she asked curiously.

"The Portal Book contains the experiences of all the Chinese Panda

Warriors before you. All of that will be transferred to you," he said.

Her incredulity was obvious as she continued listening. "Please pick up the brush. And write out the characters for *Kung Fu*," instructed the Guardian Panda.

Clara thought for a moment and brought the bamboo brush to the page and wrote out the characters for Kung Fu. She placed the brush back on top of the Portal Book as instructed.

Clara looked down at the bold black beautiful characters she brushed out, stared back up at the Guardian Panda as nothing happened. "Now what?" she asked.

The Guardian Panda smiled and continued, "Now Empress Warrior Wu, place your hands on the edges of the book and focus on the characters for *Kung Fu*"

Clara nodded uncertainly, placed her hands firmly on each side of the Portal Book. She stared at the characters for Kung Fu, when a red ember started to swirl out of each black character until it traced out the character itself. Suddenly, tendrils of flames cast outward as Clara's eyes reflected them. She steadied her hands as the warm flames gently wrapped themselves around her arms, then her torso and finally her legs.

Soon, an image of a warrior from the past emerged from the flames. He lifted from the page, performing a slew of Kung Fu moves in a dazzling show until he looked at Clara, brought his right fist into his left hand and bowed to her before disappearing. Instantly, another image of a warrior, this time a young Chinese girl, appeared as she too performed a slew of Kung Fu moves before disappearing. Then another warrior lifted off from the page, then another. Clara's mouth was agape as her eyes absorbed all the young warriors' moves while the tendrils of soft flames pulsated about her body, until finally, the last warrior gave his final lesson and respectfully bowed to Clara. The tendrils of flames brushed against her body for the last time as they receded back into the written characters from which they came. Clara suddenly looked up in awe and exclaimed, "I know Kung Fu!"

The other warriors had made similar discoveries and were spellbound for a few moments as their newfound knowledge seemed to course through their bodies as if it had always been there.

"Now, Empress Warrior Wu, you now have the Kung Fu experience of all the Chinese Panda Warriors past. You must allow your body to unleash your newfound skills," said the Guardian Panda.

Clara demanded anxiously, "Show me!"

Each of the guardians took their warrior away from the Portal Circle and began their martial arts training. Clara could feel a sense of control over every strand of muscle and was bewildered by it. She and the Guardian Panda came to a flat patch of grass, and he turned to her as his pear-shaped body came into full view.

He stared at her and said, "Now, mimic everything that I do as if I was your mirror image."

Clara nodded silently.

The Guardian Panda bowed gently toward her, and she returned the bow. Soon he lowered himself into a stance and threw out a straight right punch, which Clara mimicked. He thrusted a left punch, which she followed with her right fist. A succession of punches soon followed. He shifted his stance to the right and performed another set of punches that Clara easily followed.

Then the Guardian Panda did something she did not expect: He kicked straight up and brought the leg back down behind him. She wanted to let out a giggle as she witnessed the Guardian Panda's short leg kicking only as far as it could go, but she suppressed it. She focused ahead and effortlessly kicked upward and brought her leg back down. She was surprised by this, and the Guardian Panda asked her to do nine more before pivoting and kicking with the other leg.

The Guardian Panda was no longer performing in front of her and instructed her instead. Straight kicks turned into crescent kicks, which in turn became sidekicks, followed by a series of jumping kicks that became increasingly more advanced. What she was now learning in just hours would normally take months, if not years.

As the morning wore on, Sung, who had a few years of Tae Kwan Do training from his father, a Tae Kwan Do instructor, suddenly found himself capable of some of the most fantastic high flying aerial kicks. The fluidity and power that he felt left him in awe of himself. This was something he had never fully accomplished, to the chagrin of his father, but was suddenly something he wanted to feel again.

Yuka's hands moved in a flurry of combinations as she threw out powerful kicks here and there. She came back into the ready position and brought her hands down to her side and bowed to the Guardian Crane. Abruptly, she gleefully clapped her hands while jumping up and down lightly. Her expression of happiness was evident, and she almost couldn't contain herself.

Daniel glided his body in a series of circular movements, and he had to hold himself a few times as he found he was off balance. He was able to hold his balance and continued the moves to completion before launching his body sideways and clamping his legs together and landing in a final crouch.

"Argh… I can feel it, but it's like my body is hesitating," uttered Daniel.

"Emperor Warrior Nguyen, be patient, it will come. You have learned in hours what would have taken years back on your world," said the Guardian Buffalo.

Daniel looked over at Sung who was performing some amazing acrobatic kicks like in the movies and he envied him. He then looked toward the ground and grunted, "It's because I'm half, isn't it? If I was full Vietnamese, I would be absorbing the power faster right?"

The Guardian Buffalo spoke firmly, "Young Emperor Warrior Nguyen, it will come in time, be patient."

Daniel straightened up and said in a serious tone, "But we don't have time, right?"

The Guardian Buffalo reared his chin upward stretching the strong muscles along his neck. His eyes found the faint moon and said, "Yes, time is running out, you'll need to work twice as hard."

Daniel nodded his head and gritted his teeth. "Then teach me more."

The warriors' excitement for their newfound martial arts skills powered them through lunch, despite their guardians' insistence that it was acceptable to eat lunch. But the warriors persisted, and their stubbornness won out. By midafternoon, the guardians led their warriors back to the Portal Circle, where they stood at the ready in front of their Portal Books.

The Guardian Crane walked into the Portal Circle and looked to Yuka, who stood attentively. "Empress Warrior Satoh, please come into the center of the Portal Circle." Yuka obeyed as she looked straight ahead as all eyes were on her.

"Now show me *kata* number five," asked the Guardian Crane.

Yuka paused blankly and tilted her head up toward the Guardian Crane. "But I don't know *kata* number five," she said meekly.

The Guardian Crane looked down at her sternly and retorted, "Yes you do. Feel it within your Qi that is now intertwined with the Karate experience of the previous Japanese Crane Warriors. Show me, *kata* number five," the Guardian Crane said once again as she stepped out of the Portal Circle.

Yuka looked ahead and centered herself. She closed her eyes and searched in her mind for visions of the warriors past when one flashed before her eyes.

A warmth pulsated through her limbs, and suddenly she knew. Her body went into motion as she threw out a punch, led by turns and blocks, forceful sidekicks before she settled back into the center of the Portal Circle. She successively bowed to each guardian and warrior pair before bowing at her own guardian. She walked back to her Portal Book with a spring in her step.

The Guardian Tiger stepped into the circle and beckoned Sung to the center. Sung saw what happened to Yuka and tried searching for Tae Kwan Do forms in his mind, fretting when he drew a blank. He exhaled as he placed his arms to the side and awaited the Guardian Tiger's command.

The Guardian Tiger looked at his warrior and simply said, "Show me *taegeuk* number seven." He then walked away.

Sung felt his head go blank and looked over at Yuka. She smiled and closed her eyes while her head dipped slightly, before it rose up as she reopened her eyes. He exhaled and closed his eyes, trying to picture the number seven and panicked when nothing came to him. But then he envisioned the number seven in Korean when it became ablaze and a Korean female warrior appeared and performed a crisp and clear *taegeuk*.

Sung flung his eyes open and his body moved instinctively as he executed quick punches followed by a vicious front kick. He repeated this in all four direction and returned to center and looked up in confidence. The Guardian Tiger nodded in approval as Sung sauntered off the Portal Circle.

The hefty Guardian Buffalo walked into the Portal Circle and Daniel gulped as he followed. The Guardian Buffalo slowly circled Daniel before confronting him and he commanded, "Show me form number three."

Daniel saw Sung's prior apprehension and did what he had done. He relaxed his shoulders and closed his eyes and saw nothing but darkness. He was starting to feel an empty pit in his stomach and wasn't sure if that was hunger he felt. He exhaled again and relaxed even further when he said to himself the number three in Vietnamese. Then out of the darkness, a red ember appeared, and it soon transformed into a fiery vision of a Vietnamese warrior past who executed a flurry of moves that abruptly exploded in a flash that forced Daniel's eyes to open. He suddenly moved and without prompting, executed several circular arm gestures and launched several kicks before pivoting his body back to the center. He was beside himself in astonishment as he looked down at his clenched fists. He looked up to see his fellow warriors smiling supportively.

Finally, the Guardian Panda stepped into the Portal Circle and Clara followed into the center. The Guardian Panda looked at Clara and almost with a smile he said, "Show me form number eight."

As he left the Portal Circle, Clara focused her eyes forward, exhaled smoothly, and closed her eyes. But as soon as she did, a bold Chinese female warrior appeared in her mind alit in a fiery choreography of sweeping moves before vanishing.

Clara opened her eyes and her chin jerked strongly to the right before she returned her gaze back to center. Her arms suddenly moved in crescent arcs as her body spun fluidly, followed by spinning kicks. Her body then lowered itself into a crouched position as her leg extended outward to the side with her arm elegantly arched upward. She ended by raising herself onto one foot while her other leg retracted before extending into another crisp kick. She settled back at the center and was filled with elation as she bowed to the Guardian Panda.

She jovially skipped back to her Portal Book and couldn't believe she executed something so graceful yet so powerful.

The Guardian Crane stepped back into the circle as Yuka eagerly followed beginning the pattern all over again as the guardians called out new numbers. The warriors executed martial arts routines that they had never learned before, gracefully and solidly.

The warriors continued way into the late afternoon before they succumbed to their voracious appetites.

TWENTY

The next morning, Clara rummaged through the drawers, looking for something that could double as a scrunchie for her hair. But it seemed that such an item was not available on Azen. She found a green ribbon in one of the drawers, but it was too slender to tie up her flowing thick black hair until she came across a polished 2-inch piece of green bamboo that contained cotton. When she twisted off the cap, she realized that the bottom cap could also come off. After emptying the cotton, she was left with a hollow segment of bamboo. She looked at it along with the ribbon playfully and had an idea. She looped the green ribbon at its center, threaded it through the bamboo and pulled the loose ends through the loop. With a grin, she carefully fed the end of her hair through the bamboo, pushed it halfway up and tied it off at the bottom with the green ribbon. The bamboo slipped down and covered the knot leaving the two green ribbon strands dangling out from the bottom. She looked at her clever bamboo ribbon hair accessory and admired her fashionable resourcefulness.

Her smirk turned into a grin as she reflected that she now knew Kung Fu. She could feel confidence coursing through every muscle of her arms and legs, and for the first time in her life, she knew her body's full capabilities.

She tugged the outer side edge of her training top and let go of it playfully as it magnetically snapped into place. She smiled, looked up confidently and exhaled. *It was going to be an amazing day*, she thought as she looked down at the bow and quiver full of jade-tipped arrows. She grabbed the quiver, slung it over her back and picked up the bow and strode out of her tent.

Panda attendants were milling about, performing their routines. When Clara approached them, they bowed respectfully, and Clara bowed in return. It was a nice gesture, she thought, something to bridge the distance between strangers—so unlike New York City, where everyone pushed each other without any courtesy whatsoever.

As she approached the Portal Circle, she saw Daniel in the middle of a form. She slowed her step as she admired his tall lithe body leaping into the air to perform a double kick but double stepping on the landing. He pressed his hands to his knees to catch his breath and Clara approached.

"Morning!" she said excitedly.

Daniel looked up and smiled as he straightened. "Morning! Hey, you put your hair in a ponytail," he remarked.

"Yah… During training yesterday, my hair was just all over the place and I didn't want it going everywhere today," Clara said as she quickly stroked the end of the ponytail.

"It looks nice," said Daniel.

"Thanks," said Clara sheepishly when she asked, "Up early to practice your Vovinam?"

"Yep! I'm finding I'm a bit of off balance. It's because I'm only half Vietnamese," said Daniel wistfully.

"Does that make a difference? That you're only half?" asked Clara.

"Yep, the Guardian Buffalo even said I have to work twice as hard," he said resignedly.

"You looked pretty good to me," offered Clara.

"Thanks. I'm a swimmer more than a martial artist. Well, at least up until yesterday," said Daniel as he let out a laugh that Clara shared with him.

"I know right? Oh my god, my body feels totally entirely different even though it's the same body. It's like I know I'm capable of all these Kung Fu moves, it makes me feel so powerful!"

"Totally! When you did your form, you were so graceful and your hands sliced through the air creating that sound effect," exclaimed Daniel.

Clara's hand suddenly snapped through the air in an outright manner before withdrawing it back to her chest with her fingers pressed together in an open palm. "Like that?" she asked playfully!

"Just like that!" Daniel shouted back with a laugh.

At that moment, a winged shadow cast itself over the Portal Circle. Clara and Daniel watched the Guardian Crane gliding downward before landing gracefully.

Yuka waved from the back of the Guardian Crane and hopped off.

"You are so lucky you get to fly!" exclaimed Clara.

"I went for a morning flight with my Guardian Crane before coming here. I'm sure she wouldn't mind giving you a ride as well," said Yuka.

"That would be so cool!" said Daniel and Clara agreed.

"Hey everyone!" Sung called from the edge of the Portal Circle.

"Hey bro!" said Daniel as he watched Sung walk up with his Claw Staff held upright in his right hand.

"Is it me or do all of you feel a bit trippy like we know how to fight now?" asked an incredulous Sung.

Yuka shook her head up and down as everyone else agreed. "I feel so much more connected to my heritage now."

"I feel the same way! It's like now that I know Kung Fu, I can appreciate it so much more," said Clara.

"I didn't even know what Vovinam was until yesterday," added Daniel.

"If only you could squeeze ten years of training into one day," said Sung and everyone nodded. "My *abeoji*, oh that's what I call my father in Korean, would be so happy! He wanted me to be his prized Tae Kwan Do student but I kinda gave up on it. He wasn't happy with me."

"Your father is a Tae Kwan Do instructor?" asked Clara.

"Yep, and a Korean teacher. I just didn't feel I could live up to his expectations," replied Sung.

"Warriors, please take your place by your Portal Books. The other guardians are now approaching," said the Guardian Crane.

The warriors split up toward their Portal Books and placed their weapons into their bamboo stands. The guardians extended morning greetings and soon took up their places in front of the Portal Books.

The Guardian Buffalo stepped into the Portal Circle and started the morning lesson. "Warriors, well done on wielding your martial arts skills. For today, we are going to work on your weapons training. When the warriors of the past bestowed you with their martial arts experience, they also bestowed their weapons experience. Like yesterday, we are going to work the weapon routines to unlock what you already and don't yet know. For our honored Emperor Warrior, the mystical *Kting Voar* bequeathed his horns to the Buffalo Kingdom upon his passing and one is used as the weapon. We had discovered since then that the red jade imbued it with the power to strike with twice as much force. Therefore, this Club Horn of *Kting Voar* has been used by our warriors ever since. Emperor Warrior Nguyen, please step into the circle beside me with the Club Horn of *Kting Voar*."

Daniel nodded as he turned to grasp the club horn before walking toward the Guardian Buffalo.

At the same time, four buffalo attendants came into the circle. The first two laid down a thick stone slab while the other two put down a large melon and bowling-ball-sized rock.

"Emperor Warrior Nguyen," commanded the Guardian Buffalo. "Stand in front of the stone slab with your feet at shoulder length apart. Yes, and now firmly grip the club horn from the tapered end. Yes, just like that. When I give you the word, raise the club horn from above and strike down on that melon. Now, Emperor Warrior Nguyen!"

Daniel lifted the club horn above his head as the red jade at the top caught a glint of the morning sun. He looked at the melon and with a smooth motion, swung down, easily smashing it into pulpy bits.

"Now, do the same to the rock," directed the Guardian Buffalo.

Daniel raised the club horn above his head and instinctively brought it down harder onto the rock, which shattered into craggy pieces.

"Wow," exclaimed Daniel as he pulled back the club horn and marveled at its undamaged surface.

"The red jade will provide at least twice as much force as you exert. When used correctly, the Club Horn of *Kting Voar* will crush hard objects. It's devastating to the flesh of any creature. You may go back now," said the Guardian Buffalo.

The buffalo attendants picked up the smashed melon and the remaining pieces of the shattered rock. At the same time, four buffalos set up four stone columns opposite of Yuka. A melon was placed on each and the middle two were obscured by rice paper screens, one with a vertical slit and the other a horizontal slit.

The Guardian Crane walked up to Yuka's side and explained her task. "Your white jade has the power of replication. With your white jade moon star affixed at your waist, you can will the replication power by swiping your fingertips across the white jade outward and along your waist. Give it a try."

Yuka looked down at the moon star and placed her the fingertips over the white jade, as it glowed. She swiped on the white jade outward and around her waist as two moon stars appeared on each side.

Yuka let out an excited gasp and looked up to see the astonishment on her fellow warriors' faces.

"Easy, right?" asked the Guardian Crane. "Now, as long as you aim, the moon star will hit its target. Take off the moon star on the ends, aim for the two end melons, and throw them in whatever manner you feel comfortable. You may now begin."

Yuka gingerly held the two moon stars, one in each hand, and she could feel a slight warmth emanating from each. She eyed the melons, and though it was her first time ever throwing a moon star, she naturally lunged forward, casting outward her two hands in unison, releasing the moon stars.

Without fail, the two moon stars whisked through the air and struck each melon, level and center.

The smile on Yuka's face was unmistakable, and the Guardian Crane looked pleased. "Now, do the same thing. Hit the middle two melons through the slits in the rice paper screens."

Yuka stared down the path toward the melons and looked up at the Guardian Crane. "Um, one slit is vertical and the other is horizontal," she said.

The Guardian Crane nodded and simply said reassuringly, "Do what is natural. It's your first time."

Yuka just murmured "Mmmm…" as she pursed her lips. She plucked off the remaining two moon stars, one in each hand. She took a determined step forward, unfurled her left arm and released the first moon star. Immediately she took a second step forward, slid out her right arm, and released the second moon star. The first moon star slid vertically through the first slit, barely fluttering the rice paper before sinking into the melon. Meanwhile, the second moon star sailed horizontally through the slit into the second melon. Yuka clapped her hands gleefully while jumping up and down.

"Well done, Empress Warrior Satoh. With more training, you'll be able to throw them both at the same time. Though a smaller weapon, you'll be able to replicate at will an unlimited number of moon stars. And with their accuracy, they are ideal for the eyes or gaps in between your enemy's armor," said the Guardian Crane as she and Yuka exited the circle.

Two other buffalos set up a melon and a rock on the same stone slab. The Guardian Tiger motioned for Sung to come forward with the staff.

"Emperor Warrior Kim," said the Guardian Tiger with his low voice, "You'll learn how to master the swift motions of the staff soon enough. Like Emperor Warrior Nguyen, you must strike the melon with full force, but strike the rock only with the end of your staff. Please strike when ready," instructed the Guardian Tiger as he stepped back.

Sung exhaled, looked at Daniel, and smiled. He held out his staff horizontally outward and then twirled it at a blazing speed over each side of his body before lifting it upward and swinging it down onto the melon, smashing it apart. He immediately lifted the staff and twirled it about his waist, turning all the way around before shoving one end of the staff into the rock, shattering it.

He resumed his ready position as he brought the staff back alongside of him and looked at the Guardian Tiger. "Me and the staff, we were practicing already this morning," said Sung.

"I see," said the Guardian Tiger as the stone slab was cleaned off by two buffalo attendants. "Well done, nonetheless."

The Guardian Panda walked into the center and motioned for Clara to stay where she was. She instinctively regripped the handle of her bow and felt a reassuring warmth from it. The buffalo attendants set up three stone columns away from her and placed a melon on each. In front of the middle melon, they placed another rice paper screen with three holes, two on top and one on the bottom.

The Guardian Panda looked at Clara's gaze and simply said, "Empress Warrior Wu, hit the two end melons to warm up your draw arm."

Clara nodded and looked at each of the melons. She exhaled and with her left hand, brought the bow alongside her left arm. She reached back into the quiver and pulled out a glowing jade tipped arrow and fitted it into place. With her left eye squinted, she drew back on the bow string and released the first arrow. Then instinctively, her right hand pulled out another arrow and shot it at the second melon. Both sunk into the melons with a thud.

The Guardian Panda then said, "That was too easy. Now deliver an arrow through each hole into the center melon. You may start."

Clara reset her footing and momentarily looked down. When she looked up, she quickly drew back an arrow and released it. Followed in quick succession, with two more. They each sailed through the holes, leaving the rice paper unscathed. Before the Guardian Panda could laud her for her accuracy, Clara released four more arrows that pierced the rice paper.

The Guardian Panda looked displeased at Clara and chided her, "Empress Warrior Wu, that is a fail."

Clara nodded slightly toward the Guardian Panda, "I'm sorry but I could not help myself. If you remove the rice paper screen, I think you'll see that I did not fail."

The Guardian Panda raised one of his black eye patches skeptically while the other warriors and guardians were suddenly curious. The Guardian Panda motioned to have the rice paper screen removed. When the buffalo attendants removed the rice paper screen, everyone could see that the four additional arrows formed and upward curve.

"No way! It's a smiley face!" exclaimed Sung jovially.

Daniel chuckled while Yuka, who looked confused initially until she recognized the smiley face and grinned.

The Guardian Panda nodded his head, "Well done. You perceived the target behind what you couldn't see and landed the arrows perfectly to form, what did Emperor Warrior Kim call it, a smiley face?"

Clara smiled confidently and said, "Yes, I just felt happy this morning."

With their introduction to weapons training done, the guardians took their warriors back to the grassy spot to hone their weapons training. This they did for the rest of the day.

Later that night, as the warriors and guardians gathered for dinner, the buffalo kitchen attendants brought out servings of melon soup, melon salad, and grilled melon.

As the last plate was placed on the table, Sung muttered mockingly, "Don't tell me these are the melons we used for target practice today?"

The Guardian Buffalo looked at Sung and retorted. "But of course, we couldn't let all your prep work go to waste," as the entire table burst into laughter.

TWENTY - ONE

"I wonder where Yuka is?" asked Sung as he had just sat down at the meal table along with Clara and Daniel as the four guardians were standing about the table.

"Empress Warrior Satoh mentioned she had to get something from her tent quarters," stated the Guardian Crane as Sung nodded.

"I wonder what's for breakfast?" wondered Sung. "So far we've had Chinese and Korean. Do you think they'll serve Vietnamese or Japanese food next?"

"I hope it's Vietnamese!" Daniel blurted out. "I feel like I haven't had my *mẹ's* cooking in such a long time, I kinda miss it."

"I can have either," said Clara as she eyed the kitchen staff, as she saw a flurry of activity among several pandas and cranes.

"*Ohayo gozaimasu!*" Yuka hollered out as she pranced toward the meal table.

Sung nodded back and responded with, "*Ohayo gozaimasu!*"

"Oh, do you know Japanese Sung?" asked a pleasantly surprised Yuka.

"I know a few phrases," said Sung proudly.

Daniel gave a quizzical look to which Yuka explained, "Oh, that's how you say good morning in Japanese. Looks like Sung knows a few Japanese phrases. I guess it's just a habit but since we're all Asian, I feel comfortable saying it to all of you."

"*Joh-eun achim!*" exclaimed Sung as he bowed lightly toward Yuka. "That's how we say good morning in Korean."

"*Jo sun!*" Clara responded in kind. "But in Mandarin, it's *zao shang hao!*"

"Good morning?" said Daniel sheepishly.

Everyone laughed as Daniel added, "Man, I really need to brush up on my Vietnamese."

The guardians' attention was brought back to the warriors as they began to take their seats.

Yuka stepped in behind Clara and placed a lovely *origami* crane on her plate.

Clara's eyes lit up as she asked, "What's this?" as Yuka continued going around the table placing an *origami* crane on each plate.

"It's an *origami* crane that I made for all of you! I'm sorry that I didn't have any prettier paper," said Yuka regrettably.

"It's very pretty! Thank you!" said Clara as she admired the neat folds in the paper that created the crane.

Both Sung and Daniel thanked Yuka as they turned their cranes in their hands. The Guardian Panda and Tiger struggled to pick theirs up with their paws while the Guardian Buffalo nudged his with his hoof. Yuka came to her Guardian Crane and presented her with a red paper *origami* crane. Her beady eyes lit up while the red feathers atop her head fluttered.

"This one is for you, Guardian Crane," said Yuka as the Guardian Crane carefully picked it up with her beak and glanced at it. She carefully placed it on the table in front of her as Yuka settled into her seat while saying, "One of the other cranes was nice enough to bring me a sheet of the red bamboo paper."

The Guardian Crane looked down at her and said, "This was very kind of you, Empress Warrior Satoh. I will cherish it."

"I'm glad you like them," said Yuka as the other guardians expressed their appreciation.

"We have prettier paper back at Crane Castle," said the Guardian Crane. "You may select whatever your heart desires and fold to your heart's content."

"Ooo! I would enjoy that so much... *Tamago!*" exclaimed Yuka as a plate of *tamago* was placed in front of her. With a hunger to satisfy, she picked up her chopsticks and began to eat along with everyone else.

After the breakfast of *tamago*, seaweed and rice, the warriors with their weapons were led to the Gauntlet.

Clara had a feeling that it would be another test, so she slung her bow across her chest and ensured that her ponytail was taut.

The Guardian Panda stood before the warriors as the other guardians stood off to the side against the stone face. "Warriors, today, you will further test and hone your weapons skills. Emperor Warrior Kim and Nguyen, you will quickly test your skills against larger objects. Empress Warrior Wu and Satoh, you will target moving objects."

The Guardian Buffalo walked forward and exchanged places with the Guardian Panda as buffalo attendants worked in the background, moving two large stones into place.

"Emperor Warrior Nguyen, please step up," asked the Guardian Buffalo. Daniel reacted quickly and held the club horn over his right shoulder.

"Do you see the two large stones behind me?" asked the Guardian Buffalo just as the buffalo attendants wheeled the stones on two sturdy bamboo platforms into place.

"Yes, I do," said Daniel as he peered over the Guardian Buffalo's shoulder.

"Each of the stones weigh about one ton and measures about ten feet high. I want you to knock the one on the left off its base with the Club Horn of *Kting Voar*, in whatever way you can."

Daniel nodded, walked past the Guardian Buffalo and looked at the large stone monoliths. *This was a lot different than crushing rocks*, he thought. But he was undeterred as he regripped his hold on the solid club horn.

He exhaled and gulped in a huge amount of air. He then ran up to the stone monolith with the club horn lifted over his head with both hands. With as much strength as he could muster, he brought down the tip of the club horn as the red jade glowed, onto the center of the monolith.

It shuddered, and the rock split partially along its entire height, but it did not topple. Daniel pulled back the club horn and he felt his whole body shudder from the powerful force he had just delivered. He was amazed at the large crack in the monolith. He took a few steps back and came at the monolith once more, delivering a strike that widened the split further. However, it still failed to topple. He pulled back once more and lunged at the rock but swung at the lower right side of the monolith. It cracked on a diagonal, shifting the monolith. Then, as he walked back and glanced up to see his fellow warriors and guardians watching him curiously, the solution dawned on him. He turned to face the monolith and brought the club horn down onto its right side, causing it to slide off along the crack and crash onto the ground. He jumped up and hit the remaining upper part of the slender piece, dead center, knocking it off balance and toppling it.

Daniel walked back up with the club horn over his right shoulder and asked, "How did I do?"

"You succeeded, and as you learned, your club horn has the power to deliver immense force. But you also need to be smart about where you deliver your strikes," praised the Guardian Buffalo. "Next time, knock it down in three strikes."

The Guardian Tiger walked up with Sung and simply said, "Topple the rock."

Sung nodded, twirled his staff a few times, and exhaled. He examined the monolith, trying to find its weak points. Looking down at the center of his staff, he saw the glow of the blue jade. Shifting his gaze upward at the monolith, he ran towards it as fast as he could. He shifted to the left and swung his staff low across the monolith. A large piece of the monolith shattered from its middle, but it did not topple. Sung came back around to admire his damage and looked at the top of the monolith when he had an idea.

He sauntered back to where he had started from and ran toward the monolith. Just as he got to the wooden platform, he planted one end of this staff into the ground and pushed off it, vaulting himself upward with his legs in the air. The top of the monolith came into view as he stuck his landing on top of it. Focusing on the center of the monolith, he leapt straight up and forcefully brought the tip of the staff down onto it. The resonance created by the Claw Staff pulverized the monolith as layer after layer crumbled away.

Sung stood in a middle of rubble and pulled out the staff, his jaw open in surprise. He rushed back to the amazement of his fellow warriors and exclaimed to the Guardian Tiger, "It actually worked!"

"Bro, that was amazing!" said Daniel admiringly as Sung nodded.

The Guardian Tiger lauded Sung and remarked, "The Claw Staff is a versatile weapon that can provide great force along its length. But you realized you could also use the resonance power of the blue jade to shatter the rock. Excellent."

Sung nodded as they walked back up as the Guardian Crane walked down with Yuka.

"For your task, Empress Warrior Satoh, you will replicate your moon star *shurikens* and attempt to hit as many targets in the air as possible."

"Mmmm," Yuka replied as she looked downrange as the Guardian Crane moved out of the way. She brought her two hands along the top of the white jade Moon Star in the middle of her waist and glided them back as six moon stars magically appeared. She quickly detached two and was ready.

"That's so cool," whispered Clara as Sung and Daniel nodded their heads.

Without any warning, two melons shot into the air from each side. Just as they were about to cross each other's paths, Yuka sent two moon stars, which hit the melons square on. Two more melons were shot from the right, and she sent up another two moon stars. Then another two were sent up from each side and Yuka flicked two more moon stars slicing through the air, hitting their targets.

But then two more melons flew up. She reached down and panicked, realizing no moon stars were left. The melons started to drop just as she had replicated another six moon stars. By the time she'd snapped one into each hand, the melons had already fallen to the ground.

Yuka looked into the air. No more melons appeared. "I missed them," she said, dejected, as the Guardian Crane approached her.

"You did well, but what was the important lesson you learned?" the Guardian Crane asked.

"I need to replicate as soon as I throw my last moon stars," she said wistfully.

"Yes, you should never just have only the white jade Moon Star *shuriken*. This was an important lesson. Your aim will always be true, but your aim won't matter if you do not have *shuriken*s to throw," the Guardian Crane said kindly.

They walked back up as the Guardian Panda walked down with Clara. As Yuka passed, Clara whispered to her, "You'll get them all next time." Yuka smiled at the encouragement.

The Guardian Panda turned to look at Clara and instructed, "Empress Warrior Wu, I believe you can guess what will come before you."

"Melons?" answered Clara cautiously.

"A good guess. For this task, there are ten jade-tipped arrows in your quiver. Get ready," said the Guardian Panda as Clara quickly drew an arrow. She felt her heart race as she heard the release of a mechanism that propelled a single melon into the air. She released her first arrow and nailed it. She drew another arrow as two more melons appeared, and in quick succession, she released two arrows that found their targets. Three more melons were suddenly high in the air, and she deftly released three arrows, which found their marks. Three more melons were released in sequence and she successively drew and released three arrows, lodging one into each melon as she pulled out her last arrow.

Then two melons launched from opposite sides, and she panicked. She had only one arrow left and had to choose a melon. *Which one?* she asked as the melons both approached the top of their identical arcs. Then she reset her footing, squinted her eye and released the last arrow. It flew straight and true and sunk itself through both melons as they crossed each other, sending the conjoined melons straight to the ground with a thud.

"That was dope!" said Sung and Daniel elicited astonishment. Yuka gently clapped for Clara as she let out a sigh of relief.

"That was a trick task, wasn't it?" asked Clara of the Guardian Panda.

"It would have been fine if you had just hit one of the melons, but you were quick to reassess the situation and used your last arrow wisely," said the Guardian Panda.

With her bow slung across her chest, she brought her fist into her open palm and bowed slightly.

They were led back to the Portal Circle, and the warriors stood by their respective Portal Books. They placed their weapons into the stands by the stone columns and stood ready for their next task.

The Guardian Panda stepped into the center of the Portal Circle and spoke. "You have now been through your three phases of training, manifesting, conjuring, and invoking your Qi elemental powers, harnessing the martials arts of your heritage and wielding your jade powered weapons. You cannot learn new Qi elements all at once. So your guardians and I have been selective in your next Qi element. Emperor Warrior Kim, you will learn how to form an ice bridge that will allow you to travel over obstacles."

Sung's eyes lit up in anticipation.

"Emperor Warrior Nguyen, you will learn how to create thrust, allowing you to propel yourself through the air," said the Guardian Panda.

With a tone of uncertainty, Daniel asked, "I'm going to be able to fly?"

"In a manner, yes," said the Guardian Panda. "And Empress Warrior Satoh, you will learn how to master the air, so that you may fly."

Yuka's eyes lit up as she asked, "I'm going to be able to fly as well?"

"In the truest sense," said the Guardian Panda. "We can't have an Empress Warrior of the Crane Kingdom who can't fly."

The Guardian Panda turned and looked at Clara who was brimming with excitement of somehow soaring or traveling through the air.

"Empress Warrior Wu," said the Guardian Panda in a serious tone.

"Yes?" said an eager Clara.

"You will learn how to create a sinkhole."

All excitement faded from her face as she looked at her guardian. "There's no flying for me?" she asked.

"You are of the earth Wu element, you are earthbound," said the Guardian Panda.

Each of the warriors began brushing out their new Qi element in their Portal Book. It didn't take long before Yuka gleefully manifested the Japanese character *tobu*, to *fly*. Her elation echoed through the Portal Circle as her manifested Qi element floated toward her and seeped into her chest. She continued to manifest more as the Guardian Crane watched her.

Soon, Sung manifested the Korean word, *dali* for *bridge*, letting out an excited outburst. The Guardian Tiger watched him as he manifested additional Qi elements.

Clara was next, willing the fiery embers of the Chinese character *tei hum*, *sinkhole*, to lift off the page and seep into her body as she watched unenthusiastically. She let out a sigh. She wished her Qi element was more uplifting.

Daniel was still learning the Vietnamese language, and the Guardian Buffalo patiently coached him through it. Though it took some additional time, he was able to manifest the Vietnamese word *đẩy*, for *thrust*. Once he had done so, a sense of validation filled him. He was coming into his own and starting to reclaim his Vietnamese heritage, something that he had been indifferent to for most of his teenage years.

Clara watched Sung as he bounced toward a patch of open grass. The Guardian Tiger was gesturing from Sung's feet to some distance away as Sung nodded. As the Guardian Tiger took a few steps back, Sung conjured up the Qi element for bridge, and an arched ice bridge suddenly appeared. It was beautiful, and Clara admired how the ice glistened in the sunlight. Soon, Sung invoked his Qi element to evaporate the ice bridge. The Guardian Tiger came back to Sung and after a bit of coaching, he stepped back and Sung tried again. He excitedly licked his lips, looked ahead, and then down at his feet. He conjured up the Qi element for bridge, pointed to his feet, and cast it out.

The ice formed at his feet and built up behind him, pushing him along the ice bridge to his surprise as he lost his balance. His arms flailed as he fell to the ground with a thud. As the fifty-foot-long ice bridge finished forming, Sung laughed heartily and sat up. He looked over and saw Clara looking at him, and he pointed to the ice bridge with a big grin. She nodded casually as she turned away to watch Daniel.

The Guardian Buffalo was coaching Daniel in an open clearing. There was a look of apprehension on Daniel's face as the Guardian Buffalo stepped back. His face said it all as he huffed and puffed a few times before looking down at his feet. He conjured up the Vietnamese word for thrust, and the Qi element ignited what looked like fire beneath his feet. Suddenly, it propelled Daniel about twenty feet up as he let out a few screams of fright and delight. Almost immediately, however, Daniel's upward flight stopped and he started to freefall back down to earth, where the Guardian Buffalo stepped in and caught him. Daniel leaned back, pointed upward and shook his fists back and forth in excitement. He leapt out of the Guardian Buffalo's arms, eager to try again.

Clara heard the Guardian Crane behind her and she turned to see Yuka gracefully hovering about ten feet in the air. She was poised and her arms were outstretched, giving her balance. There was not a worry on her smiling expression, and she caught Clara looking at her. She gently waved to Clara, who waved back. Yuka was a natural, and the Wu element air was perfect for her. Yuka invoked her Qi element and swooped upward, immediately whooshing through the air, defying all tethers to the world of Azen.

"Are you ready to try invoking your new Qi element?" asked the Guardian Panda.

Clara turned back to the Guardian Panda with a sigh and nodded. He led her back to the beginning of the Gauntlet, where there was a large clearing.

"When invoking the Qi element for a sinkhole, the stronger the fist, the larger and deeper the sinkhole will be. Do you understand?" the Guardian Panda asked.

Clara nodded.

She focused on the clearing in front of her and imagined a sinkhole appearing about fifty feet out. It would be a small sinkhole, maybe about ten feet across and deep she thought. She exhaled and conjured the Qi element for *sinkhole* and it appeared, dancing on her fingertips. She heard the glee of her fellow warriors and jealously clenched her fist. She invoked it as she flung it from her hand.

The Qi element sped away and seeped into the ground, where a loud rumbling emerged. The ground around Clara and the Guardian Panda shook. He quickly turned to Clara and threw her over his shoulder before she could react. Her eyes widened as the ground behind her started to sink away as the crumbling earth raced toward her and the Guardian Panda. The rumbling soon stopped and the Guardian Panda put Clara down as he turned around.

In front of them was not a small sinkhole but a massive sinkhole that was about thirty feet wide. How deep it was, they did not know. The Guardian Panda looked down at her and asked, "I thought we agreed on a small sinkhole?"

Clara who was still taking in the large sinkhole before her, sheepishly shrugged her shoulders and muttered, "Sorry?"

The Guardian Panda gently nodded and said, "Empress Warrior Wu, you may now fill it."

A patch of ice suddenly appeared to the left of Clara's feet startling her as Sung suddenly slid to a stop on it. She looked behind him and saw a sloping ice bridge. Soon Daniel awkwardly floated downward as he controlled his thrust while Yuka gracefully floated in as they looked at the large gaping hole in the ground.

"Holy moly," said Daniel. "Did you create that, Clara?"

Clara nodded and said, "I guess I don't know my own strength."

Yuka looked on in astonishment, "Thank goodness I can fly now."

Everyone laughed, but secretly, Clara wished that she could fly somehow as well.

TWENTY - TWO

Clara found herself mulling at the end of the table where the Guardian Crane usually sat. After another delightful dinner that showed the numerous and creative ways eggs could be cooked, the guardians were nowhere in sight.

The illumination jades gave the area a peaceful glow, and the moons were radiant in the night sky. They were different than the white pearl in the sky back on Earth. These moons had different hues, from blue to salmon to pink and green. They were beautiful, but she feared what they portended. The closest moon was almost full as she stared upward.

"Clara," blurted out Sung as he surfed over from his ice bridge. He stepped off it, turned around and evaporated it. "Pretty cool, right?"

Clara looked at him with a frown and nodded.

"Hey, what's wrong?" asked Sung as he took the seat opposite of her.

Clara turned to him and in a grumpy tone, blurted out, "Why couldn't I fly like you guys?"

Sung's empathetic eyes lit up, "Oh I see. Well, if it makes you feel any better, I'm not really flying but kind of surfing on this ice bridge."

"Well, it's still way cooler than making big holes in the ground," said a despondent Clara.

"But you are the earth element, which really can't fly."

"Sure it can!" exclaimed Clara.

"How?" asked Sung.

"Dust! Dust flies through the air!" said Clara happily.

"So, you're telling me, you want to be known as the Dust Empress?" asked Sung.

A moment of silence passed before they broke out into laughter.

"Well, when you say it like that, it doesn't sound that impressive anymore," said Clara with a smile.

There was a stumbling of feet as Daniel landed with an awkward thud by the table's edge. "Whoa, still working on those landings," he said.

However, Yuka gracefully flew over and floated down effortlessly.

"Looks like you're a natural at this," remarked Daniel.

"It just feels so right, like I was meant to fly."

"Lucky you," said Clara with a hint of grumpiness.

"What's wrong?" asked Yuka as she stared at Clara.

Sung interjected on her behalf, "Oh nothing…"

"I wish I could fly like you guys! All I can do is make big holes in the ground or split it!" said a bitter Clara. "Why couldn't I fly on a bed of dust?" asked Clara rhetorically as she stood up with one arm shot straight up into the air with her chin held up high.

There was an awkward silence until Sung said, "I almost wanted to call her the Dust Empress."

Clara's flying pose collapsed into laughter as everyone else joined in.

"But that's a great idea! Let's give ourselves superhero names!" exclaimed Daniel. "I mean we have all these powers; we might as well be superheroes."

"Yah, that's a great idea!" said Sung.

But Clara interjected, "I don't know about that. I mean we do have official titles already. Emperor or Empress Warrior that, Warrior of the Wu element earth, air, fire and water."

"Right but that's the point. Those titles are officially boring. These names are just for us, for fun," said Daniel.

"I kinda like my title, 'Empress Warrior of the Wu Element Air,'" said Yuka proudly.

"There's nothing wrong your title. Come on, just play along, like I'll go first. Hmmm, let me think," said Daniel as he pondered.

"Hothead!" said Sung to everyone's laughter.

"Very funny," said a smiling Daniel. "No, I was thinking, 'Scorch.'"

"Scorch," said Sung. "I like that. Then I'm going to call myself 'Iceman!'"

"Very original," said Daniel sardonically. "How about you, Yuka?"

Yuka looked at her three friends and gracefully invoked her Qi element, floated about a foot off the ground and said, "Airess."

"See, she's a natural. She didn't even think about it," said Daniel. "And what about you Clara?"

"Definitely not Dust Empress," said Sung.

Clara glanced at Sung with a smile. She stood up and looked at her three friends, "You can call me 'Quake,'" she said.

Sung looked at Clara with wide eyed surprise as Daniel rushed over to him, grabbed Sung's arm feigning fear and blurted out, "Save me Sung, I'm quaking in my shoes!"

Everyone laughed heartily and Yuka turned to Clara, "I like it, it sounds really strong."

Clara pursed her lips and nodded at Yuka, who said underneath her breath, "Quake."

"So these are our secret superhero names, right?" asked Yuka.

"Yep!" answered Daniel.

"You know what else we should have?" asked Sung.

"What?" asked Daniel curiously.

"A secret bow or handshake!" said Sung.

Yuka clapped her hands gently as she gleefully said, "Yes! It'll be our secret."

"How about this one?" asked Daniel as he folded his arms over each other and nodded sternly.

"Too serious!" said Sung. "How about this? A secret first bump?"

Sung thrust his fist toward Daniel, who did the same. Sung quickly performed about five additional hand gestures that Daniel was able to mimic with enthusiasm.

"Too hard," said Yuka, looking dismayed.

"I know," said Clara.

"Really? What's your idea, Clara?" asked Yuka.

"Yah, what you got, Quake?" teased Daniel.

Clara looked at her fellow warriors. In a simple motion, she brought her clenched fists together, with the back of her hands facing outward at chest level with her elbows along her sides. She then nodded slightly and looked back up.

Daniel looked at Sung and they both did the same, followed by Yuka and they all nodded to each other.

"With our arms like this, it looks like an A," said Clara. "For Azen."

"That's smooth," said Daniel as he nodded approvingly. With everyone still holding the pose, in unison they nodded and said to each other, "For Azen."

TWENTY - THREE

The Guardian Panda's nose twitched in the darkness as he had just fallen into a sound sleep. His body heaved heavily and let out a low slow breath when abruptly, the seam to the entrance of his heavy cloth tent split open. Muffled footsteps rushed in as the light from an illumination jade torch filled the tent.

"Guardian Panda!" a panda guard exclaimed.

The Guardian Panda's eye opened wide as three panda guards approached the edge of his bed. His second eye fluttered opened as he pushed himself into an upright position and asked, "What's the matter?"

The three panda guards immediately bowed, and the lead panda simply said, "Empress Warrior Wu is missing."

The eyes of the Guardian Panda opened wide, and he asked, "What do you mean she's missing? Have you checked the kitchen area? Perhaps she wanted a snack?"

"Yes. As instructed, we have been discreetly peeking in on the warriors to ensure their safety and in this check, she was missing. We confirmed that all the other warriors are safe. We have checked the Portal Circle as well as the Gauntlet and felt you needed to be told immediately."

The Guardian Panda was up on his feet and reached for his bamboo staff. He took a step toward his wardrobe and plucked from it, a bamboo stalk about 2 feet long. With a twist, the light from the illumination jade torch within escaped from the slit and filled the room. He securely fitted the jade torch over his bamboo staff.

He faced the lead panda guard and instructed, "Let's form search parties immediately. We'll radiate out from her tent quarters. It's dark, let's give word to the cranes to enlist their help as they can cover more ground more quickly."

"Yes," the panda guard retorted. "The Guardian Crane is already aware and is assembling a search team."

"Good," said the Guardian Panda as he walked around and past the other guards who followed him, "Let's find our empress warrior and hope the Warlock has not worked his conniving powers into Azen."

Pandas fanned out in search parties of five. They were instructed to re-check all inspected areas again and once an area was searched, one panda was left behind in case Clara returned. The tigers and the buffalos were also on alert but stayed within their tent compounds. Cranes launched into the night sky to canvas the ground from above.

The Guardian Panda's eyes were tense as he led a search party with the three guards who had come into his tent. He focused as his padded feet muffled the sounds of his anxious footsteps. The light of the jade torch brightened the way, but he still meandered carefully among the grassy knolls, bamboo stalks, boulders, and trees. He was quiet, not wanting to reveal his anxiety to the panda guards, who must have felt guilty for not keeping a better eye on Clara.

The Guardian Panda came upon the boulder where he had first met Clara and where she had startled him. He squinted a few times and looked about. No sign of Clara. He walked past the boulder as one panda guard stayed behind. He took the barely lit path that Clara had followed, and soon came to the grassy spot where he believed the Portal Book had materialized her. He looked up as he heard the flutter of a crane's wings and realized that they had expanded their search area.

He turned back to the two pandas, who looked anxious as he nodded to them to continue onward, leaving one guard behind. He took about ten steps when he abruptly stopped. His snout turned northerly and there was a glint in his eye. He marched off silently in that direction as the lead panda guard followed him.

They trudged through another grassy patch and came upon another path. The Guardian Panda looked down and with his jade torch, he thought he could make out depressions. "Shoe prints," whispered the Guardian Panda. He looked up with anticipation, "Hurry!"

The path soon became overgrown in tall bamboo stalks until it ended at a large clearing, encircled with bamboo stalks. In the middle was a low circular wall of neatly assembled rocks. It was topped off with a flat piece of stone shaped in a slight arc. Together they formed a neat circular stone wall. The Guardian Panda's eyes blinked a few times and along the side was a young girl, whose elbows rested on the stone wall with an illumination jade placed atop of it. It was Clara.

"We've found..." whispered the lead panda guard but he stopped mid-sentence as the Guardian Panda brought his finger to this mouth. He turned toward Clara and just watched her. He turned to the lead panda guard and whispered for him to go back and let everyone know that Empress Warrior Wu was found. He alone would bring her back to the compound he added. The lead panda guard nodded and sauntered off.

The Guardian Panda stepped into the clearing toward Clara. He saw that she had her bow and quiver leaned up against the low stone wall. Soon enough, his muffled footsteps caught Clara's attention as she turned her head and she saw the Guardian Panda approaching.

"Guardian Panda," she said. "Why are you up?"

He stopped and settled down next to her in a big ball of white and black fur. He turned to her with his tranquil eyes and said, "Empress Warrior Wu, we were looking for you when it was discovered you were missing from your tent."

Her eyes widened in surprise, "Oh! I'm so sorry! I didn't mean to make you worry."

"No concerns, Empress Warrior Wu. It was only a small search party and I've sent them back," said the Guardian Panda convincingly. "As long as you are safe. However, if you should wander off next time, please inform one of the guards."

"I will. I didn't mean to. I've been exploring a bit for a couple of nights now, usually when everyone is asleep. I would have returned earlier, but then I found this pool."

"The Origins Pool," muttered the Guardian Panda.

"The what?" asked the inquisitive Clara.

"The Origins Pool," said the Guardian Panda more clearly. "And why did you decide to stay?"

Clara looked out into the very still pool of water. She could see hers and the Guardian Panda's reflection, along with two moons reflected behind them, looking back at her. "It was so peaceful and I guess… I needed to get away from everything for a little bit. I miss my parents."

The Guardian Panda's ears fluttered, "I understand," he said. "Do you know why we call it the Origins Pool?

Clara looked up curiously, "No."

"Well, throughout Azen, we have come across small bodies of water like this, and we discovered that some of them have strange characteristics."

Clara's body straightened up a bit as her curiosity grew.

"This peculiar body of water has the odd power to show you your parents," said the Guardian Panda.

Clara's eyes widened, "No way! Really? How?"

"Well, let me finish. We first discovered its peculiar powers entirely by accident. When one day long ago, a Guardian Panda waded into the water with his warrior nearby. He happened to think about his mother and suddenly, an image of his mother appeared in the pool, and he was scared right out of his fur. What we discovered was that a powered jade invoked some unknown intrinsic power in the body of water. That's when we also discovered that the warrior could see his parents. When we discovered this peculiar power, we studied it as much as we could, knowing that our warriors' time was limited in our realm. Since then, we built this wall around the body of water, to honor it. Thus we call it the Origins Pool."

"Wow, that's so cool! So, I can see my parents?"

"Well, only one parent. It seems a warrior can only summon one parent at a time, and then a day or two later, the other parent. Our panda researchers could only theorize that the immense power to traverse the distance between our realm and your earthly realm must tax the pool. That reminds me, it seems that when either of your parents appear, there is usually water involved."

"Really? Do you think somehow water connects our worlds?" asked Clara.

"We think so, but we can't be sure. But in all the images, there is usually water," stated the Guardian Panda.

"I see. Can we try now?" asked an eager Clara.

"Certainly," said a smiling Guardian Panda.

The Guardian Panda leaned over and onto his forearms of the stone brim of the pool as Clara cautiously did the same. He gestured at the bow and Clara nodded. She brought up the bow, rested it on the stone brim cap and looked up toward the Guardian Panda.

"Now, think about who you want to see, your mother or your father," asked the Guardian Panda.

"This is so hard. I don't want to decide," she said grumpily.

"You must for now. We'll return in a couple of days to see your other parent."

"Fine. I choose my mom. I'll see you soon, *Baba*," said Clara sadly.

The Guardian Panda continued, "While touching the jade on the bow, dip your fingers into the water and think of your mother."

Clara nodded her head and looked into the dark calm water of the Origins Pool. With her fingers deftly on the Bamboo Jade, she dipped the tips of her fingers into the cool water and whispered, "Mom."

For a few seconds, the water remained black until an ethereal image started to float to the surface, causing Clara to stare at it with spellbound awe. The image seemed out of focus, like a blurred silhouette, but as it rose from the depths of the pool, it sharpened into an image of her mother. Clara crooked her neck a little as she seemed to be looking upward toward her mother.

Despite the angle, Clara could see that it was a still image of her mother. She had on her apron and was holding a knife in one hand and a leek in the other.

"It's my mom!" exclaimed an elated Clara. "But this angle is so odd, and it's blurry."

"What is she doing?" asked the Guardian Panda.

"It looks like she's cooking dinner?"

"And where does she usually cook dinner?" asked the Guardian Panda.

"In the kitchen, of course," said Clara mischievously.

"Of course, but I meant, think about where the water is, as that is how the Origins Pool connects to your earthly world."

Clara looked at the perspective of the image again and gasped, "I know! It's the water faucet! I'm seeing her from the water coming out of the water faucet! Wow, that is strange."

"Your mother looks fine," said the Guardian Panda. "She looks rather young for a mother."

"Yah," said Clara as she added with a sardonic tone. "She says something about Asians don't raisin."

"Raisin?" asked the Guardian Panda.

"Never mind," answered Clara with a grin as she looked back down into the water. "Mom, I'm sorry for the other day. Oh I wonder what she is making! What I wouldn't do for her dumplings! Oh, nothing wrong with the dumplings here on Azen. It's just that my mommy's dumplings are special…" but before she could finish, a voice bellowed from above.

"We found you!" exclaimed Yuka as she and the Guardian Crane spiraled downward. The Guardian Crane landed, and Yuka promptly hopped off and ran toward Clara.

Clara rose and before she could flick her fingers of the water, Yuka threw herself at her and hugged her.

"I was so worried about you!" said Yuka.

Clara was surprised by the hug but smiled as she hugged Yuka back. "I'm okay. Really, I am. I went for a walk and found this pool and stayed a bit. I guess I lost track of time. I didn't know that I was going to cause such an alarm."

The girls pulled back from each other as Yuka smiled and wiped away her blurry eyes.

"Empress Warrior Wu is unharmed?" asked the Guardian Crane of the Guardian Panda.

The Guardian Panda nodded his head, "Yes, she is all right. She found the Origins Pool and was distracted by it."

"What's the Origins Pool?" asked Yuka.

Clara explained the peculiar and singular powers of the Origins Pool to her, and Yuka blurted out, "I want to see my father!" A sense of urgency filled each of her words as she turned toward the Guardian Crane.

The Guardian Crane's eyes looked down at Yuka, "Certainly."

Yuka then looked at Clara, "If you don't mind, I'd like to see my father alone."

Clara detected something heavy in Yuka's request as she looked at the Guardian Panda. "Sure. We'll leave you alone with you and your Guardian Crane..." but she couldn't complete her sentence.

"Just me, please," pleaded Yuka as she looked up toward the Guardian Crane. "Can you just show me how?"

"As you wish, Empress Warrior Satoh," said the Guardian Crane.

Clara gently picked up her bow and quiver as Yuka detached her Moon Star. Her head was slightly downcast, and the atmosphere became awkward as Clara mumbled, "I'll see you tomorrow?"

Yuka nodded and looked up at Clara with a soft smile, "Thank you."

"Come now, Empress Warrior Wu, we need to return you to your tent," said the Guardian Panda reassuringly. Clara nodded and walked alongside him as she turned for one more look at Yuka, who appeared unnerved. She saw the Guardian Crane giving her the same instructions in the soft glow of the illumination jade that she left on the brim of the pool. Soon the Guardian Crane bowed and took her leave of Yuka, staying by the edge of the bamboo stalks that encircled the Origins Pool.

Yuka looked cautiously into the dark water before her. She could see her dark image reflected in the water. She kneeled and with her white jade moon star in one hand, she reached out into the water with the other. She closed her eyes and in a fraction of a thought, she opened them. She waited and nothing appeared. She bit her lip and closed her eyes once again and reopened them. Then from the depths of the dark water, an image started to float upward as her fingers trembled. The image became larger and clearer until she gasped.

Tears seeped in around Yuka's eyes and against her choked voice, she blurted out *father* in Japanese, "*Otosan!*"

TWENTY - FOUR

"Whoa!" exclaimed Sung. "You got to see your mom? How is she?" Sung asked Clara the next morning at the meal table.

"She looked good. Making dinner as usual. What I would do for some spicy wontons just about now!" said Clara hungrily.

"Let me get this straight: The water in this Origins Pool is somehow connected to the water on Earth, and if our parents happen to be near water, we can see them?" asked Daniel.

"Yep. Don't ask me how, but I saw my mother, and I'm happy," said Clara with a smile just as Yuka flew down and landed softly.

"*Ohayo gozaimasu!*" Yuka greeted as she skipped over to her fellow warriors as they echoed back in an awkward chorus of, "*Ohayo gozaimasu!*"

Yuka giggled and said, "Your Japanese is getting much better! From here on, let's greet each other in our Asian languages and say it back. It'll be so fun to learn your languages!"

Daniel looked around at Clara's and Sung's smiling expressions and said, "I'm down with that."

"What are you down with?" asked Yuka.

Everyone chuckled, "You know, 'down with that,' I agree with you," explained Daniel.

"I see," said Yuka with a smile.

"Yuka," Clara asked in a cautious tone, "Did you see your father?"

Yuka's eyes lit up and she responded, "I did! He's fine. I… I… just hadn't seen him in a while and he looked good. I hope he's home when I return to our world."

"Awesome! I'm glad you saw him," replied Clara.

"Man, I want to go the Origins Pool too!" said Daniel. "I really miss my mẹ."

"I miss both of my parents," said Sung, to which Daniel replied, "Well at least you have two parents, it's just my mother and me."

"Oh, sorry man," said Sung regretfully, but Daniel interjected, "Oh, I didn't mean to make you feel bad."

Clara was about to say something when the voice of the Guardian Panda bellowed over to them. "Warriors, please come to breakfast. We have a long training session for you today."

After a light breakfast of congee, salted eggs, slivers of seaweed, and *tamago*, the warriors were led back to the Gauntlet. They were met there by four additional armored soldiers, one representing each kingdom.

The warriors looked at these new soldiers in awe. Their armor was impressive. Holding a bamboo jade tipped spear, the panda soldier was slender and muscular. His bamboo armor fit across his chest and back perfectly. Across the front of his chest was a glowing green jade, and his Clawdium shoulder guards looked imposing. A cap from a bamboo stalk fit neatly atop his head, acting as a helmet. A red streak ran along the front of the helmet with a green jade in the middle. Along the sides of the helmet were Chinese characters marking a high rank of some sort.

Down the entire length of the buffalo's back was an interlocking system of armored plates, like the scales of a fish. The buffalo's entire torso was covered in flexible Clawdium chain mail. Across his chest was a single red jade.

Being the most agile, the tiger soldier wore a flexible bodysuit that fit him like a wetsuit. His furry limbs protruded from the bodysuit in an imposing manner. Across his chest was embedded a blue jade. Armored gauntlets covered his forearms, where three slender razor-sharp blades extended his reach by about a foot.

The large battle crane had little armor other than the Clawdium mesh that ran down its feathered chest and belly. A white jade glistened at the center. But what was most impressive were the gleaming blades that ran down the outer edges of its wings. When the winged blades caught glints of sunlight, they looked even more impressive.

"Empress and emperor warriors," said the Guardian Panda as he stood in between the four warriors and four kingdom soldiers. "I'd like to introduce to you to the heads of our elite battle teams in our kingdoms."

The four kingdom soldiers bowed to the warriors who reciprocated in kind.

"The tiger soldier, *Hanro*, is Head of the Prowlers, an agile and ferocious group of tiger soldiers. The buffalo, *Vo*, is Head of the Rammers, who are trained at ramming and goring their opponents. The majestic crane who you see, *Sho*, heads up the Top Talon program that develops the most gifted and agile of all crane combat aviators. And finally, the panda who you see before you, *Xi Peng*, is Head of the Pandemonium Squad," the Guardian Panda announced as he continued.

Sung leaned slightly into Clara and whispered, "*Hanro*, he's like Wolverine."

Clara looked up at Sung and then at the three Clawdium blades that extended beyond Hanro's fist and nodded in agreement.

"They, along with soldiers from each of their teams they command, have created an obstacle course that runs down the Gauntlet. However, the Top Talon cranes will not take part, as all the Warlock creatures are earthbound. They will be observers instead. And this is a good opportunity to show you their *katana* wings.

"As you look down the Gauntlet, you will see a white line before you and a white line at the end. Your goal is to use all your training to cross that line. Are there any questions?"

"Won't our weapons hurt them?" asked Sung with a concerned tone.

"The battle armor that you see on our soldiers is protected by their jades. They will be fine, as long as you aim for their armor," said the Guardian Tiger as Sung nodded in understanding.

"What if we fail?" asked Yuka.

"No warrior has ever failed the final Gauntlet run, as the Portal Book has chosen you as our empress and emperor warriors," said the Guardian Panda. "Trust in your abilities and capabilities."

"Very well, then. Elite soldiers, please prepare your attacks," said the Guardian Panda as the elite soldiers nodded and headed into the Gauntlet.

Clara felt some apprehension and wondered if her fellow warriors felt the same. But they all looked so calm. Even Yuka looked confident, but it was apparent that out of the group, Yuka was the natural master of her Qi elemental powers.

The Guardian Crane walked in front of the young warriors, studying them, and said, "You'll all do fine. Trust your instincts."

The warriors let out a collective sigh as Daniel rolled his shoulders back and forth. "This is how I loosen up before swimming, but this is not swimming," he said casually.

An echoey squawk was heard from somewhere down the Gauntlet, and the Guardian Panda's ears perked up. He walked toward the warriors and guardians and motioned for everyone to move behind a bamboo screen. He reached into a pouch and pulled from it four bamboo disks. Carved into each one was the shape of each animal. After placing them back in, he looked up at the Guardian Crane and asked if she wouldn't mind picking out the first disk.

The Guardian Crane nodded and placed her beak into the pouch as the bamboo disks rattled. She pulled out the first disk and turned to show it to the others. "Buffalo!" announced the Guardian Panda. "Emperor Warrior Nguyen, you are first. Please go with your guardian."

Daniel exhaled and looked to his fellow warriors. "Wish me luck," he said. He walked slowly to the start of the Gauntlet with the Guardian Buffalo. "Now remember, Emperor Warrior Nguyen, it's not always about strength. Trust your instincts and you should be fine."

"Thank you," said Daniel as he stared down the Gauntlet, where he saw nothing. The sporadic number of boulders along the sides of the Gauntlet were still there. But what was new were the number of bamboo walls erected strategically along its length, where he surmised the soldiers were lying in wait. Along the sides of the stone wall were several ledges, where he spotted more bamboo walls.

"You may begin once I reach the end of the Gauntlet," said the Guardian Buffalo as he began to walk toward the other end.

Once Daniel saw the Guardian Buffalo had reached the end, he looked left, then right and back to the center. He exhaled and steeled his nerves as he tightened his grip on the club horn. He crossed the white line.

His senses tingled as he held the club horn in front of him and the red jade glinted in the sunlight. He cautiously approached the first set of bamboo screens on each side. His ears perked up as the bamboo screens crashed to the ground, revealing a large buffalo-shaped wooden creature on wheels. The wooden attack dummy charged towards him, pushed from behind by two large buffalos. He was turning towards it when a crash from behind made him glance back at a second attack dummy bearing down on him. He re-focused on the first attack and ran towards the charging dummy. With his club horn raised above his head, he brought it down on the dummy's wooden forehead, shattering it and burying it into the ground. He turned backwards toward the second attacker, but it was already too close.

Invoking his *thrust* Qi element, *đẩy*, Daniel soared upward as the attack dummy came to a halt. As the two buffalos pulled it back, Daniel now had the advantage. He flipped midflight and came charging down on the wooden attack dummy with his club horn, caving it in. The four buffalos knelt on their knees, and Daniel landed on the ground and continued his advance down the Gauntlet.

He regripped his club horn as he approached another set of bamboo walls on each side. He rushed past the walls, hoping to get a jump on the next attack, but there was nothing behind them until he heard a bow string. He instinctively swung around as he invoked a Qi element and a thick fire wall appeared. The arrow travelled through it and reappeared as a charred sliver of itself that fell to the ground with a whimper.

A line of panda archers suddenly appeared, releasing several arrows behind Daniel. He swung around, throwing up a second fire wall that burned the incoming arrows. The two fire walls burned bright and shielded Daniel as he sent several fireballs toward the first set of archers, who ducked down. He spun around to send up another flurry of fireballs, forcing those archers to duck down as well.

Daniel once again thrust himself upward and sent several fireballs into the chests of each panda, knocking them harmlessly onto their haunches. He quickly flew left as an arrow barely missed him. As he came out of the arc, he flew toward the second set of panda archers just as they took aim. He quickly invoked three fireballs, which hit each panda squarely in the chest and knocked them against the stone wall with a thud. One of the soldiers tilted his bamboo helmet backward and blinked a few times as Daniel nodded at him.

Daniel had just landed on the ground when four tigers came running at him at full speed. He threw up two fire walls, but the tigers nimbly ran around them and launched themselves at Daniel. Daniel sidestepped as the ferocious tigers scattered when one amazingly flipped and twisted backward toward Daniel.

Daniel's eyes lit up as he intuitively swung the club horn. It connected with the tiger's head as he fell to the ground. Meanwhile, the other three had circled back, and one leapt at Daniel, its broad chest exposed. Daniel executed a spinning back kick, and his foot connected with the tiger's chest, knocking him back. Before the next tiger could react, Daniel crouched down and invoked a fireball, which sent him flying backwards. The final tiger lunged at Daniel, who he evaded by quickly thrusting upward. As the tiger looked up, he was met with a fireball that flew down onto his back, forcing him onto his stomach.

As Daniel hovered in the air, marveling at his work, something strong caught the back of his heels, turning him upside down in mid-air as his thrust Qi element sent him into the ground. Dirt scraped across his chin as his chest got the brunt of the landing. He quickly shook it off and rose into a crouch as the Head of the Rammers charged at him, horns lowered. There was no time, and Daniel barely sidestepped the massive buffalo as it spun around for another charge.

His heart rate quickened as he brought the Club Horn of *Kting Voar* up and downward onto the powerful buffalo's horn and the thud reverberated through Daniel's forearms. The Head of the Rammers stumbled and took a couple of steps backward before falling onto its bottom in a daze with its tongue popping out.

A worried Daniel took a couple steps toward the buffalo. It gazed up at Daniel with its eyes and raised its right hoof at him and nodded. Daniel stopped and knew the buffalo was fine. He looked to this right and quickly covered the last ten feet to cross the white line as the Guardian Buffalo looked at him.

"Well done, Emperor Warrior Nguyen, you have successfully navigated the Gauntlet," said the Guardian Buffalo.

Behind the bamboo wall, the three guardians listened calmly with their heads bowed as the three warriors cringed upon hearing the calamitous sounds coming from the Gauntlet. A loud and long squawk was heard, and the guardians lifted their heads. The Guardian Panda then said, "Emperor Warrior Nguyen has crossed successfully."

The warriors' eyes lit up as they let out a collective sigh of relief. "I'm so nervous," said Yuka as she brought up her clasped hands.

"Guardian Crane, will you pick out the next warrior?" asked the Guardian Panda as he lightly shook the pouch.

The warriors watched with anticipation as the Guardian Crane reached into the pouch with her slender beak and plucked out the disk with a winged and beaked silhouette.

Yuka's eyes widened as she muttered, "It's me."

The Guardian Crane plopped the disk into the waiting paw of the Guardian Panda and stated, "Yes, Empress Warrior Satoh. Please follow me."

Yuka pursed her lips and looked at her two fellow warriors as they smiled encouragingly to her. She turned and followed the Guardian Crane to the white line.

"Trust in your training, Empress Warrior Satoh. I'll be waiting for you at the end," said the Guardian Crane.

Yuka exhaled, and with both hands on the Moon Star, she fanned back along her waist replicating four stars on each side. She plucked two moon stars, one in each hand and looked at her Guardian Crane and said firmly, "Ready."

Yuka kept her eye on the Guardian Crane as she rose and flew away. When she reached the end of the Gauntlet, Yuka could see the silhouettes of Daniel and his Guardian Buffalo. A squawk breached the air and with her moon stars at the ready, she crossed the white line.

She stepped timidly into the Gauntlet, approaching it cautiously. The two bamboo walls on each side crashed to the ground as she approached them. Two wooden attack dummies shaped like large dogs, each pushed by a buffalo, approached her from each side. She immediately looked left and right, releasing a moon star in each direction that sunk into the center of the foreheads of the attack dummies. But they did not stop, so Yuka instinctively invoked the *fly* Qi element, *tobu*, and flew upward. She plucked another pair of moon stars and watched the buffalos pushing the wooden structures in a looped path like an infinity symbol. Yuka then remembered where she had to aim her moon stars. She swooped in and released two stars that embedded themselves in the attack dummies' eyes. She spun around again and plucked and released two more moon stars, which found their mark on the others' eyes. With moon stars in all their eyes, the buffalos flipped the attack dummies onto their sides.

Yuka landed back on the ground, replicated two more pairs of moon stars, plucking one in each hand. Her heart racing with excitement, she continued down the Gauntlet when the bamboo screen on her right plopped down, revealing a panda throwing a heavy bamboo spear at her. She instinctively released a moon star. It merely deflected the spear as it flew harmlessly past her. Before she could pluck another moon star, the panda released another spear. With her free hand, she invoked an air wall and the bamboo spear sunk into it.

"Wow," exclaimed Yuka at her skill when she heard a crash behind her as the other bamboo wall came down, revealing three panda archers. They released three arrows and Yuka threw up another air wall. The arrows simply sunk into it and hung in mid-air.

Yuka quickly invoked a gust of wind that knocked down the three panda archers before they could reload. The sputtering feet of the panda with the spear just rounding the invisible air wall made Yuka turn toward him. A gust of wind from Yuka sent him backwards as well.

She walked briskly down the Gauntlet and eyed two more bamboo walls as she plucked out two more moon stars. She approached the walls cautiously. As she expected, they came crashing down as two tigers raced toward her from each side. Her heart skipped a beat as they growled ferociously. She launched two moon stars into the side of one tiger before flying upward just as the other tiger barely missed her with his claws. She smirked as the three unscathed tigers circled below her, so she simply invoked a strong gust of wind that rolled all three away. She looked left and right and saw no other attackers as she floated downward and crossed the white finish line.

"Well done, Empress Warrior Satoh, you have successfully navigated the

Gauntlet," declared the Guardian Crane.

Clara and Sung stood awkwardly near one another with anticipation and looked up as they heard the gleeful squawk. The Guardian Panda said, "Empress Warrior Satoh has crossed successfully."

Clara and Sung looked up and breathed a sigh of relief. The Guardian Panda shook the pouch lightly and pinched one of the disks. The Guardian Tiger held out his paw and the Guardian Panda let the loose disk fall out. They looked down at the disk and back at each other.

"Who's next?" asked Clara.

The Guardian Tiger lowered his paw for the warriors to see and it was the tiger disk.

Sung looked up, nodded, picked up his staff, and walked with the Guardian Tiger out to the Gauntlet.

"Good luck!" hollered Clara.

"I'll see you on the other side," responded Sung as he turned to her and smiled before disappearing from her view.

"Now remember, Emperor Warrior Kim, speed and agility are your friends. And trust your training," advised the Guardian Tiger.

Sung nodded and added, "Thank you, Guardian Tiger, I have to admit, I'm a bit nervous."

"You're nervous? How do you think I feel?" said the Guardian Tiger smartly. "Wait until I travel down the Gauntlet. Once you hear the squawk, you may begin."

Sung nodded as he came up to the white line and watched with awe as the Guardian Tiger dropped to all fours and swiftly raced down the Gauntlet. From afar, Sung could make out the Guardian Buffalo and Crane waiting with Daniel and Yuka.

Sung twirled his staff around him a few times to loosen up and peered over the glowing blue jade. A quick squawk zipped through the air and he looked up. He firmly tapped the bottom end of the staff onto the ground as he stepped over the white line. He kept his right hand free as he came up to the bamboo walls.

As he expected, both walls dropped, and he lowered his stance. The same large attack dummy rolled toward him while three of the smaller doglike dummies came at him from the other side. Sung assessed the situation and immediately invoked a long ice wall blocking off the three smaller wooden attack dummies. He spun his attention to the larger and more menacing attack dummy. As it came charging toward him, he tossed his staff into his right hand and twirled quickly before lunging at the wooden attack dummy, driving the staff's tip into its head. The crackling of the wood pierced the air as he forcefully maneuvered the staff downward, tipping the dummy onto the ground. The two buffalos behind it looked astonished at Sung's strength and nodded as he pulled his staff out.

Then two of the dog-sized dummies rounded the closest end of the ice wall as the third rounded the far corner. Sung raced to close the gap and swiftly swung the staff at the closest attack dummy, knocking it onto its side. He quickly spun his head as the second attack dummy sprung up onto its hind legs from some spring mechanism. Sung skillfully sunk the tip of his staff into its wooden belly, causing it to buckle.

With the staff still in the wooden attack dummy's belly, he turned to the third attack dummy and invoked an *icicle* Qi element, *godeuleum*, which flew into its head. The buffalos all knelt as he pulled his staff out and continued down the Gauntlet.

As he approached another set of bamboo walls on either side, he glanced upwards along the ledge, where three panda archers stood on each side and released their arrows. His heart racing, he invoked an ice bridge, which carried him upward. As he rose, he curved the ice bridge toward the archers on the right. But before they could shoot their next round of arrows, he invoked an ice wall at the base of the ledge, causing them to fall back into the stone wall behind them.

With the first three archers locked behind the ice wall, he veered the ice bridge around to face the three remaining archers, who released their arrows. He maneuvered out of the way and ice-surfed quickly toward the three archers, who had almost reloaded. Sung swung his staff and hit each bow out of the archers' hands as he whizzed by them. He stopped and turned to see the disarmed panda archers, then quickly invoked three dagger size icicles into the bamboo chest plate of each archer. The panda archers nodded as Sung ice surfed back onto the ground.

He stepped off the ice bridge and continued to walk down the Gauntlet. He was thrilled that he was almost at the end when suddenly he froze. The roars of two tigers reverberated from behind the bamboo wall on each side of him, before they appeared. The tigers were fast approaching, their eyes bearing down on him as they showed off their ferocious teeth. He steadied his stance.

The first tiger lunged at him, and Sung sidestepped him, whopping him on the side of his torso and sending him to the ground. Sung spun around to face another tiger, who swiped at him with his powerful paw as he ducked out of the way. The tigers were big, and their fur bristled.

Sung took a step backwards, lobbed his staff into his left hand, and invoked an ice wall to block them. He ran to the closest end of the ice wall as he swung his staff, which connected with the mid-section of a tiger who appeared unsuspectingly from behind. The tiger stepped back as Sung ran to the center of the ice wall and invoked an icicle that caught the re-emerging tiger in the chest, shattering on impact. As the second tiger reared its head from around the ice wall, Sung sent an icicle toward him, which missed as he pulled away from view.

Aware that the two tigers were behind the ice wall contemplating their next move, Sung invoked an ice bridge and soared almost straight up, allowing him to stare straight down at the two tigers prowling the edges. He whistled to them, and as one tiger looked up, an icicle slammed and shattered along its back, sending him onto the ground. The other tiger roared but was helpless as Sung invoked an ice wall that encircled the tiger. The ice wall trapped him and acknowledging this, he bowed to Sung, conceding defeat.

Sung was smiling when suddenly his footing slipped. He started to fall as the ice bridge beneath him crumbled away. He turned his head and saw that Hanro of the Prowlers had hacked away at the ice foundation with his razor-sharp blades. Sung did the only thing he could and invoked another ice bridge from below that rose to catch him, allowing him to glide away.

As he hopped off and onto his two feet, he spun around, and Hanro swiped at him with his blades. Sung instinctively deflected the attack with his staff. Sparks flew off as the two metals clanged. Sung blocked the second swipe from the tiger's powerful paw, and he pulled back onto all four paws with his haunch in the air.

Just as Sung had steadied himself, the head prowler lunged at him with both set of blades extended before him. Sung reacted by dropping onto his back while deflecting the blades with his staff. He caught the tiger's belly with his feet and pushed him over. As the tiger flipped in the air, Sung spun his legs to push himself into an upright position, then ran toward the tiger who had just landed on his back with a thud.

Sung grunted as he swung his staff overhead, which the tiger blocked by crossing his two set of blades. Sung then flipped the other end of the staff and split apart the two set of blades, quickly flipping the other end of the staff onto the tiger's chest. The impact knocked the breath out of the tiger, and Sung stepped back, panting. Hanro, the head prowler, crooked his head toward Sung and nodded.

Sung nodded as he rested one end of the staff on the ground and slightly leaned against it. He peered over to the Guardian Buffalo, Crane, and Tiger, along with Daniel and Yuka, before walking over the white line.

"Well done, Emperor Warrior Kim, you have successfully navigated the Gauntlet," exclaimed the Guardian Tiger.

Sung looked up and nodded while catching his breath. "Thank you, Guardian Tiger, that wasn't easy."

"No, it wasn't meant to be easy, but your prowess was exciting to watch," said the Guardian Tiger proudly. "Before we call Empress Warrior Wu, would you mind removing your ice sculptures?"

Sung looked down the Gauntlet and saw the ice structures that he had left behind and nodded his head as he invoked his Qi elemental power to evaporate them.

Clara paced in place, shuddering at each clang of metal or the sound of ice blocks seemingly crumbling to the ground. But it was the roars of the tigers that shook her until finally, her eyes lit up upon hearing the squawk.

"Are you ready?" asked the Guardian Panda as he looked at her from his black furry eye patches.

Clara let out a breath and straightened her shoulders as she followed the Guardian Panda toward the Gauntlet. It looked even bigger than before, and anxiety gnawed at the pit of her stomach. She stopped at the white line and looked up at the Guardian Panda.

"Trust your training, let your intuition be your ally," the Guardian Panda reminded Clara.

She nodded and watched the Guardian Panda waddle down the Gauntlet. She looked down at the Bow of Destiny in her left head. She turned the green jade upward just as her own green jade bracelet slid down her wrist a bit. She reached back toward her quiver and ran her fingers along the feathery ends of one of her thirty arrows before drawing one out. She cocked the arrow into place and looked up as she heard the squawk echo from the Gauntlet.

Clara closed her eyes and listened to her breathing, then opened them as she stepped over the white line. She trotted gingerly toward the first pair of bamboo walls, expecting full well that something would be waiting behind them. Her suspicions were confirmed as both walls dropped and hulking buffalo-shaped attack dummies from each side charged at her.

She aimed and released an arrow, which sunk into the center of the attack dummy's forehead and spun around as she reloaded. Without hesitation, she released another arrow that sank into the forehead of the other dummy, and both came to a stop. But before she could think, two smaller attack dummies converged on her, and one launched into the air toward her. With her right hand, she invoked the *wall* Qi element, *ten-bing*, and trapped the attack dummy in midair. The second attack dummy charged at her, and she was forced to sidestep as the buffalo pushed it passed her. As the buffalo turned the dummy, Clara confidently unleashed an arrow into its forehead, stopping it in its tracks. The buffalo nodded to her, and she proceeded down the Gauntlet while reloading an arrow.

She had passed one phase, she thought. It was like taking a multipart exam. She approached a second pair of bamboo walls, and her senses perked. Her eyes glanced upward as two sets of three archers appeared along the opposing ledges. They fired simultaneously, unleashing two sets of three arrows from both directions. Clara gasped but managed to quickly invoke a dirt wall that arched over her, giving her protection from both sides. When the six arrows sunk harmlessly into the arched dirt wall, she emerged and fired three arrows in succession at the three panda archers on her left. She quickly retreated into the arch as the tips of the arrows sunk into the ground where she had just been standing. She pulled out three arrows and loaded them simultaneously. With a quick step, she exited through the other end of the arched dirt wall and fired her arrows. They sunk into the chests of the three panda archers' bamboo armor.

Before she could even feel relieved for taking out the archers, two more bamboo walls dropped, and a large panda soldier with a spear came at her on each side. With her free hand, she easily invoked the Qi element to split the ground in front of the panda closest to her, and he tumbled into the resulting hole. She turned quickly to deflect the spear coming at her with her bow, but its force caused her to take a couple of steps backward.

She regained her footing just as he swung the spear toward her, and Clara bent backwards just as the spear brushed up against her chest. She straightened up and leapt backwards as she pulled out an arrow, cocked it and released it. The arrow sunk into the middle of the panda soldier's chest. The panda stopped in his tracks, looked up at and nodded to Clara who had landed on her two feet. She smiled and continued down the Gauntlet.

She cocked another arrow and stealthily approached the next two bamboo walls. As she expected, they collapsed, and a pair of spear-toting panda soldiers lumbered forward. She looked left and turned right and successively fired off two arrows, which stopped them. She quickly turned to face the other two pandas, who were now almost on top of her, and quickly split the ground before them as they tumbled into another hole. They both looked up and nodded.

As she took a couple of steps back, thinking she was finished, something barreled into her from behind. She flew onto her stomach and instinctively turned onto her back when a mass of white and black fur fell on top of her. Clara brought up the bow as his paws pressed down on it. The strength of the Head of the Pandemonium Squad was overpowering Clara. She shook her head just as she made eye contact with him when suddenly he snarled ferociously at her as he bared his teeth.

"No!" she screamed as she released the grip on her bow, which he abruptly pulled away from her. She crossed her forearms to shield her face from the onslaught, which never came.

"You are not the Panda Warrior!" the Head of the Pandemonium Squad declared. "The Portal Book is mistaken, you cannot be our warrior, you are a…"

"Enough!" as the sharp voice sliced through the air. The Guardian Panda pulled the Head of the Pandemonium Squad off Clara, who shuddered behind her crossed forearms.

"Clara!" from multiple voices blurted out. Sung slid to her side and placed his hands on her forearms, which made her jerk them away slightly as she peered upward into the concerned looks of her fellow warriors.

Daniel came to the other side of Clara and along with Sung, they gently lifted her into an upright position as Yuka asked, "Clara, are you okay?"

Clara's lips trembled as she looked all around. She looked up into the dark brown eyes of the Guardian Panda. Devastated, she mumbled, "I failed."

TWENTY - FIVE

Clara drew her knees up toward her chest and wrapped her arms around them, resting her head on top of them. She rocked back and forth in the middle of her bed as her mind replayed the fear she felt back at the Gauntlet. The bared teeth of the Head of the Pandemonium Squad and the ferocity in his eyes unraveled her confidence.

Her eyes stared down at the Bow of Destiny and quiver. The green jade glistened back at her, and she remembered her first night inside the dangling bamboo, when the white light spiraled outward, indicating she was the Panda Warrior. The words of the Panderess echoed in in her mind until newly sown self-doubt took over. *What if I'm not the Panda Warrior?* she wondered.

The heavy flap to her tent opened, and the Guardian Panda cautiously lumbered in, stepping around her shoes. He saw that she quickly looked up, then diverted her gaze from him. As he approached, he could feel a heavy cloud of despair in the air. Looking at the table, he saw that she had barely touched her dinner.

"Empress Warrior Wu," the Guardian Panda said softly.

She didn't respond immediately. He said once more, "Empress Warrior Wu."

"I know what you are going to say. 'I failed. I'm not the Panda Warrior,'" said Clara shamefully.

The Guardian Panda sat down on the corner of the bed, which creaked from his weight. He looked at her with his dark brown eyes. She couldn't resist his adorable white and black fur face and turned her head slightly toward him.

"That is not true. The Portal Book chose you and the Bamboo Jade confirmed it," said the Guardian Panda confidently.

"What if the book made a mistake?" asked Clara.

"The Portal Book doesn't make mistakes."

"Well, what if I made a mistake, and that's why I failed?" asked Clara sadly.

"It's just one mistake…" but before the Guardian Panda could continue, Clara interjected.

"But that big Pandemonium soldier said that no warrior has ever failed before, is that true?"

There was a moment of silence when the Guardian Panda responded, "That is true. No warrior has ever failed... I meant not finished the Gauntlet."

"See, maybe he's right. He's a real soldier. Not me. I'm just a fifteen-year-old Chinese American girl from New York City."

"No, that is what your earthly world tells you, but here on Azen, you are the Panda Warrior," he said firmly.

Clara let out a sigh, "Then why did I fail? Do you how hard it is for an Asian American girl like me to fail? We're not supposed to fail. We're supposed to bring home all As."

The Guardian Panda's eye widened, and he asked, "What's an A?"

Clara looked up at him and grinned. "Never mind."

"When the Head of the Pandemonium Squad knocked you down, do you remember what it was that startled you?"

"I don't know. It was the way he showed his scary teeth, and I never seen such scary eyes before. Pandas are not supposed to be scary," Clara said despondently.

"I see. We are not like the comfortable pandas on your earthly world, though we all eat bamboo," said the Guardian Panda.

"That is true, you both love bamboo a lot," said Clara with a chuckle. She continued, "I just don't know. Maybe I'm not a true warrior. I've never been in a real fight in my life."

"I see. But certainly, you must have imagined fighting. Have you not ever gotten mad at anyone before?" he asked.

"Clarissa," said Clara with a grumble.

"Who?" the Guardian Panda asked.

"Clarissa Hobart, the school meanie," said Clara with contempt.

"Clarissa, Hobart, the school meanie. Is this an official title?"

Clara looked up exasperatedly and started to rant, "No, that's my title for her. Can I tell you how mean she is? She's this blonde girl who think she's all pretty and that. She picks on all the kids not inside her circle of arrogant friends. But she's really mean to us Asian students. Every time when she sees me, she always throws out 'Hey ching chong!' Oh, how I want to punch her in the face sometimes, no, all the time!"

"This Clarissa Hobart seems very evil," said the Guardian Panda seriously.

"She is evil!" Clara said as she let out a laugh.

The Guardian Panda eked out a smile and continued. "Being a warrior isn't easy. You will never know if you can kill until you actually do it. But you are the Panda Warrior, this much I do know."

"The other warriors before me, could they kill too?"

The Guardian Panda's eyes lit up as he hopped off the bed and asked, "Empress Warrior Wu, follow me."

"What is it?" she asked with a startled look.

"You shall see. Bring the Bow of Destiny and slip into your boots. We are going to Bamboo Tower," commanded the Guardian Panda as he walked toward the tent's entrance.

Clara picked up the bow and quiver and slipped into her boots. She asked, "But won't it be a long walk to Bamboo Tower?"

The Guardian Panda pulled back the flap, and before her was a new type of bird. It was a larger bird, big and muscular, and covered in black and brownish feathers. It had a much shorter beak than the cranes, and its eye flickered at the Guardian Panda and Clara.

"No, because we will be flying there," said the Guardian Panda.

TWENTY - SIX

That night, Sung's mind was distracted by the thought of Clara's experience in the Gauntlet. She was doing so well until the Head of the Pandemonium Squad pounced on her from behind. *Did she let her guard down because she thought she was almost finished?* he thought to himself.

That's when his eyes caught a Qi element floating in the air before seeping into Daniel's chest. Sung took the last few steps to the perimeter of the Portal Circle.

"Manifesting?" asked Sung.

Daniel looked up and waved, "Hey, yep. Gotta manifest as many Qi elements in preparation for the battle. I don't want to be caught empty handed when I have to go up against some demon creature."

"I hear ya. It's why I came up too," said Sung as he walked up to his Portal Book and picked up the Clawdium brush. "It's a shame what happened to Clara."

"Yah. A real disappointment, and she's one hundred percent Asian," remarked Daniel slyly.

Sung's brush froze, and he turned to Daniel's back, "What's that supposed to mean?"

Daniel, who continued brushing, replied, "Her being one hundred percent couldn't save her, so I guess being one hundred percent Asian doesn't make her one hundred percent Chinese."

"Clara is totally one hundred percent Chinese!" said Sung tersely as he turned toward Daniel.

Daniel put his brush down and turned toward Sung as his dark brown hair swayed a bit. "Then how come she failed earlier today? All my life, I was told that I was only half Vietnamese and that I would never be good enough to be Vietnamese. But look what I did today! I kicked butt and that confirms that I'm the warrior to represent the Buffalo Kingdom!"

"Hey! Whatever stuff you dealt with from other guys about you being only half Vietnamese has nothing to do with Clara," retorted Sung as he clenched his fist.

"Well, it's not fair that I was born half Vietnamese and had a lousy father who didn't care for raising me. But here and now, I'm proving my Vietnamese is just as strong as you full-blooded Asians!" yelled Daniel.

"Yah? That may be, but it's your other side that is being a real jerk right now!" said Sung hurtfully.

Daniel traced into the air and invoked the fireball Qi element at Sung. But Sung was ready and invoked an icicle that met the fireball in midair, neutralizing it.

Daniel invoked another fireball that balanced on his fingertips as Sung invoked a larger icicle in his hand. As Daniel was about to cast out his fireball, its fire dwindled and vanished just as Sung's icicle evaporated away.

"What the?" exclaimed Daniel as someone screamed from above, "Stop it!"

Daniel looked up and saw an angry Yuka floating down with her finger pointed at him.

Out of frustration, Daniel invoked another fire Qi element, but it would not alight, and he was befuddled at how his Qi elemental powers were being extinguished.

"Stop fighting!" scolded Yuka as she landed in the Portal Circle.

"What did you do to my powers!" demanded Daniel of her.

"I created a vacuum around your fireball. Without oxygen, there cannot be fire," said Yuka confidently.

Daniel was annoyed and came toward Yuka as he tried to invoke another fire Qi element. But Yuka immediately snuffed it out and sent a gust of wind into Daniel's chest, which sent him up against the Portal Book.

Yuka took a step toward him, her finger pointing at him menacingly.

"I guess air conquers fire," Daniel said frustratingly.

"No, you just have to be quicker than me, I've been learning Japanese all my life, so I'm simply faster than you," said Yuka confidently.

Sung sauntered toward her and coyly said, "I guess I shouldn't get you mad, either."

"No, you shouldn't," Yuka said teasingly before looking back at Daniel sternly.

"Can we stop your immature talk and think about Clara? We're about to fight some warlock army, and we need all of us to be battle ready," implored

Yuka.

"You saw how she froze," complained Daniel. "What do you think is wrong with her?"

"I don't think anything is wrong with her. I think it's all in her head," said Yuka.

TWENTY - SEVEN

Clara was disappointed that her Qi elemental power did not give her the power to fly but being harnessed to the back of a large Japanese eagle with the Guardian Panda was close enough. For a while, all the heavy guilt and shame she felt for failing the Gauntlet lifted away as they glided through the air.

As she stared around her, she could see the clouds floating against the backdrop of the dark blue night sky. The Guardian Panda raised a dark furry paw to catch her attention. She looked down as he pointed to Bamboo City. The same sense of wonderment that she felt upon seeing it for the first time, came rushing back.

From the bird's eye view, she could see how large the bamboo was and how impressive the engineering that went into the majestic city's construction.

"It's always a sight to see," said the Guardian Panda.

Clara nodded in agreement, distracted by a crane that flew by in the opposite direction on her left.

"As the day of battle draws near, the Ascendant of the Crane Kingdom extends to all the engaged kingdoms a squadron of cranes and a team of eagles for heavy lifting," explained the Guardian Panda.

"Wow. So, there's like a whole fleet of Japanese birds flying in between the kingdoms?" asked Clara.

"Yes, there is. We're all in this together," said the Guardian Panda.

From the front, Clara's attention was distracted by the Japanese eagle's instructions, "We're on approach to Bamboo Tower. Be sure to hold onto your harness straps. Guardian Panda and Empress Warrior Wu."

Clara nodded as she regripped the bamboo strap and readied herself for the descent.

The eagle widened his large wingspan to catch more air and slow itself down. The eagle aimed for the large opening on the side of Bamboo Tower, which was alit with illumination jades. A panda was on one side of the opening, waving an illumination jade baton, helping to direct the eagle through the opening. As the eagle drew nearer, Clara and the Guardian Panda leaned forward, and they passed through the opening smoothly. The eagle came to a stop with a few hops of his feet before lowering his body to allow them to disembark.

Clara shot both of her hands into the air and hollered, "So cool!"

The Guardian Panda was elated to see that Clara was happy and then gestured for her to carefully slide off. After she did so, the Guardian Panda slid off and said to the eagle, "We'll be back. Please make yourself comfortable in the hangar."

The eagle nodded and began to walk toward an open bin of bamboo nuggets.

"Let's go see the Panderess," said the Guardian Panda.

"Are we taking the same lift?" asked Clara as she readjusted the bow and quiver across herself.

"Yes, we are," he responded.

"Oh cool," said Clara as she admired the happenings inside the hangar. There were a few other cranes about who were relaxing and conversing with other pandas who were minding the hangar. Otherwise, all was quite calm.

They arrived at the opening to the lift and as soon as one arrived, they carefully hopped into it. As the lift ascended, the other floors whizzed by until they arrived at the floor where the Panderess was waiting. They hopped off and walked down the length of the red silken path. Clara took in the ambiance once more and admired the stoic panda guards lining the path.

The Panderess was at the center. As they approached, they both bowed, and the Panderess bowed in return.

"Panderess, I'll will leave Empress Warrior Wu in your care. Let me know when she's ready to return," said the Guardian Panda.

"*Xie Xie*, Guardian Panda, I'll take her from here," said the Panderess. "Empress Warrior Wu, how are you today?"

Clara nervously looked up, and all the shame that seemed to have just flown away, suddenly rushed back like a heavy weight in the pit of her stomach. "I'm doing okay, though I don't know if I deserve the title of Empress Warrior Wu any longer."

"Yes, I heard what happened today," said the Panderess. "You mustn't dwell on the setback, but rather find a solution to it."

"I know, but what happens if I'm not a warrior? What happens if I can't kill?" asked Clara.

"Do you think all warriors were born to kill? Do you think your Guardian Panda knew he could kill and become the great warrior that he was before he became the Guardian Panda?" asked the Panderess soothingly.

Clara looked over her shoulder at her Guardian Panda. He was just the most adorable panda with his plump body covered in lush white-and-black fur. She would never have assumed he could fight, but she could sense that her Guardian Panda was a seasoned warrior.

"Your Guardian Panda fought for what is righteous and true. He fought for Azen, the Panda Kingdom, and other kingdoms, and he also fought alongside previous warriors to protect your home. Knowing the existence of the Warlock, would you not fight for your home and your parents?"

Clara's eyes lit up as she thought about her parents, and yes, she knew in her heart that she would fight for her parents. Especially now that she knew Kung Fu. "Yes, I would."

"And would you not fight for justice?" asked the Panderess.

"If it's true justice, that needs to be fought for, then yes, I guess I would fight for it," responded Clara.

"Is there any injustice that is going on back in your earthly home?" asked the Panderess.

"Yes, Clarissa Hobart. She's an injustice all right," exhorted Clara.

"And what injustice does she commit?"

"She's a big bully, and the way she picks on all the Asian girls is really mean. I can't even tell my parents since they just tell me never to get into a fight and to walk away. But if I could, I would pound her into the ground to teach her a lesson," said Clara with pleasure.

"From your clenched fists, I see you are summoning the warrior spirit," noted the Panderess.

Clara looked down and noticed that she unconsciously clenched both of her fists in anger and released them.

"What you just felt is but an ounce of your warrior spirit. Be aware of it and channel it. Embrace it, and it will be your ally when you do battle with the Warlock's armies. Once you prevail over his armies, then you may dispatch this Clarissa in your earthly world," said the Panderess.

Clara laughed and responded, "Oh no, I can't do that to Clarissa. I would be suspended from school!"

"Come, follow me. I want to show you something," said the Panderess.

Clara straightened up and followed the Panderess to a set of stairs that led into the floor below. When Clara reached the base of the steps, she looked upward and noted a totally different feel to the space. It felt almost sacred. She was again in a circular room and standing along the outer wall were a handful of guards. But in the middle was a bright green circular room, and she followed the Panderess through the round entrance. A fire glowed in the middle as they entered.

The Panderess turned around and faced Clara. "This is the Warrior's Circle. It is where we honor all the empress and emperor warriors that led us to victory in the past wars with the Warlock."

"Whoa," Clara let out as she scanned the wall's inner perimeter, and she could see people carved out of bamboo.

"In the center is the Bamboo Flame that honors the warriors for eternity," said the Panderess.

Clara glanced over it as the Panderess walked over to one of the statues against the bamboo wall. "This is Yi Wu-Fei, our first Panda Emperor Warrior," she said.

Clara stood in front of the amazing statue, caved from a block of bamboo. He was a young and tall Chinese teenager, standing proudly in an elaborate battle outfit. He had a strong face and his eyes bore down on her.

The Panderess moved over to the second statue of another Chinese teenaged boy of about the same height. The intricate carving had him holding the Bow of Destiny in one hand and he looked rather bold. Clara could feel his warrior essence. "This is Zhou Feng."

The Panderess then moved to a third statue, which was a teenaged girl. Her hair was long and flowing, and she wore a warrior's attire as she held her bow. Her armor was fitted to her feminine figure. Clara felt an immediate admiration for the Chinese Panda Empress Warrior that fought so long ago. "This is Hua Mulan," said the Panderess as she moved on.

Clara froze and looked at the statue of the teenaged girl up and down and uttered, "What? Who is she again?"

The Panderess turned back, looked at Clara's awestruck gaze at the statue and restated, "This is Hua Mulan."

"The Hua Mulan? The same Hua Mulan that took her father's place in the emperor's army to save him?"

"I do not know of her trials on your home world," said the Panderess with fondness. "She was an incredibly gifted warrior imbued with raw talent. We helped her to hone her natural skills even further. Her Qi was very strong. But I can see her honoring her father in that manner."

A few moments of silence passed when Clara uttered, "I'm related to Hua Mulan?"

The Panderess blinked a few times and responded back, "Well not exactly but…"

Clara repeated even more slowly, "I'm… related… to… Hua… Mulan?"

The Panderess sensed Clara's building confidence and decided to use it. "Perhaps in some small way, you may be."

"Oh my god! I'm related to Hua Mulan!"

TWENTY - EIGHT

Daniel kicked at the ground beneath his feet as he waited in the morning sun along with Sung and Yuka. Sung dawdled as he balanced his staff across his finger, and Yuka shifted her feet in place with her hands clasped behind her back.

"Do you think she'll show up?" asked Daniel.

"She'll come," said Yuka with a hint of annoyance at Daniel for asking.

"There she is!" exclaimed Sung as he looked up the path to see Clara with the Guardian Panda by her side.

Yuka's glum expression changed to one of joy as she ran toward Clara. As Yuka closed the gap, she gently extended her hands, and Clara warmly took them, smiling at Yuka. Daniel and Sung fell in behind Yuka moments later.

"How are you feeling?" asked Yuka.

Clara smiled. "I'm good. I am." Clara looked up at Daniel's and Sung's smiles, but she could see the anxious concern behind them. "I'm sorry about yesterday. I didn't mean to let you down."

"Hey, don't be too hard on yourself," said Sung reassuringly.

"Yah, we all make mistakes. Well, not all of us," said Daniel disdainfully.

Yuka shot Daniel a look and he suddenly regretted his snarky remark.

Yuka turned back to Clara, "I believe in you. You're going to do great, I know it," said Yuka as she gently grasped Clara's fingertips.

Clara looked at Yuka and then to the guys. "I promise I will do my best today," she said confidently

"Empress and emperor warriors, thank you for your support of Empress Warrior Wu. Please make your way to the end of the Gauntlet, where your guardians are waiting. Empress Warrior Wu will then commence this morning's trial," said the Guardian Panda.

Yuka gently shook Clara's fingers and when she let go, she said, "Hey."

Clara looked up as Yuka caught the boys' attention. She looked firmly at Clara and brought her fists up as her forearms formed an "A." Sung and Daniel quickly did the same and Clara giggled as she mirrored them. As they bowed to each other, they all whispered, "For Azen."

Smiles and soft giggles were all around as they began to turn away from Clara but Sung turned back toward Clara.

"Good luck out there!" said Sung as he made eye contact with her as she smiled back. Daniel then nodded in Clara's direction.

The Guardian Panda walked up to the white line with Clara, noticing that her stride was confident. They stared down the Gauntlet, where all was deceptively peaceful. He turned his fluffy white and black head and stared down at Clara as she looked up into his black eye patches.

"Empress Warrior Wu, be the warrior that you know not but that you already are."

"I will," said Clara as she removed the Bow of Destiny from her chest.

The Guardian Panda nodded and began to trot down the Gauntlet.

Clara inhaled the morning air, cocked her head from side-to-side, and lifted each foot a couple of times. When the Guardian Panda was almost at the finish line, she knelt, placed her palm against the ground and reached out. She felt the earth, and for a moment, she almost felt the entire terrain around the Gauntlet. Her ears perked up as her eyes shot open upon hearing the squawk. She raced forward as she cocked an arrow. As she passed the first set of bamboo walls, they fell to the ground. And not two nor four attack dummies, but at least eight appeared.

She immediately drew back her arrow and sunk it into the eye of the large attack dummy on the right. She let fly another arrow, which sunk into the eye of the large attack dummy on the left. But neither stopped as the buffalos pushing them from behind turned towards her.

The six smaller attack dummies were closing the gap as she slid an arrow onto the bow's rest and held it in place with her left hand. Using her right hand, she invoked the Qi element to split the earth beneath the three attack dummies on the right, forcing them to fall in. She quickly did the same with the three remaining attack dummies. The two large attack dummies were raging towards her as she invoked a Qi element. A thick wall of dirt shot up from underneath the attack dummy on the right, propelling it into the air before it came crashing back down onto the earth. As the last large attack dummy approached, she stood her ground and stared it down as she invoked a Qi element. A dirt wall arose in front of the large attack dummy and grew towards it, pushing it and the buffalos backwards, helpless to stop it. The buffalos sprung out of the way as the dirt wall pushed the wooden attack dummy against the stone wall, crushing it into hulking pieces.

The Head of the Pandemonium Squad wasn't going to make it easy, Clara thought.

Clara turned and raced to the next set of bamboo walls. As expected, they dropped with a thud. Behind them were panda spearmen and archers. Three large spears were launched into the air, and Clara invoked the wall Qi element as the spears sunk into them with successive thuds. Instinctively, she invoked another dirt wall on her exposed side as the arrows sunk in harmlessly. Without looking, she invoked a small sinkhole under the feet of the spearmen and the archers, swallowing them up. She emerged from between the two dirt walls protecting her and looked up at the ledges to see a set of three panda archers on each side.

With her right hand, she invoked the Qi element as a towering dirt wall rose, blocking the archers' views. The three other archers released their arrows, and Clara easily sidestepped them. Her hand pulled out an arrow from her quiver and released it. She quickly repeated these two more times. Each found their mark in the center of a panda's chest plate.

Without giving them any more attention, her fingers pulled out three arrows, which she rested on her bow as she invoked the Qi element to collapse the towering dirt wall. The three panda archers each released an arrow, which was split in half by each of Clara's three arrows. Before they could reload, Clara sent up three more arrows, and each lodged itself in the center of the panda archer's chest plate. Clara, satisfied with her work, looked down the Gauntlet and moved on as she loaded two arrows onto the bow.

As she approached the last pair of bamboo walls, they collapsed as two pairs of angry pandas charged at her with spears. She didn't slow down or hesitate as she shot two arrows at the pandas on her left, lodging each into their bamboo helmets. She turned around to see the other two pandas were almost on top of her. She dodged the first spear that passed her waist and she arched backwards to avoid the thrust of the other. She spun out of her predicament and somersaulted away. She landed in a crouch and invoked a Qi element, causing the earth beneath the two spearmen to split open, swallowing them up.

Her ears twitched as she heard rustling behind her. She immediately spun around, catching the cheek of the Head of Pandemonium Squad with the tip of her bow. He was caught off guard as she suddenly landed a solid sidekick into his chest, but his heavy body absorbed the blow. The Head of the Pandemonium Squad quickly flicked the bow out of Clara's grasp as it flew behind him landing a few feet away.

Clara was undeterred as a force of will welled up from deep within her. She grabbed the spear from his grip and launched her body sideways, landing a double kick on the panda's jaw, sending him back. Clara's body spun upward in an arc before she landed on her two feet. Intuitively, she invoked a dirt wall that rose upward and cradled her bow. She summoned it as the low dirt wall rolled toward her and delivered the bow firmly into her left hand.

She loaded an arrow and walked toward the Head of the Pandemonium Squad as he recovered from his momentary daze. She released an arrow toward him, which he confidently deflected with his spear. She released another arrow, which he also deflected but his eyes widened as three arrows came toward him. They found their destiny as they sunk into his chest plate with a forceful thud. He simply stared at Clara. She had her bow drawn with a loaded arrow not more than three feet away from his helmet. He stared at her and brought his spear upright to his side and nodded respectfully to her.

Clara relaxed the draw string and placed the arrow back into her quiver as she walked toward the guardians and her fellow warriors, who were looking at her in utter amazement.

Sung turned to within earshot of Daniel and said quietly, "My mother said, 'Never piss off an Asian girl.'"

Daniel simply nodded as he stared at the bold and fearless Clara.

As she crossed the finish line, she simply said to them, "I'm Empress Warrior Wu."

TWENTY - NINE

The laughter from the meal table was lighthearted as Daniel continued, "And the look on Xi Peng's face was like this," as Daniel stared up blankly and continued. "And he's got three arrows sticking out of his chest, and Clara is simply aiming another at his head. What was he going to do?"

Everyone laughed and despite her newfound confidence, Clara was blushing from the adulation.

"And the way you used the dirt to push things away and bring things to you, insanely genius! Who taught you that?" asked a boisterous Sung.

Clara smiled in his direction and humbly answered, "I don't know, I just felt that I could. I suddenly have this stronger connection to the earth, and I just knew."

"You were so much stronger today! Where did you find the strength to fight the Head of the Pandemonium Squad?" asked Yuka.

Clara paused and simply uttered, "Clarissa."

There were blank faces all around until Yuka asked, "Who?"

"Clarissa, she's this blonde bully at school. She bullies everyone but especially me and my Asian friends. She calls us... chinks," said Clara resignedly.

After a moment, Yuka followed with, "Japs. They call us Japs and say that we are not wanted."

"Gooks... they call us gooks," said Sung as his shoulders drooped along with his chopsticks onto the table.

"Why are White people so mean?" asked Yuka as a tear formed at one end of her eye.

"Not all White people," said Sung.

"My... my White father called me a gook," said Daniel under his breath.

Everyone's eyes looked up at him as they were taken aback by his admission.

"Yeah. My father married my mom, a Vietnamese woman, and when I was born, he didn't like seeing my Vietnamese features in me. He had hoped that I would grow out of it. Like I could really control that, and when my Vietnamese features started to become clearer, he lost it. All I remember when he left, as my mom cried and pleaded with him, was he said, 'I didn't marry a *gook* to raise a *gook*!'" uttered Daniel with clenched fists.

His fists suddenly slammed down on the table shaking everything that was on it and startled everyone.

"Hey, hey," said Clara soothingly as Daniel pulled back his hands disarmingly and revealing his teary red eyes.

"I'm sorry. I didn't mean to…" offered Daniel as he wiped his eyes with the back of his hands.

"Bro, man, it's okay. We're all Asian here, we get it," said Sung as he placed his left hand reassuringly on Daniel's shoulder.

"It's just so hard, you know… when your own father tells you he hates a part of you… and then I begin to hate that part of myself… but at the same time, I cherish my mom, who is everything I hate," said Daniel as he choked back on his words.

Yuka stared off silently, not knowing what to say as Clara spoke, "You don't hate your mom. She loves you so much."

Daniel sniffled and shook his head, "You're right, I love my *me*. She is everything to me. I think I'm letting my father's words mess with my head."

"Right, we need to stop letting White people mess with our heads, we're pretty awesome Asians!" said Sung to approving looks from Yuka and Clara.

Daniel looked up and nodded a few times under his tears. "Ugh, I can't believe I'm crying like a baby. But you know, I've never felt prouder to be Vietnamese, than among my Azen friends. I just had to be transported to some faraway place with talking animals to realize it."

Everyone looked at each other in a moment of silence and suddenly let out a laugh.

"You're right, I never really appreciated my full potential as a Chinese girl until I came here and was almost beaten up by a scary panda soldier," said Clara.

Another round of laughter rang through the group as Sung added, "Yo, I can't tell my *eomma* that a white tiger makes better *kimchi* than her. She'd hit me so hard that it'll send me to Korea!"

"Maybe it'll be hard enough to send you back here to Azen," said Daniel with a smile.

"Yah, it could be that hard! She's the real tiger mom!" Sung agreed with a hearty laughter.

"I'm glad I met all of you," said Yuka appreciatively. "It's nice and I feel that we're doing an honorable thing here on Azen."

"I know it's only tea, but let's pretend like we're older and toast," said Clara as everyone brought in their cups of tea. "To the *awesomest* Asian Warriors of Azen!"

As the warriors drank from their tea, Yuka caught sight of the four guardians coming down the jade illuminated path toward them with a somber demeanor. She nudged Clara who looked up, which caught both Sung's and Daniel's attention as they turned to see the approaching guardians themselves.

"Empress and emperor warriors," said the Guardian Panda seriously. "We need you to follow us to the Portal Circle as the lunar eclipse is imminent."

The warriors looked up at each other gravely, put down whatever was in their hands and picked up their weapons as they got up. The warriors paired up with their guardians and walked in somber silence to the Portal Circle. As they arrived, Clara took up her place at her Portal Book and everyone else followed suit.

As each guardian stood behind their warrior, the Guardian Panda entered the Portal Circle and pointed to the full moon just cresting over the horizon. The other not-yet full moons were in different places along the night sky.

"The first moon, which is called, *Jinju*, will be in our shadow shortly. It will last only a few minutes. As this is your first time witnessing an Azen lunar eclipse, please observe in silence. But you may watch the eclipse itself. Yes, Emperor Warrior Kim?"

"*Jinju*? Is that Korean for pearl?"

"Yes," replied the Guardian Panda. "All of our moons are named after pearls."

The Guardian Panda walked toward Clara and stood behind her. The tone of the moment turned ominous as the warriors fidgeted a bit, but soon, the full moon crested over the horizon. It was larger than usual with its pinkish aura creating a spectacular sight. Its rocky surface was almost visible. Soon, the planet's shadow started to crawl upward from the lower left corner of the moon's surface. As the moon arced higher into the sky, the shadow became bigger as the pink moonlight around it dimmed to black. Clara looked around, and her friends' eyes glistened in the darkness. Finally, the shadow completely enveloped the moon, dampening its pearly radiance. Then as soon as it began, the moon crept out of the world's black shadow until finally, its pink radiance was restored as it soared higher into the night sky.

The Guardian Panda re-entered the Portal Circle and announced, "It's done. The Warlock's first army has been teleported. Our scouts from each of the cardinal points will report in within a couple of hours. We'll reconvene at that time. For now, feel free to have this time to yourselves."

The warriors looked at each other as the guardians traveled down the path, and as if they read each other's minds, they turned to their Portal Books. Clara flipped to an open page, picked up her brush and started to manifest more Qi elements, starting with wall. Sung, Yuka, and Daniel followed suit.

The guardians returned within a couple of hours to the warriors diligently manifesting Qi elements. The guardians admired the sight of their four warriors brushing feverishly, manifesting fiery Qi elements that seeped into their chests. As their footsteps became audible, the warriors looked up from their Portal Books and put down their brushes, giving their weary hands a rest.

The guardians took up their usual spots by their warriors, but this time, the Guardian Crane entered the Portal Circle. She summoned from the Wu air Portal Book and fiery streams sprung forward, weaving into a fully three-dimensional terrain in the middle of the Portal Circle.

"Empress and emperor warriors, our aerial scouts have returned. The first Warlock army has teleported to the eastern location. This location has a natural chokepoint formed by a crack between a tall mountain range. We call this, Jagged Pass," elucidated the Guardian Crane. Fiery streams formed the image of the rocky mountain with the crack down its middle as the warriors watched in intense awe.

"Beyond the chokepoint is a swath of open barren land that rises up to a ridge that the Warlock's army will surmount before descending toward Jagged Pass. It has been our experience that it's best to eliminate as much of the threat as possible before they pass through Jagged Pass. This will be the task for the buffalos and the tigers, with my cranes providing attacks from the air. Behind Jagged Pass is the valley, which is lined by a rocky formation on each side. This is where the pandas will attack from. The buffalos and tigers will retreat to this point at the end of the valley, and this is the point that we must hold at all costs," said the Guardian Crane sternly.

"Do we know what creature makes up the Warlock army?" asked Sung.

"Yes, we do," said the Guardian Crane as she waved her wing into the fiery streams, dispersing them. They recombined into a ferocious looking dog with fiery eyes and fire coming from its mouth. It suddenly came to life, jolting the warriors and they continued to watch the dog rear its head as bursts of fire shot out from its mouth.

"This is the fiery demon dog, the *Huo Dou*," said the Guardian Crane. "It should not be confused with the kinder domesticated dogs of your world. These creatures are pure evil and are loyal to the Warlock. These dogs are larger, their fur is thick and bristled. Their canines are powerful, and their claws even more so. But their most nefarious weapon is their ability to shoot fireballs from their mouths."

"How many of them will there be?" asked Yuka?

"Several hundred, possibly a thousand, maybe more," answered the Guardian Crane.

"That seems a lot," said Yuka concerningly.

The Guardian Tiger stalked into the Portal Circle as the Guardian Crane exited. "It may seem that way, but remember, our combined kingdom armies is of equal if not a greater match. But what these demon creatures lack in the power of the jade and your Qi elemental powers, they certainly make up in ferocity and an insatiable, unrelenting desire to kill and to serve their powerful Warlock."

Daniel asked, "With the jade armor, will you be protected from death?"

"No, we are still mortal, but the power of the jade strengthens our armor and gives us a better than excellent chance at surviving the demon creatures' attacks."

The warriors were silent as the enemy's capabilities were explained. The Guardian Tiger pointed his paw at the fiery demon dog image as a new image appeared, showing a fully three-dimensional landscape. Pointing with one of his outstretched claws, he said, "We are here, the journey to Jagged Pass is one day's journey for us, while it is a two-day journey for the demon dogs. We will leave tomorrow morning."

The Guardian Buffalo stepped in as the Guardian Tiger exited. He waved away the fiery image with his massive horns and waved in another. It was a fiery recreation of the Portal Circle along with the stone pedestals with the Portal Books. He looked at each of the warriors and finally said, "This is what we must protect, the Portal Books. It is the only mechanism for reaching your world. If we fail, the Warlock will use the books to invade your world, to enslave it and to plunder its resources. It is our duty to protect the Portal Books at all costs."

THIRTY

The next morning, the warriors met at the Portal Circle. They could feel a sense of agitation in the air. The sky was filled with more cranes than usual. The air was filled with noises that the warriors had not heard in the preceding days. It was coming from the east, and as much as the warriors wanted to explore, they were told explicitly to meet with their guardians first thing in the morning.

"I wonder when we'll be moving out," asked Sung as he shifted in place. "Guardian Tiger told me last night that we'll be advancing first due to our speed."

"My Guardian Crane told me that we'll be flying out to secure Jagged Pass," said Yuka.

"Man, I hope I manifested enough fireballs and walls. Hundreds, maybe thousands of these demon dogs… I don't want to run out of Qi elements," said Daniel anxiously.

The wind blew through Clara's hair as it tangled around her face. She tucked her bow between her legs. She removed the bamboo ribbon hair accessory from her pant pocket. Her hands gathered up her hair neatly as she slipped it through the bamboo. Then she tied it off with the ribbon at the bottom. She picked up the bow, glanced down at the Bamboo Jade, and slung it across her chest.

"I'll see you guys when I get there. I'll be taking up the rear with the panda army, from what I am told," remarked Clara as she exhaled. "Oh, here come the guardians."

The guardians approached and greeted everyone. They asked the warriors to follow them as they set out in an easterly direction along a dirt path. The path soon widened out and sloped upward. After walking about a mile, they crested the gentle hill that oversaw a wider expanse.

There, formations of pandas in battle armor were checking the bamboo wagons, filled with jade-tipped spears and arrows, bamboo shields, crates of supplies and battle emplacements. Buffalos were being fitted with rigging to pull the wagons forward. Beyond them stood a large number of pandas in neat formations, some with spears and the others with bows slung across their chests.

The next sections were formations of buffalos in their elaborate cladded armor. Dirt flew up as thousands of hooves dug into the ground. Agile tigers were stalking in place, impatient to move on, with their bodies sleek in their mesh body armor.

Finally, at the very front were hundreds of cranes and eagles. Some were spanning out their wings, readying for the flight ahead of them. As the cranes' wings moved, the edges of their *katana* wings caught the light and glinted. Multiple battle banners swayed slightly in the wind, each one designating a formation's purpose.

"Wow," said Clara as she admired the convergence of the four kingdom's armies in one place.

"You can say that again," said Daniel as he admired the military strength before him.

"Impressive, isn't it?" asked the Guardian Panda.

"It is," said a still awestruck Clara.

The guardians led their warriors down the slope and arrived on level ground. The strange noise that they heard back at the Portal Circle—the agitation of the final preparation of thousands of troops and armaments—was now amplified.

The Head of the Pandemonium Squad was in full battle armor and gear and approached the Guardian Panda. But when he saw Clara, he stopped, stared at her after catching her attention, and offered a respectful bow. Clara appreciated the bestowed respect and reciprocated in kind. He then turned his attention to the Guardian Panda in hushed consultation.

"This is starting to feel real," said Sung. "Guardian Tiger told me that I will be riding on his back the entire way as he does not want me to use any of my Qi elements. What am I going to say to him during the march there?"

Before anyone could answer, the Guardian Panda let out, "Empress and emperor warriors, please give your attention to our kingdom leaders."

The warriors turned and could see that the Panderess, Tigeress, Ascendant, and the Horn Protectoress, were walking toward them with their visible entourage in tow.

The warriors quickly lined up in front of their guardians as the kingdom leaders came before them. Each of them was wearing elaborate attire from their Chinese, Korean, Japanese, and Vietnamese heritage. The Ascendent came forward as her beak seemed to nod to each warrior.

"Empress Warrior Satoh, Empress Warrior Wu, Emperor Warrior Kim, and Emperor Warrior Nguyen, on behalf of the kingdom leaders and the council of the entire kingdom leaders, I want to thank you for your courage and sense of duty to be here today. I know that the expectations being asked of you are vastly different from the lives you led back on your earthly world. But you are so much more than what you know of yourself. You are our kingdom warriors, and if you believe in that, your fullest potential to live up to your status will come true. We trust you to protect Azen from the forces that would want to do harm to us and abscond with the Portal Books. We wish you the strength that we know is in you and the courage to prevail. For Azen!"

At that moment, everyone within earshot of the Ascendant echoed back, "For Azen!"—except for the warriors, who had not been aware of the battle cry. But without missing a beat, Clara quickly looked at each of her fellow warriors and they echoed back, "For Azen!"

The kingdom leaders nodded and turned back to where they came from as their attendants followed.

The emperor and empress warriors relaxed as they turned toward their guardians. Without hesitation, their marching orders were given.

"Empress Warrior Satoh, you will fly with me," said the Guardian Crane. Yuka quickly waved to her fellow warriors and climbed onto the back of the Guardian Crane. Once the harness was secure, the Guardian Crane's great wings unfurled magnificently, and she flew upward. As they reached the formation of the cranes idling on the ground, they came alive in a cacophony of excited squawks. Soon orderly groups of cranes and eagles lifted into the air. They formed into the distinctive V formation and began their flight to Jagged Pass.

The Guardian Tiger came to Sung, lowered himself onto all fours, and asked Sung if he was ready.

"Ready as I'll ever be, Guardian Tiger. Okay, see you guys at the battle front."

"Be sure to strap yourself in and press your body into mine when I sprint ahead," admonished the Guardian Tiger.

Sung did as he was told, and when the harness was secured about his waist, he magnetically slapped the Claw Staff onto his back. He pressed his body into the thick fur of the Guardian Tiger and patted his right shoulder. In an instant, the Guardian Tiger jolted off.

"Emperor Warrior Nguyen, come with me," said the Guardian Buffalo. "We'll be traveling in the forward battle chariot."

Daniel looked at Clara and hollered out, "I'll see you at the battlefront!"

Clara echoed the sentiment as Daniel and the large Guardian Buffalo walked away.

"That leaves us, Empress Warrior Wu," said the Guardian Panda. "Follow me to the rear battle chariot."

"Yes," replied Clara as she hurriedly followed the Guardian Panda. She could see up ahead as formations of buffalos started to move out along with buffalo-drawn bamboo carriages. The winged squadrons were already out of sight, and the sprinting tigers were already gone as well. Soon, they arrived at the closest battle chariot. It was quite spacious, manned by a panda and drawn by two buffalos. It had a bamboo bench on each side, and behind it were bamboo spears fitted into slots. At the rear of each corner of the chariot was a bamboo pole with a battle banner swaying slightly in the wind.

Clara looked up at the green banner on the left and saw a bamboo stalk with eight leaves. She tilted her head to look at the banner on the right and on that was a bamboo bow and arrow. *Cool,* she thought.

The Guardian Panda stepped into the chariot and gestured for Clara to sit on the opposite bench. He spoke into the ear of the panda manning the chariot, and soon he sat down as well. The chariot started to roll forward, and Clara marveled at the number of battle chariots, wagons and formations of battle pandas that moved in unison behind her.

She was finally going into battle.

THIRTY - ONE

The march was long and uneventful. There was little conversation between Clara and the Guardian Panda as he busied his eyes over battle plans drawn on bamboo paper scrolls. Though he was a seasoned warrior himself, he probably had many thoughts to reflect on. The long monotony was interrupted by a simple lunch fetched from within the storage area under Clara's bench.

Clara focused on herself as she steadied her thoughts and focused on putting aside any imagined idea about how the battle would unfold. She had to trust her skills and Qi elemental powers. During the march, she happened to look over at the chariot riding along the left side. She saw that it was the Head of the Pandemonium Squad. But she noticed that her battle chariot was surrounded by several other battle chariots holding battle pandas with distinctive red stripes across the center of their helmets. *She was being guarded by the Pandemonium Squad*, she realized. She could see about twenty of these specialized battle solders, and she felt honored by their protection.

As the sun started to set, the chariot rumbled more slowly. Clara got up and steadied her hand on the rail and saw before her, far off in the distance, a high rock formation with a jagged crack running down the middle. The valley was wide and long and was flanked on each side by several rocky ledges. At the top of the ledges were hundreds of cranes who were settling in as they squawked to each other. There was much bustling and movement in the valley floor among the tigers and the buffalos.

Directly ahead of her was a flattened plateau that marked the natural end of the valley before it sloped away onto the wide path that she was on.

"Welcome to Jagged Pass, Empress Warrior Wu," said the Guardian Panda.

"Whoa. I didn't think the rock would be so tall," Clara exclaimed.

Just then, Sung and Daniel sauntered up and waved to Clara. She jumped out of the chariot and turned to them when a voice from above caught her attention.

The Guardian Crane gracefully glided downward and tucked in her wings as she bowed with her beak. Yuka jumped off and said, *"Domo arigato."*

"This place is amazing," Yuka said as the guys approached.

"Hey," said Clara. Everyone offered a greeting.

"I've been here for a while already," Yuka said. "Beyond the chokepoint, I saw an open expanse that ends at a ridge. Beyond the ridge is a wide swath of land, and these thick old trees on each side. That's where the Warlock army of demon dogs will be coming from," Yuka explained thoroughly.

"Wow, you know so much already, Yuka," said Sung. "I'm impressed."

Yuka smiled and continued, "There's more. The Guardian Crane told me a lot. So, you guys will be in the lead formation with the tigers and buffalos beyond the chokepoint. From prior experience, once the Warlock's army crests the ridge, they'll survey our defenses. Once they are ready, they'll pour over the ridge and down toward you guys. But before you engage them, me and the cranes, along with the eagles, will perform our aerial assault by dropping heavy jade-tipped darts. There will be formations of heavy panda archers who will launch a lot of arrows. Hopefully we can take a lot of them out before you guys, along with your buffalo and tiger armies, engage them head on. Then depending how many are left, the buffalos and the tigers will pour through the chokepoint and hopefully draw in the remaining demon dogs so the hundreds of panda archers will take care of the rest. That's the plan, at least."

"That's intense," Daniel let out. "But wouldn't the chokepoint also slow down the buffalos and the tigers?"

"Oh, I forgot to mention this! I couldn't believe it when the Guardian Crane told me. Once we start our retreat, the cranes will land to allow the tigers to hop on. Then the eagles will fly over the buffalos, grab onto a special harness under their armor, and carry them away. They will be flown to the top of the ledge so they can run to the back of the valley. Isn't that crazy?"

"Totally crazy!" said Sung.

"Well, I need to work with my Guardian Crane on additional preparations, but let's meet up for dinner later?" said Yuka.

"That sounds good," said Clara as Yuka hopped back onto the back of the Guardian Crane and flew off.

"Wow, when did Yuka get so military?" asked Clara aloud.

"I don't know but I'm impressed," said Sung admiringly. "But yeah, we need to see what we can do to help. But Azen Warriors dinner later?"

"Sounds good to me," said Daniel. "See you later."

Clara nodded as everyone left, leaving her looking for the Guardian Panda. When she found him among the throngs of pandas moving about, he was looking down at a group of three red bearlike creatures. They were about a third of the height of the Guardian Panda, with fluffy striped tails, white furry snouts, and eye patches. She grinned at their cuteness as she went to them. All three turned their heads toward her with the cutest expressions.

"Oh, how cute!" exclaimed Clara.

The lead red bear looked insulted as he recomposed his expression and introduced himself, "Good evening, Empress Warrior Wu, I am Xiang Xiang, leader of the Red Panda Scouts. It is an honor to fight alongside you. If you shall excuse me, we shall now depart. Guardian Panda."

As the three red pandas bowed, the Guardian Panda and Clara reciprocated, and they scurried off.

"Red pandas?" asked Clara. "I never knew there were any such pandas!"

"Yes, we call them cousins. They are the forward ground scouts. They will be passing beyond the chokepoint tonight to scout out the advancing Warlock army and relay any vital tactical information that may be useful," answered the Guardian Panda.

"Wow, they're scouts. They're going into the night all by themselves?"

"Better them than three big fluffy white and black pandas," replied the Guardian Panda slyly.

Clara let out a chuckle and agreed with his assessment. She looked up at the Guardian Panda and said, "Everyone has their part in this battle, it seems."

"Yes, though we have won every battle and kept the Warlock at bay, we can never be complacent," responded the Guardian Panda gravely.

"What can I do to help?" asked Clara as she looked up into the brown eyes of the Guardian Panda.

THIRTY - TWO

The fire crackled, its lively flames dancing among the rocks surrounding it. Empty bamboo boxes were all that were left to show how the *baos*, rice paper spring rolls, *kimchi* pancakes, and *tamago* had been devoured with abandon. The four warriors looked into the fire in silence and Clara held out her hands for warmth. The air was chilly, and the night sky was dark as the moons traced arcs overhead as the large shadowy ring planet loomed over.

"Man, what I wouldn't give for Korean barbecue right now," said Sung as everyone laughed. "The fire is perfect for it, throw a grill over it, instant Korean barbecue setup."

"*Thit bo voi bo,*" said Daniel as he smacked his lips.

"What's that?" asked Sung.

"It's this Vietnamese beef dish that is sizzled over a hot pan, oh the smell is amazing!" said a hungry Daniel.

"*Yakitori!*" said Yuka gleefully!

"Yes, *yakitori!* What's your favorite?" asked Sung.

"I love the chicken liver," answered Yuka with a smile.

"Oooo… what I wouldn't do for chicken liver. How about beef tongue?" asked Sung.

"Yummy!" said Yuka as her eyes smiled at the thought of sizzling *yakitori*.

"Do you think hot pot can be placed over an open flame?" asked Clara.

"Do you think water will boil over an open flame?" asked Sung sarcastically. "Hot pot is so much fun!"

"Man, if our guardians could hear us talking now, they'd kick our butts," said Daniel as everyone laughed.

"Well, we can imagine for a little bit," said Sung as his eyes got lost in the blaze of the flames.

"Tomorrow is the day. We're going to be fighting for real against some demon dogs," said Daniel.

"*Huo dou*, that's what they are called in Chinese," said Clara.

"Yah, the *Huo Dou*, demon dogs," Daniel repeated. "Are you guys scared?"

The silence was deafening as everyone looked up at each other.

"I am, but I'm more worried for all of you," said a concerned Yuka.

"I'd be lying if I said I wasn't nervous about tomorrow," Sung said.

"Yah, me too," said Daniel as he looked at Sung. "But me and you, we're like fire and ice," as Daniel pushed out his fist toward Sung.

Sung's eyes lit up and he fist bumped Daniel and pulled it back, flashing his open fingers, "Don't you know it, we'll sweep up these demon dogs."

"How about you Clara?" asked Daniel.

"Huh, oh… I am. But I know we'll pull through. We're the Azen Warriors, right?"

"That's right!" said Daniel confidently.

"Don't get cocky, Daniel!" admonished Clara as she stared up at him.

"You're right… Quake," said Daniel with a smirk.

Clara smiled and said teasingly, "Did you just call me by my secret superhero name?"

"Hey, you named yourself, Quake, I'm just regular Scorch and mister unoriginal here is Iceman," said Daniel.

Sung blurted out, "Hothead would have been better!" as everyone laughed.

Clara moved onto her knees and got closer to the fire. She motioned to everyone else to do the same. All eyes were on Clara anticipating her next move.

Clara looked at everyone and started, "Let's promise we'll fight our best tomorrow to protect our guardians and all the battle animals that are here. They are depending on us so much. And let's promise that once we win, we will have dinner again. We may be scared now, but we are the Azen Warriors and we will defeat the Warlock army!"

Everyone looked at each other and then Clara brought up her two clenched fists to her chest. Everyone smiled and did the same, feeling the power of their secret gesture. As tiny embers danced upward, Clara looked up at everyone and quietly said, "For Azen."

Everyone nodded and looked at each other with smiles and said, "Azen Warriors!" in resounding unison.

As they let their clenched fists drop, Daniel remarked, "That was pretty dramatic… Quake."

Clara smiled as Daniel picked up his dinner box and continued, "Okay, I'm going to bed. Guardian Buffalo told me to get a full night's rest as we need to be up at the crack of dawn."

"Me too," said Sung as he reached for his dinner box. "Have a good night! Coming Dan?"

Clara and Yuka waved as the two guys walked away.

"Hey," said Yuka curiously.

"Hmmm?" replied Clara as she stoked the fire with a thin bamboo stalk.

"Want to take a ride?" asked Yuka?

Clara looked up and asked, "What do you mean?"

"Follow me," said Yuka.

They walked back to Yuka's tent, and she gave Clara a smile. "Watch this," she said as she whistled lightly.

In a few seconds a handsome crane swooped down and landed in front of them. He blinked at them with its beady eyes.

"I have a crane! I'm not supposed to use any of my Qi elemental powers until battle so to get around, Takeshi is my ride."

Clara's eyes lit up and let out excitedly, "Oh cool! But will he be able to take the both of us?"

"If I'm expected to fly a tiger on my back tomorrow," Takeshi replied, "I'm certain I can take two human girls on my back."

Yuka and Clara laughed at his unexpected answer.

* * *

They soared silently through the night sky, and Clara was even more impressed with the unobstructed view of the gaseous planet and its large ring looming in the night sky. They stayed silent, as it was the eve of battle and the Warlock army of demon dogs were approaching from a distance, though still many hours away.

They flew past the ridgeline where the horde of demon dogs would cross before racing toward Jagged Pass. Despite the anticipation of the battle, the flight was uplifting, and all of Clara's and Yuka's worries were lifted away.

"This is amazing," whispered Clara as she pressed the side of her face into

Yuka's back while gripping onto the bamboo harness that held her in place.

Yuka murmured and patted the crane gently on the nape of his neck. He reared his beady eye as she said, "Time to return."

"As you wish, Empress Warrior Satoh," said the crane as his beady eye suddenly reflected fire. He immediately faced forward as Yuka suddenly looked up and saw a burst of fire coming at them!

"Hold on!" Takeshi shouted as the girls tightened their grip as he violently banked left. The fire burst shot up past them, but another came at them and he turned even harder as it brushed up against his right wing. A third fireball exploded upon the mesh armor on the underside of his belly, and he let out a grunt. Then a fourth exploded on the exposed front of his neck, and a painful shriek shattered the night sky.

Takeshi mustered his last strength despite the searing burn on his neck, sputtering through the air toward the chokepoint. He flapped with all his remaining strength before two more fire bursts hit him from behind, forcing his tail end to buck upward in a flash of fire.

"Oh no!" screamed Yuka as she yelled out, "Hold on!"

Clara suddenly felt them plummeting as her stomach rose into her throat. The crane tried to rally once more before his neck went limp. He began to freefall, beak first into the treetops. Yuka frantically invoked the wall Qi element in front of the falling crane, and it slowed his body down as he crashed through it. She invoked another and the crane's body went through it until finally, they were at the mercy of the tree branches.

"Hang on!" screamed Yuka as the crane's body crashed into the branches with Yuka and Clara desperately holding on while harnessed to the crane's limp body. Tree branches violently snapped away and breaking the eerie silence as Clara's arrows fell from her quiver.

Clara braced herself by pressing into Yuka's body as branches and leaves violently brushed up against them as they fell until finally, the crane's body hit the ground with a thud.

Still dazed from the fall, Clara leaned back as she brought her hand to her forehead, but Yuka was already unfastening her harness as she whispered repeatedly, "Oh no."

"Clara, you need to unclip your harness," Yuka whispered frantically as she tried to feel about the harness that kept Clara strapped in. Clara's eyes refocused in the dim light of the forest. She started to work at the harness and soon unclipped it. She slid off along with Yuka, who immediately ran to cradle the head of the dead crane.

Clara then walked around the massive crane and saw a couple of her glowing jade tipped arrows on the ground. She gasped as she reached into her quiver. Empty. All her arrows were strewn about the dark forest floor. She quickly picked up the two she saw, returned one and cocked the other. She ran to Yuka and knelt beside her as she was tearing up. Yuka looked down at the closed eyes on the crane's head as her heart cried for him.

Clara placed her hand on Yuka's shoulder, "Yuka, we need to get out of here now!" she whispered urgently.

"But what about Takeshi? We just can't leave him like this," complained Yuka.

"We have to. We need to get back to the others. They can come get him once we get reinforcements. Do you understand?" asked Clara.

Yuka looked down at the crane's head and looked back up and nodded. She placed the crane's neck on the ground and whispered in Japanese for *I am very sorry, "moushi wake arimasen deshita."*

Yuka got up and suddenly, surrounded by the tall dark trees in the eerie silence, she could feel the danger that she and Clara were in.

"Do you think you can fly both of us out of here?" asked Clara.

"I can try," said Yuka as she allowed Clara to climb onto her back. Once Clara's legs were wrapped around her waist, Yuka invoked the fly Qi element and they soared into the air—all of ten feet before they floated down.

"Let me try again," said Yuka as she clenched her fists tighter. They soared about fifteen feet in the air, but again they floated down. Clara climbed off Yuka's back as she turned to face her. "I don't think my Qi element for flying was meant for more than one person," said Yuka hopelessly.

Clara's shoulders drooped as she looked at Yuka, "Go get help."

"I can't leave you!" said Yuka urgently.

"You have to! Yuka, we're behind the ridgeline. Obviously, some of the demon dogs are already here, and they are probably looking for us now. Takeshi was able to fly us away far enough to buy us some time to escape. You need to go back and bring back help. With your flying, you'll be there in no time."

Yuka nodded reluctantly, "I'll be back soon. Hide, okay?"

Clara nodded and though she was trying to look confident, fear started to well up from within as her fingers trembled. "Go now."

Yuka nodded, stepped back and invoked the fly Qi element as she soared off into the night.

I wish I could fly, thought Clara as she scanned the forest floor and found another three arrows. As she picked up the last arrow, she heard a low bark in the distance.

She quickly cocked her bow and looked about her, surrounded by the dark trees, all alone.

THIRTY - THREE

The trees were old and their bark thick and crusty. Some trees were tightly clumped together, leaving open patches of clearing. Clara quietly made her way up a slight slope toward a larger tree while keeping the downed crane within view. Every step she took crushed the underbrush beneath her, and the sound seemed to be amplified in the dead of the forest night. She pressed herself against the large tree and peered over her left shoulder. She could faintly make out the dark navy silhouette of the crane's bulbous body.

A snap pierced the forest silence and sent a shiver down her spine. She held her breath and carefully peeked over her right shoulder. Then she saw them.

A fiery pair of glowing eyes was scanning the forest floor. Then another pair and another, until she could make out at least five pairs of fiery glowing eyes. But it was the fire burning in their mouths that made her heart jolt.

They were moving slowly, and she could barely make out their bodies as their dark fur blended into the night. They were carefully exploring. The attention of two of the demon dogs was piqued, and they scurried from view. Clara exhaled slowly, then inhaled deeply as she looked over her left shoulder.

The demon dog pack found the body of the dead crane. Two of them began sniffing the body. She felt helpless. Then one of them came to the crane's crooked neck, sunk its fiery jaws into it, and began desecrating the poor crane's body.

Untamed anger rose within her as hopeless tears started to form at the corner of her eyes, causing her to bring up her arrow hand to her mouth. She couldn't help the dead crane, so she turned her head way to avoid the gruesome ordeal as her foot snapped a twig.

Her eyes widened as she quickly placed her hand on the end of the arrow and pulled taut the bow string. She slowly peered over her left shoulder and saw that the dogs had peeled away and were coming in her direction. They were sniffing the air and the ground.

Clara's heart raced. Finally, when they were ten feet away from her, she appeared from behind the tree just as the demon fire dogs looked up. They let out a loud bark as the fire within their mouths grew. Clara's first arrow drove itself through the mouth and head of one dog as the other two dogs raced toward her, expelling fire bursts from their mouths.

A second arrow took out one of the oncoming dogs, but the third veered to her left, obscuring itself behind the trees. Clara trained her bow on it and released it, sending the third arrow into the dog's side, forcing it to stumble into a heap of dark fur. But while she was focusing on the third demon dog, the other two demon dogs returned, something that she didn't have time to notice. The tips of the dogs' fur glistened with fire making them more menacing. She didn't have time to load another bow, so she invoked the *wall* Qi element as she yelled, "*teng bing!*" The dirt wall broke through the ground, pushing them back momentarily.

Clara panted as she took a couple of steps backwards. She wondered where Yuka was. She loaded her fourth arrow just as both demon dogs appeared from both ends of the dirt wall. She couldn't take them both out, so she aimed for the one on the left. The arrow sunk into its head. But the second dog lunged at her as she gasped. She immediately ducked, but one of the dog's claws snagged on her top, causing her to roll over onto the ground.

As she landed, her head hit the ground with a thud. In a daze, she struggled to push herself up onto her side. She reached back into her quiver but panicked when she felt nothing.

She trained her eyes back on the fire demon dog, which was on all its paws, claws extended, haunches raised, its fur bristling in fire, as fire glared from its eyes and flared from its snout. In a split second, it lunged into the air at Clara. She screamed as she brought her forearm up to her face.

Her breathing was shallow in anticipation of jaws and claws upon her. But there was nothing. She only heard a deep growl as she peered over her forearm to see the fire demon dog floating and struggling in midair. In another split second, the body of a large crane whisked by. The demon dog went lifeless as the front of its body fell away, leaving the bloody innards of its back half exposed in midair.

"Clara!" screamed a familiar voice as Yuka landed in front of her, with nine moon stars strapped to her waist. She rushed to Clara and without a word, pulled her up. A heavy flutter was heard along with a thud as a crane landed. It was the Guardian Crane.

"Empress Warrior Wu, climb aboard quickly!" she ordered.

Clara did what she was told without question and climbed aboard the feathery back of the Guardian Crane. Yuka quickly strapped her in and firmly pressed herself into Clara's back.

"Go!" yelled Yuka as the Guardian Crane soared upward with its great wings as two other cranes flanked her.

"You're safe now," whispered Yuka.

Clara let out a sigh of relief, closed her eyes and uttered, "Thank you," as they flew back to Jagged Pass.

THIRTY - FOUR

The chilly wind whisked about Clara's face as her senses came back to her. She realized that the Guardian Crane was flying faster than she ever thought was possible. She took notice of the two other cranes flying in formation on either side of them. Finally, she felt Yuka's presence behind her.

"What happened back there?" asked Clara. "The last thing that I remembered was coming out of my daze and the demon dog lunging at me."

"It was so dark from above, we couldn't find you easily. But the Guardian Crane saw the fire from the demon dogs' bodies. Their fur only ignites when they are about to attack. We swooped in and saw you had just taken out one of them. But then you fell as the other leapt over you. As soon as he tried to lunge at you, I invoked a wall of air and trapped him inside of it and well, you saw what the Guardian Crane did next with her *katana* wing."

"Whoa," said Clara when she panicked, "Where's my bow?"

"I have it," said Yuka. "Do you want it back now?"

Clara nodded as Yuka unslung it from her body and slung it over Clara's head from behind. Clara grabbed the grip of the bow with both hands and looked at the glowing green jade, finding comfort in it. "Thanks."

Soon they crossed over Jagged Pass. They flew silently toward the plateau at the end of the valley, and she could see several battle animals there, including Sung and Daniel, who were waving.

The Guardian Crane gently glided downward and landed. Sung and Daniel rushed over as Yuka unclipped their harnesses. As Yuka slid down the back of the Guardian Crane, Daniel reached upward with both arms. Yuka braced her hands onto his strong shoulders as he gently grabbed her by the waist, eased her off the Guardian Crane and onto the ground. Sung reached up toward Clara as she pushed back her hair and reached down toward him as he eased her onto solid ground by her waist.

"Are you all right?" Sung asked Clara whose head was downcast as she nodded quietly.

"Empress Warrior Wu, are you unharmed?" asked her Guardian Panda, which made Clara look up at him with his concerned brown eyes buried in the black eye patches.

"I am, thanks to Yuka and the Guardian Crane," said Clara gratefully.

Yuka recapped quickly what happened, which elicited awed expressions from Sung and Daniel. When she mentioned the slicing of the demon dog in half by the Guardian Crane, Sung's and Daniel's eyes turned toward the Guardian Crane and saw the residual blood on her right *katana* wing. They were speechless.

"Clara got first blood," said Daniel respectfully.

At that moment, Clara realized that she had the will to kill within her, as long as the cause was just. She looked up at her fellow warriors and spoke. "Guys, let me tell you. Those fire demon dogs, they are not like the dogs that we love back home. They are ferocious and they are relentless. Don't think twice about killing them. I could feel it, they are pure evil."

Her tone struck a chord with each of them, and they embraced her words and the gravity of the situation that lay before them.

Their attention was distracted by the loud flapping of wings not far away. It was two cranes, who had stretched out a large, bloodied cloth between their talons. When they set it on the ground, the cloth fell open, exposing the crumpled and bloodied body of the dead crane.

Yuka's hands went to her face as tears welled up in her eyes and she raced over. Clara was about to go as well when the Guardian Panda's voice told her not to.

Clara stopped along with Sung and Daniel, who stood in place, feeling helpless.

"Let her grieve," said the Guardian Panda.

"It was our fault; we were curious, and we just wanted to fly…" Clara said as her voice trailed away.

"His death was tragic, but it also told us something. That the demon dogs are closer than we thought. It may explain why the red panda scouts never returned."

"Oh no! What happened to them?" asked Clara.

"They may have fallen, since the demon dogs have advanced further than we thought, or they could be hiding," said the Guardian Panda.

"What does that mean?" asked Sung as he sensed some concern.

"We had thought we would fight a noon battle with the sun high over us, but if we are to fight a morning battle, the sun will be in front of us."

"Does that change our battle plans?" asked Daniel.

"It means we may have to lure them through Jagged Pass earlier than anticipated, so the walls of the rock formation can shield our eyes. But the valley can only absorb so many enemies at once before we are overwhelmed."

There was silence as the warriors mentally worked through battle scenarios in their minds that they had never experienced firsthand.

"Warriors, please do not worry. Trust your guardians along with the leaders of each elite battle team. They are very experienced and will be able to direct the battle as it unfolds," said the Guardian Panda.

Yuka came back to rejoin the group looking gloomy.

Clara went over immediately and embraced her gently. As Yuka rested her chin on Clara's shoulder, she said, "He has a wife crane back home."

Clara's eyes widened in shock. It wasn't something that she thought about: That the battle animals may have families of their own.

Yuka stepped back and looked at her warrior friends, "He sacrificed himself by veering away as far as possible to buy us time. We need to fight those fire demon dogs to the end!" Yuka exclaimed as her voice reached a crescendo.

The warriors nodded in unison and reflected on their earlier pact, which was made even more urgent with the new details.

"Empress and emperor warriors," said the Guardian Panda. "I know that it has been a tragic night, but the bigger battle is tomorrow. We need all of you to get a full night's rest. Attendants will wake you tomorrow to prepare you for your first battle."

THIRTY - FIVE

The sun had just broken over the horizon as sun beams raked over the forested terrain. Clara was putting on the final touches to her morning routine. She pulled over the front flap of her top and allowed it to magnetically snap into place. She gathered her hair, slipped it into her bamboo ribbon hair accessory and tied it off, allowing it to hang over her shoulder. She slung the quiver full of green-jade-tipped arrows across her back. She had just gripped the Bow of Destiny when the flap to her tent opened.

She looked up as the Guardian Panda entered, in full bamboo battle armor and with his green bamboo helmet under his left arm.

"Good morning, Empress Warrior Wu. The attendants told me that you were already up," he said calmly as he stood at full height.

Clara looked down briefly at her boots before looking back up and replied, "I wanted to prepare, and thought I'd get dressed before the battle."

The Guardian Panda gave her a quizzical look as he looked at her up and down. "You didn't think you'd be wearing your training gear into battle, did you?"

"Well, I..." said Clara before the flap to her tent opened yet again. An ornate bamboo wardrobe was wheeled in by two other panda attendants, who propped it up behind the Guardian Panda.

"What is that?" she asked.

"Your battle armor, befitting a Panda Empress Warrior," he said. He stepped aside, and the two wardrobe doors opened.

Clara's eyes lit up as she uttered incredulously, "Oh wow!"

* * *

"Sung, your battle armor looks dope!" said Daniel as he admired Sung's attire. His chest armor was a system of multiple interlocked matte metallic plates. It ended at a wide belt, and a finer mesh armor hung below his waist. Emblazoning his belt buckle was a silhouette of a tiger's head with blue jade eyes. A second, larger blue jade was embedded into the top of the chest armor. His forearms were protected by a mesh-like gauntlet. His boots were protected by an exterior shin guard, whose tips were embedded with a small blue jade. A black skull cap fit neatly atop his head, giving him an unexpected athletic look.

"Bro, I feel like I'm in one of those traditional Korean dramas, but this battle armor, it's so much more functional. Guardian Tiger told me that this chest armor and my battle cap were created using Clawdium."

"That is so cool!" said Daniel.

"And look!" said Sung as he angled the Claw Staff behind him when it suddenly snapped against his back. "Magnetic!"

"Now *that* is cool," marveled Daniel.

"And yours, man!" said Sung. "That chest armor with the molding, all seems to fit together making it look tight!"

Daniel moved his chest to show the interlocking plates of metal that formed a battle armor system with shoulder guards. Metallic mesh fabric extended below his belt line to protect his thighs, and he wore gauntlets and boots similar to Sung's. A red jade glowed slightly in the center of his battle armor.

"Check out the helmet," said Daniel with a smile as he finagled his left hand under the black metallic helmet he'd been cradling under his armpit. He slid it over this head, and it covered his ears. At the top was an insignia for a buffalo where a red jade was embedded just above it.

"*Ohayō gozaimasu!*" someone cried out from above. Sung and Daniel looked up to see Yuka floating down. When her white boots lightly landed, she saw the guys gawking at her and couldn't help smiling at the attention from them.

Her entire battle armor was made up of intricate interlocking white plates wrapped around her chest and back. At the center of her chest was a sizeable white jade. Below her waist was a three-section system that protected her lower thighs. Matching the colors of her crane, she wore a bodysuit of black mesh, sewn from silken-bamboo threads and intertwined with Clawdium fibers. Her shoulders were protected by another layered armor system, and she too wore gauntlets and boots outfitted with shin guards. At her waist was a wide white belt where her Moon Star *shuriken* was fastened.

"Whoa!" said Sung. "You look amazing!"

"Let me add the final touch," Yuka said as she pulled out her white helmet. At the top of the helmet was another white jade, but the front was emblazoned with a red flare that swooped over the top of the helmet. She slipped it on and looked at the guys.

"Red! Like the top of the crane's head!" said Daniel as he saw the entire color ensemble.

Yuka pointed at Daniel while shaking her head enthusiastically.

"Oh wow! Cool battle armor, Yuka!" exclaimed Sung.

Footsteps crossed the plateau, and the three turned their attention to Clara.

Her chest plate was molded to her torso in a blend of light gray and green. The light green came from jade dust collected during the polishing phase of the jades. Across her chest plate was a green jade. A plated protection system also extended from her waist to her mid-thighs, and her shoulders were similarly protected. Underneath everything, she wore a black body suit, woven from silken-bamboo thread and interwoven with Clawdium fibers. Like the others, she wore gauntlets and boots with shin guards, but covered with swirls of jade dust that followed the contours of her calf muscles. Her form-fitting light gray helmet had green jade dust that splashed backward with a panda logo etched into the top.

"You look amazing!" said Yuka as all four of them walked towards one another.

"Thanks!" said an excited Clara. "You look amazing yourself," she added, admiring Yuka's battle armor.

"Wow, both of you girls look so amazing right now!" said Sung as he admired his two female warriors.

"You guys look really great too! Your muscles really show!" said Clara as she admired Sung's arms and then turned away when she realized she was making it too obvious.

"Wow, when my Guardian Buffalo came in with that wooden wardrobe, I didn't know what to expect," said Daniel.

"Me too!" said Clara humorously. "And I had just gotten dressed too."

"Those green swirls?" asked Daniel as he pointed to the green inlay within Clara's battle armor which was different than everyone else.

Clara looked down at the green jade dust that followed the contours of her body and responded, "Jade dust."

"Jade dust?" asked Sung.

"Yep!" Clara said enthusiastically.

"You are the Dust Empress!" said Sung as everyone burst out laughing.

"Look at us! I feel like we are real warriors now," said Yuka with a confident smile.

Sung noticed the four guardians approaching and hurriedly shot everyone a look. As if on cue, they each brought up their clenched fists to their chest with their elbows to their sides, nodded and whispered in unison, "For Azen."

"Warriors of Azen," said the Guardian Tiger as he crept up on them. "Please face me and your fellow guardians."

The Guardian Tiger stood up and he looked at everyone with his steely blue eyes. "We hope that your battle armor suits you, and we know that it will also protect you. From now, until we are victorious over the Warlock's *Huo Dou* demon dogs, you must wear your battle armor at all times. On behalf of your fellow guardians, we believe in you and we will always protect you. Now, our aerial observations tell us that the enemy is almost at the ridgeline so we must move into place. Empress Warrior Satoh, you and the Guardian Crane will take to the air. Emperor Warriors Nguyen and Kim, you are with Guardian Buffalo and me. And Empress Warrior Wu, the battle for the valley is yours, please follow the Guardian Panda."

Without any further oratories, the warriors looked at each other one last time and followed their respective guardians into battle.

* * *

Sung rode atop the Guardian Tiger as he looked at the neat formation of buffalos before him with impressive armor cladding across their back. There were hundreds, and he could easily make out Daniel, riding atop the Guardian Buffalo. He stuck out like a sore thumb. It was the task of the buffalos to ram through the horde of demon dogs and to scatter them, sending them into the claws of the white tigers.

He could feel his chest tighten, but he continued to breathe as he held onto the harness. The silence of waiting was deafening. He looked to this left and saw hundreds of white tigers, breathing steadily, eyes focused on what was about to come. His head turned backwards and saw more neat formations of white tigers. Behind the last white tiger formation were regiments of panda archers. Behind them were multiple squadrons of cranes and eagles. He tried to locate Yuka, but he could not see her in the sea of black and white feathers.

His eyes rose as he felt a dull rumbling. He cast his eyes along the ridgeline and the sun was already above it. *This was going to work against them*, he thought.

"Remember, Emperor Warrior Kim, once we engage the enemy in battle, lift off of me and trust your battle instincts," reminded the Guardian Tiger.

"Yes, Guardian Tiger," replied Sung.

The rumbling started to amplify and all eyes along the battlefront looked up. Buffalos by the hundreds stomped their hooves into the ground in anticipation as Daniel leaned atop the Guardian Buffalo who stared outward with his red eyes.

Yuka saw the panda archers pull taut their first arrows of many and admired the tight coordination among them. She looked left and right and saw that the cranes were gently flapping their *katana* wings, catching the glint from the sun. She looked down and their talons were twitching and balancing about large leather sacks filled with heavy jade tipped darts. The tension was building all around. She wondered what Clara was thinking behind Jagged Pass.

* * *

"I wonder what's going on?" Clara wondered aloud.

The Guardian Panda's eyes did not stray as he simply said, "Carnage."

Clara nodded. She had seen firsthand what the *Huo Dou* fire demon dogs were capable of doing, but she also had faith in all the battle animals, the elite battle teams, the guardians, and of course her warriors, though it was their first battle.

Clara, eyes fixed beyond the crack of Jagged Pass, knelt down and placed her hand on the dirt ground beneath her. She flattened her palm against the earth and closed her eyes. Reaching outward, she sensed it; the open valley in front of her, the open ground beyond the chokepoint and the thousands of talons, paws, and hooves upon it. Further out she sensed the ridgeline and she felt them, thousands of fiery paws. Her eyes shot opened as she whispered, "Oh my god."

Dark shaggy figures crested the ridgeline, and a long line of snarling dogs with fiery animus in their eyes and mouths appeared. They looked down at the armies of the animal kingdoms and soon, they moved forward, and more demon dogs appeared until the forward formations were ten deep and three hundred across.

"There are thousands," uttered Daniel as he surveyed the evil forces before him.

"When we engage the demon dogs, Emperor Warrior Nguyen, fly high and trust your Qi training," said the Guardian Buffalo.

Daniel's eyes rose as he saw a tall dark shadowy figure arise from the center of the formation of the demon dogs. With the sun in front of him, Daniel could not make out any of his features except that he held a trident upon his shoulder. When the shadowy figure turned his head to survey the flank of demon dogs, he thought he could make out a snout, similar to a buffalo.

"Is that the Warlock?" asked Daniel.

"No, that is one of his demon lords, the Ox Demon Lord. He is considered a traitor among my people," said the Guardian Buffalo. "A very distant cousin, we'd like to say."

The Ox Demon Lord was unfazed by the combined armies of the animal kingdoms of Azen. He looked to his left to survey the bristling fire demon dogs and was happy that the spawning session yielded more of them. He looked down at the lead demon dog, who shook his head in reverence. It sat on its haunches and howled loudly into the air, and all the fire demon dogs snarled and snapped their fiery canine teeth. Silence then fell as the lead demon dog howled ominously, and in an instant, all the fire demon dogs raced forward in a howling rumble.

A drum suddenly rang out a quick succession of three beats and a panda yelled out *release* in Mandarin, "*Fang jian!*"

In unison, the panda archers released their first volley of jade-tipped arrows. They arced high and with the power of the jade, they each found their mark, eliciting guttural snarls among the fire demon dogs. The drums pounded out another three beats, and another volley of arrows whizzed through the air. They too found their marks, and cries of pain and death rang throughout the battlefield.

Daniel's heart was racing as he saw hundreds upon hundreds of the ferocious fire demon dogs go down. He saw a third wave of arrows flying overhead and finding their marks. As the fiery furry masses went down, a sense of gratified excitement welled up within him.

The stampede of demon dogs had covered about a third of the distance to the kingdom armies when the drums pounded out five beats. The Guardian Crane looked at Yuka and commanded in Japanese, the word for *ascend: jōshō suru!*

The first row of cranes took off in an orchestrated formation, carrying in their talons leather sacks holding the jade-tipped darts. Meanwhile, the pandas started their coordinated retreat through the crack of Jagged Pass.

Yuka invoked her fly Qi element and soared alongside the Guardian Crane. From her vantage point, she could see the waves of fire demon dogs. Many had already passed over the fallen, and the path was open. She looked to her left and right and saw that the cranes had efficiently organized into several V formations, with the Guardian Crane in the lead. She glanced backwards and saw a similar line of eagles. As they neared the mid-point, the Guardian Crane squawked, and the first wave of cranes released the heavy darts.

As the darts fell, they righted themselves as the feathers caught the wind, aiming the jade tips downward. With impressive accuracy, they lodged into all areas of the fire demon dogs' bodies. Hundreds of dogs fell grunting in pain if the strikes weren't immediately fatal.

But the fire demon dogs continued to plow ahead relentlessly. The fire along their backs splintered into shards as it rose into the air. The first wave of cranes arced backwards, and the second wave released another volley of heavy darts.

Yuka hovered in the center and plucked a moon star into each hand. When she could see the fiery eyes of the fire demon dogs, she released them. They sailed through the air, twisting and turning until they sunk into the fiery eyes of two fire demon dogs, causing them to wince in pain. But they continued until she hit their second eyes, blinding them. Other fire demon dogs plowed into them but soon righted themselves, racing toward the buffalos with vile intent.

Yuka knew her moon stars were having limited effect, so she invoked gusts of wind that blew back packs of the fire demon dogs. But they merely got back up and continued racing onward. As she screamed out "*kabe*" while invoking scores of invisible air walls onto the battleground, the fire demon dogs clumsily plowed into them head on. But they were tenacious and merely plowed along the length of the wall until they came to the end and their bodies whipped onward, followed by more fire demon dogs.

The Guardian Crane hovered alongside and screamed out, "Good, you're slowing them down and confusing them…" she was cut off as she veered off as a fire burst shot up between her and Yuka.

Yuka invoked another fly element to reenergize her ability to fly and saw below her a line of fire demon dogs shooting up more fire bursts. She soared even higher and looked down to see that about half of the fire demon dog army had been decimated. They were about to cross the halfway point. The third wave of cranes had already released their last volley of heavy darts and were flying back to the buffalo and tiger formations. That's when she heard the drums pound out a succession of seven beats.

The Guardian Buffalo stared at the imminent clash with the fire demon dogs. He looked to his left and right. He then snorted as he hollered out *horns* in Vietnamese, "Sừng!"

Daniel looked around in confusion as all the buffalos' heads fluttered for a moment. Then he looked down in horrified amazement as the muscles around the base of each of the Guardian Buffalo's horns pulsated. With incredulous eyes, Daniel watched as the horns rotated forward until they locked in place.

"What the hell?" asked Daniel as he witnessed the buffalo battle soldiers bearing down in anticipation with their forward-facing horns.

"It's much easier to gore when our horns are facing front," said the Guardian Buffalo. "We only do this before we ram."

"Gotcha," said Daniel as he was still in awe as the Guardian Buffalo reared his head once more with his massive horns now facing forward.

"*Thù lao!*" screamed out the Guardian Buffalo in Vietnamese for *charge*! Instinctively, Daniel let out a scream as loud snorts were exhorted. Suddenly the ground beneath them rumbled as thousands of hooves stampeded forward to engage the seemingly hundreds of remaining fire demon dogs.

"White Tigers of Claw Mountain… *Gong gyuck!*" growled the Guardian Tiger in Korean for *charge*! Sung leaned forward as the Guardian Tiger sprang ahead.

Daniel's eyes stared down the hordes of black fur and fiery ember eyes and mouths. His breathing quickened as he gripped onto the harness with his left hand and the Club Horn of *Kting Voar* in his right.

The gap was closing. One hundred feet, eighty feet, sixty feet, forty feet and Daniel focused on one of the oncoming fire demon dogs. Its fur bristled in fire as copious amounts of hot saliva whipped behind him from his snout.

Twenty feet came and Daniel raised his club horn as the fire demon dog leaped into the air. Zero feet, and the club horn caught the fire demon dog in the torso. The power of the swing sent the dog flying backwards at least twenty feet. He tossed the club horn into his left hand and invoked the thrust Qi element and soared off the back of the Guardian Buffalo.

The clash was horrific as bodies of creatures crashed into each other. The violent growling and snapping of teeth shattered the air as the demon dogs pounced onto the buffalos' armored back. Others were being rammed by the buffalo's massive horns.

Daniel threw down fireballs at the fire demon dogs who were coming in from the rear, and soon Yuka flew alongside him. He nodded. She nodded silently and worked her Qi elemental powers, throwing down gusts and walls.

Sung saw ahead of him packs of dogs teaming up on one buffalo and the bloody carnage that was unfolding. His heart was pounding like mad, and while still astride the Guardian Tiger, he invoked several icicles that found their marks among the pack of fire demon dogs on the buffalo. But it was the same scene everywhere. The buffalos broke up the waves of fire demon dogs, scattering them. Yet further back, hundreds of fire demon dogs were stymied as they navigated an invisible and fiery maze. He looked up as Daniel sent down fireballs and saw Yuka casting out her airy Qi elements.

"Now Emperor Warrior Kim!" ordered the Guardian Tiger as Sung immediately invoked the bridge Qi element and surfed away on an ice bridge. The Guardian Tiger sprung out his sharp claws. Along with hundreds of tigers in attack mode, they dug them deep into the first fire demon dogs in their path.

The chaotic scene was one of buffalos ramming and goring, tigers clawing, and fire demon dogs snapping, and to the horror of Yuka, Sung, and Daniel, the fire demon dogs started to leap over the air and fire walls. The first invoked walls started to dissipate, and Yuka and Daniel started to throw down more: *Kabe! Tường!*

The fire demon dogs were living up to their name as they started to unleash fire bursts at the buffalos and tigers. The tigers' agility was their advantage, but for the buffalos, not so much: Many were lit aflame, forcing them to run blindly until they collapsed.

Sung shot icicles toward the buffalos in flames while Yuka flew down and tried to snuff out the flames, but their chaotic movements made it hard for her to focus her Qi elemental powers.

The cranes flew down and easily dispatched the few fire demon dogs who had made it past the buffalos and the tigers. Their halved bodies pulsated slowly as their blood soaked into the ground.

Despite the carnage on the battlefield, the combined kingdom armies were gaining the upper hand. As fearless as the fire demon dogs were, the last remaining ones were scattered about and were either having their throats clawed out, their sides gored, or their entire bodies halved, impaled by icicles, blown asunder or blasted by fireballs.

Everyone started to feel the exhaustion as their concentration was focused on hunting down every straggling fire demon dog.

Then it came, a howl. A howl louder than before and all eyes turned onto the ridgeline. There were only two silhouettes, the Ox Demon Lord and the lead fire demon dog. He howled once more as he lowered his snout.

The collective eyes of Yuka, Sung, and Daniel widened as the ridgeline filled with more dark figures. They crept over, hungry and angry as another line of fire demon dogs followed, then another, until they were another ten deep.

"Oh no," Yuka let out hopelessly.

The drumbeat rang out loudly and this time, it wasn't a set number but a continuous fast beat. "Fall back to the pass!" was the order that came from the

Guardian Crane.

The Guardian Tiger looked at the bloodied horns of the Guardian Buffalo and said, "I hope the pandas are ready."

"Me too," replied the Guardian Buffalo as he and the Guardian Tiger raced back.

The Guardian Crane raced to where Yuka and Daniel were. "There's too many of them!" screamed Yuka.

"Yes, but right now, we need to buy our fellow battle soldiers time. Lay down as many air and fire walls as possible and as high as possible," ordered the Guardian Crane.

"What about me?" asked Sung.

The Guardian Crane looked at him and said, "Head to the crack of Jagged Pass and I'll meet you there."

The second wave of fire demon dogs furiously descended, undeterred by the air and fire walls, leaping over them if possible and sending more fire bursts toward Yuka and Daniel, who were furiously invoking Qi elements.

The tigers raced down the open ground and with agility started to slip through the narrow crack of Jagged Pass. The buffalos were slower, but as planned, the eagles descended upon them, lifted them up by their special harnesses, and flew them to safety over the rock formation. Cranes and eagles picked through the morass of mangled bodies, finding injured tigers and buffalos and airlifted them to safety.

"Hurry!" Daniel called out as he could only assume that thousands of new and fresh fire demon dogs were making their way through the maze of Qi walls and the mangled bodies of their canine brethren. Yuka invoked a thick air wall in midair to protect her and Daniel from the onslaught of fire bursts. Without an offense to challenge them, this second wave was moving more quickly toward Jagged Pass.

The Guardian Crane screamed out, "Back to Jagged Pass!"

With that, both Yuka and Daniel invoked a new Qi element for flight and thrust and raced back to the chokepoint.

* * *

"So many are coming," said a worried Clara.

"Did you feel a third wave?" asked the Guardian Panda.

"No, this is the only wave but it's smaller," said Clara.

"The first wave was a sacrifice, to wear down our initial battle troops. But they underestimated us," said the Guardian Panda. "It looks like the last of the tigers are coming through now."

"What happens now?" asked Clara as she tightened her grip on the bow.

"Watch. With Emperor Warrior Kim, the Guardian Crane has a trick she likes to employ," said the Guardian Panda with a hint of mischief in his voice.

Clara sighed with relief as she saw the Guardian Crane and her friends soaring over the rock formation. Yuka and Daniel hovered near the crack and the Guardian Crane seemed like she was gesturing to Sung. However, her eyes soon fell into the crack as she saw masses of rolling darkness interspersed with fire. The fire demon dog horde was undeterred: There were still hundreds.

The mechanical sound of spinning gears and creaking wood caught Clara's attention as she spied, large bamboo crossbows aimed downward from along the top ledge

"Repeating crossbows, a panda invention," said the Panda proudly.

"I thought it was the Chinese?" asked Clara.

"Who do you think the Chinese learned it from?"

Suddenly, Clara was drawn to the crack as Sung stood atop a steep ice bridge and started to invoke an ice wall into the crack itself. The ice wall was a third of the way up when one fire demon dog flew over it, but it was met with an arrow from a panda archer with deadly accuracy.

The ice wall was two thirds of the way up and the sounds of bodies crashing into ice was heard. Panda archers along the top of the rocky ledge of the chokepoint fired arrows after arrows. Finally, the entire crack was filled with ice. *It was actually beautiful*, thought Clara, seeing the ice wedged inside of Jagged Pass just as the sun was cresting over it. However, the beautiful scene started to crumble as something bright flashed behind the ice wedge. Fire.

The fire demon dogs were throwing hundreds of fire bursts into the ice wedge, which was splattering spectacularly on the other side.

"It's only a matter of time," said the Guardian Panda.

Clara nodded, then pulled out an arrow and loaded it into her bow.

A crack appeared at the bottom as Sung watched with worry as he stood on the steep ice bridge, which was also beginning to melt.

A second crack appeared as Yuka and Daniel flew to either side of him. "Hey, can you just reinforce the ice wall?" asked Daniel.

Sung looked at Daniel and said, "I think I used up all my wall Qi elements and I'm sure I'm low on icicles."

Daniel looked at Yuka, and they both realized they may be down to their last few as well. A sinking feeling settled into the pit of their stomachs as they all turned to Clara, who was probably at full strength.

The crackling sound was sudden and horrific as the ice wedge shattered and large blocks of ice crumbled downward.

"We need to get out of the archers' line of sight!" yelled Yuka as the first packs of fire demon dogs spilled through. Yuka and Daniel soared high as Sung invoked a new ice bridge toward the top ledge.

As the fire demon dogs streamed through, they became agitated, releasing fire burst after fire burst. But the panda archers were relentless, releasing a barrage of arrows. The automatic cranking of winches and twang from the release of bow strings from the repeating crossbows were impressive.

The panda spearmen, with their interlocked bamboo shields, kept at bay any fire demon dogs trying to scurry up the sides.

A wall of buffalos and tigers formed at the end of the valley separating the horde of fire demon dogs from the Guardian Panda and Clara.

But the sheer number of fire demon dogs was overwhelming. They started to leap through the crack, despite the large blocks of ice and fallen bodies of demon dogs scattered about the entrance.

Clara watched in awe at the battle but let out a gasp as fire demon dogs appeared at the top of the rock formation, which they'd somehow managed to reach. Several cranes descended and disappeared below the rock formation as panda archers furiously fired away.

The Guardian Crane swooped in and hovered, exclaiming, "There are hundreds of them. They are piled up on top of each on either side and climbing over each other to breach the wall. Oh no!" squawked the Guardian Crane as scores of fire demon dogs poured through the crack along the entire height of the opening.

"The two piles of fire demon dogs converged on the crack, prepare yourself, Empress Warrior Wu!" warned the Guardian Panda as he pulled down his bamboo helmet and braced his bamboo spear.

Clara pulled taut on her bow as her fears came true. Tens, if not hundreds of fire demon dogs were pouring through the entire height of the crack in frenzied determination and racing ahead. Many were cut down, but they were flooding the valley while releasing fire bursts after fire bursts. They were climbing up the sides and slamming into the bamboo shields, forcing the panda spearmen to engage them. As if on cue, the wall of buffalos and tigers rushed forward to engage the onslaught. Seeing a fire demon dog being gored and somersaulting through the air was suddenly invigorating for Clara.

Still a fire demon dog got through and came at her with its fiery eyes, and she sunk an arrow into its forehead. Two more came through, and she launched two successive arrows, felling them. Suddenly, it was no longer one or two, but tens of fire demon dogs breaching the gap and from afar, she could see that more were seeping through.

A fire demon dog leapt at her, but the Guardian Panda whacked it on the head with the butt end of the bamboo spear. He turned to battle another one. Two more came at Clara. She invoked the wall Qi element, but they simply ran around it. She sunk an arrow into one with authority, but there was no time to reload as the gaping jaws of the second fire demon dog lunged at her. She brought up the bow crosswise and the demon dog's canine filled jaw clamped down on the Bow of Destiny with immense force. She could feel the heat of the fire from its demonic breath. It was strong and clawing at her as she struggled while her heart raced. When suddenly, the growling fire demon dog repositioned its canine and came down on the Bamboo Jade in the Bow of Destiny.

It cracked and an explosion of white light erupted from the jade as it shattered.

"No!" screamed Clara as the Guardian Panda looked back to see what happened. His eyes suddenly lit up larger than she had ever seen as his own jade's glow subsided. He spun around and stabbed an oncoming fire demon dog as he screamed out, "Protect the Empress Warrior!"

Clara was still struggling with the insatiable fire demon dog when the back of its head was pierced by a bamboo spear. Clara looked up and saw the Head of the Pandemonium Squad beaming down at her as he echoed, "Protect the Empress Warrior Wu!"

Pandemonium Squad Pandas encircled Clara as she reached downward to pick up the green shards of what remained of the Bamboo Jade. In the chaos, she realized that without the power of the jade, the battle armor of all the pandas were no longer protected. The jade tipped arrows were no longer unerringly accurate, either.

She looked up as the Head of the Pandemonium Squad, shoved his bamboo spear down the throat of a fire demon dog, but a leaping fire demon dog swiped at his mid-section, slicing through the bamboo armor as red blood splattered through the air.

"No!" screamed Clara as she reached out with her bow hand and saw the Guardian Panda smacking his end of the bamboo spear onto the head of that fire demon dog. And that's when she saw it. The jade bracelet on her left wrist. She looked at the hollowed inset on the Bow of Destiny that mirrored the hopelessness that set in. Then her eyes focused on the size of the bulge of the Bow of Destiny above the grip. Without thinking, she quickly pulled off the draw string from the top of the bow and placed it on the ground. Each panda that encircled her was engaged with at least one fire demon dog. She slipped off the end of her gauntlet and grasped at the jade bracelet with her right hand. With all her might, she pulled on it. It got stuck at her thumb and she pulled with even more might until it slipped off. While ignoring the pain on her left thumb, she set her bow upright. She frantically pulled the jade bracelet over the bow's bulge until it was snug. She let out a gasp and stared at it as splashes of red, white and black blurred in the background. Suddenly, a white light grew out of a singular point and raced around her jade bracelet. Then a bright white light radiated outward until it touched every green jade in its path.

The claws and teeth of the fire demon dogs were no longer easily ripping away the bamboo armor. When the Guardian Panda realized that the power of the jade had been miraculously restored, he looked at Clara, who was still holding the unstrung Bow of Destiny upright. The jade bracelet around the bow caught his attention and he understood. He turned forward to all the pandas and ordered, "Fight on!"

Clara quickly reattached the draw string and without thinking, successively released ten arrows and took down ten fire demon dogs. The Pandemonium Squad pushed them back further. She looked afar and saw the valiant buffalos and tigers beginning to succumb to fatigue as the panda archers were running out of arrows. Daniel, Yuka, and Sung were fighting down to their last Qi elements. They were on the precipice of victory or defeat.

The last of the fire demon dogs struggled into the valley, and she was not going to let her friends and fellow kingdom soldiers suffer defeat. She knelt down and placed her palm firmly on the ground. She could feel all the dirt in the valley floor. With her eyes furrowed, she stood up and screamed out in Cantonese, "*teng bing!*" as she traced the character for *wall* into the air. A high and thick wall erupted from the earth, separating the fighting buffalos and tigers from the fire demon dogs.

With the wall in place, Clara screamed once again as she invoked the wall Qi element. Earth suddenly shot upward from the chokepoint, pushing up any fire demon dogs as the wall flowed toward the back and connected with the first wall that Clara threw up. The fire demon dogs, confused at first then turned around and rushed toward the other side when another similar wall suddenly appeared.

The fire demon dogs became angry and with only one way out, they rushed to the crack of Jagged Pass when it suddenly and violently filled with dirt. The remaining fire demon dogs snarled angrily in all directions when they felt a tremble beneath their feet. They all went silent as their ears perked up and their feet pattered in place. Suddenly, the earth beneath them opened, and they fell through. As the fire demon dogs looked upward seeking the light, falling through the sinkhole, its opening sealed shut as blackness enveloped them.

Clara with her right hand still outstretched, suddenly fell to one knee as the Guardian Panda rushed to her side. She was still gritting her teeth and simply asked, "Did I get them all?"

The Guardian Panda looked toward the massive wall as the bloodied Head of the Pandemonium Squad met his gaze in astonishment. He nodded his head toward the Guardian Panda, who then turned to Clara, "You got them all, Empress Warrior Wu. You may relax now."

Clara released her clenched fist and suddenly felt exhaustion. She gripped her bow with both hands as she exhaled and looked up at the black eye patches of the Guardian Panda who looked curiously down at her.

Yuka swooped in and landed next to Clara. Daniel flew in and Sung ice surfed in.

"Clara! How did you do that?" asked Yuka?

"I thought we couldn't create such massive and continuous walls?" said Daniel.

"Neither did I," said Clara as she smiled up at her friends.

"Hey, why is your bracelet on the bow?" asked Sung stupefied.

The Guardian Panda looked at the broken shards of what was once the Bamboo Jade and then looked at the jade bracelet around the Bow of Destiny and uttered, "This shouldn't be possible."

Clara looked up at the Guardian Panda and retorted, "Don't ask me, but I had to try something."

The Guardian Crane flew in and tucked in her wings. "It looks like the battle is won. We've dealt with any stragglers and we're clearing up the battlefield. Once Empress Warrior Wu is up to it, she can collapse the walls so that we may survey the valley," said the Guardian Crane with a wink of her beady eye.

The Guardian Tiger and Buffalo came up to the plateau and nodded at everyone in silence.

"Well done, all," said the Guardian Panda and everyone exhaled in relief.

* * *

The Ox Demon Lord stood silently at the ridgeline with only the lead of the once formidable *Huo Dou* demon dogs. The last demon dog opened his jaw and licked his lips before closing his jaw shut. The Ox Demon Lord turned about and started to walk away with the fire demon dog along his side. He then let out, "The jade may be destroyed. This has never happened before. The Warlock will find this bit of news to his liking."

THIRTY - SIX

Clara kept an eye on the Guardian Crane, who was carrying a weary Yuka. She looked to her left and saw Sung rejoicing at the experience of flying atop a crane and she looked to her right to see Daniel pressing himself into the crane's nape, afraid of extreme heights—a strange phobia for someone who could fly. She peered behind her to see the three other guardians on the backs of a crane except for the buffalo, who was atop an eagle.

As she looked straight ahead, she was glad for the flight home. A twelve-hour trek back to the Portal Circle would have been exhausting and she was sure that it was the same for the others. *Well, except for Yuka*, she thought, *she always gets to fly*.

As she looked back on the past few hours, everything seemed like a blur. The actions of the day seemed to have been fast forwarded in her mind and she rewound everything back to replay slowly. But she was amazed that a teenaged Asian American girl like herself had fought against an army of fire demon dogs. The despair she felt when she saw the Bamboo Jade shatter and the new hope alit, when the jade bracelet her mother gave her, erupted in the protective power. But it was the wielding of the Qi elemental powers that astonished her the most as she caused the destruction needed to help win the battle.

She was told by the Guardian Panda that previous warriors had exceptional skills, but none came as close to her for wielding the earth Qi elemental power. Clara didn't know what to make of it, she'd never been a warrior, let alone one wielding powers through her Chinese language. All she was joyful for was that it was all over.

A squawk from her crane distracted her from her mind's wanderings as she looked up. Another squawk came from the crane carrying her Guardian Panda. The Guardian Panda pointed downwards, and Clara saw the faint outline of Bamboo City and understood. They were not going to the Portal Circle, and she looked at her fellow warriors who turned to look at her. They all gave a fond wave to her as her crane and the Guardian Panda's crane dove down toward Bamboo City.

The two cranes took the same approach as the massive eagle who had flown her to Bamboo City. Her exhilaration began to build up once more as she leaned into the crane's nape and gripped the harness tighter as the crane aimed for the bamboo hanger opening. With a whoosh, she was through. The crane tilted his wing to slow himself down and came to a three-step standing.

The crane squatted as Clara undid her harness and carefully climbed down. As she landed on her two feet, the crane turned to her with his two beady eyes and nodded slightly, "It has been a pleasure to serve with you, Empress Warrior Wu."

Clara nodded and uttered, "Thank you. Thank you for being so brave."

The crane nodded once more and abruptly looked downward. Clara's eyes followed the crane's gaze and before her was a rather large light brown rabbit, on its haunches staring back up at her.

Clara's heart melted as she immediately reached down and picked up the rabbit into both of her arms and exclaimed, "Oh my god, you are so cute!"

The rabbit suddenly writhed within her grasp until it let out, "Please unhand me!"

Clara's expression went blank as she was not expecting the rabbit to talk back to her as she gently put him back down. But the rabbit looked offended by the hug as it stepped back and mumbled, "How rude." As he patted his fur down, the Guardian Panda came up to them and looked at the rabbit and then at Clara.

"I see you met our top medicinist and herbalist, JuJu," said the Guardian Panda awkwardly.

"Oh my god, I'm so sorry. I didn't mean to pick you up like that…" said Clara as a deep sense of embarrassment rushed up within her.

The rabbit exhaled and thumped his foot a couple of times before looking back up at Clara. "Let's try that again. Empress Warrior Wu, it is an honor to meet you, though I wish it was under different circumstances. I am JuJu, the top medicinist and herbalist assigned to the Panda Kingdom's army. I and my trained staff are here to care for you and any other pandas from the battlefront."

Clara wanting to start over bowed to the rabbit and offered, "Thank you for overlooking my bad manners earlier. It's an honor to meet you as well."

"JuJu, it's good to see you again," said the Guardian Panda.

"I assume we were victorious in the first battle?" inquired JuJu.

"Yes, we were, and Empress Warrior Wu here was instrumental in securing our victory," said the Guardian Panda with pride.

"I did what I had to do," said Clara suddenly as she felt she had to diminish the compliment considering the enormity of it.

"Empress Warrior Wu," interjected JuJu sternly. "Do not decline a compliment especially if your deed was extraordinary. You are the Panda Empress Warrior and it is expected that you would do great things as only you can wield the power of the green jade. Through your acts, the rest of us will draw inspiration and courage. Do you understand?"

Clara was a bit taken by his forceful tone and acknowledged his words with a nod.

"Good," said JuJu as he looked up at the Guardian Panda, "A humble one we have here."

The Guardian Panda nodded as the sound of fluttering wings were heard behind him as additional cranes ferrying pandas landed.

"Very well then, it looks like you have not sustained any injuries, so my team and I will now look after the injured. It looks like the Pandemonium Squad just arrived. Good day," bided the rabbit as he hopped away.

"I'm so embarrassed," said Clara as she looked relived. "And why does he talk like he's British?"

The Guardian Panda looked down quizzically at Clara and asked, "What's a British?"

Clara looked up and simply said, "Never mind," and giggled.

"Guardian Panda, Empress Warrior Wu," asked a panda attendant who appeared and bowed at them.

The Guardian Panda and Clara nodded back at the attendant of the Panderess who requested that they follow her to see the Panderess.

Clara felt disheveled as she checked her battle armor to make sure everything was in place. Then she looked down sadly at the Bow of Destiny and the bereft hollow from where the Bamboo Jade once was. She sighed as her eyes fell onto her green jade bracelet that fit snugly above the rest. She looked at the Guardian Panda who assuaged her by saying, "Don't worry. The Panderess will understand."

Upon arriving at the same room where she had always met the Panderess within Bamboo Tower, the Guardian Panda recapped the battle. Clara could only listen in awe and disbelief as he described her actions in vivid detail. At the end of the summary, the Panderess nodded and looked down at Clara.

"Empress Warrior Wu," she said calmly. "You are to be commended and though you were always the warrior that you knew not but the Portal Book knew you could be, it is always necessary for me to say, on behalf of Panda Kingdom and the other great kingdoms of Azen, thank you for your bravery and courage."

Clara bowed to the Panderess who also nodded back and asked. "The Bow of Destiny, may I see it?"

Clara nodded and unslung the bow from her chest and with both hands, extended it to the Panderess who took it gently with both of her paws.

She looked at the Bow of Destiny itself and saw no apparent damage to the smooth hewn bamboo. She looked at the dark green jade bracelet, turning it over and scanning its entirety with utmost curiosity.

"And you saw a white light spiral and radiate out?" the Panderess asked.

"Yes," said Clara.

The Panderess brought the Bow of Destiny close to her right eye with her left eye closed and peered ever so deeply into the dark green jade. "And where did you get this green jade bracelet?"

Clara uttered, "My mom gave it to me."

The Panderess put down the bow, looked at Clara and then at the Guardian Panda. "This should not be possible. Mystical jades should not exist in her world."

The Guardian Panda shrugged and stated, "It's a mystery to me as well."

"Empress Warrior Wu, may I keep your bracelet for further inspection? Our top Jadeologist would be fascinated by this."

"Of course," said Clara as she suddenly felt bereft of the jade bracelet that she had not taken off since her mother had given it to her.

The Panderess then handed the Bow of Destiny to another attendant, who took it away as Clara's eyes trailed after it.

The Panderess caught Clara's concern and added, "Of course, we will fashion you with a replacement bracelet that will pass off as the jade bracelet that your mother gave to you."

Clara let out a sigh of relief as she said, "Thank you. I wouldn't know what to say to my mom or dad if they asked."

"Very well. Please rest for the remainder of the night as tomorrow, you will be going home," said the Panderess as Clara's eyes lit up.

"Really?" Clara asked excitedly.

"Yes. With our first battle victory secured, your Guardian Panda will now explain the next phase of this Warlock war, as it will be some time before the next lunar eclipse is upon us," the Panderess announced. "Guardian Panda, please show our empress to her quarters. For at least this night, you don't have to be a warrior. Good night."

"Good night, Panderess," responded Clara as she watched her turn and walk away with an air of confidence.

"Shall we go to your room?" asked the Guardian Panda as they started to walk back to the lift.

Clara mumbled a bit as she walked alongside the Guardian Panda.

"Your meal will be plentiful, and I'm sure you want to get out of your battle armor," said the Guardian Panda.

Clara looked down at her gauntlets and felt the snugness of the bodysuit that her battle armor was clinging to.

"Why so gloomy?" asked the Guardian Panda.

Clara looked up and simply said, "I kinda like the battle armor."

The Guardian Panda chuckled, "Always the warrior."

THIRTY - SEVEN

Clara laughed with her fellow warriors, who had become her newfound friends. But their friendship would be a special one, one that would be out of this world.

Sung gingerly picked up another piece of the Korean omelet that was served to them at breakfast that morning along with a bevy of Asian items. Daniel joked that he never enjoyed rice so much in his life, and everyone teased him that rice and being Asian were intertwined.

Daniel looked up and his tone turned more soulful, "You know, before I met you guys, I never knew how much fun it was to be Asian. I've been missing out."

Sung looked at Daniel like how an older brother would and extended a fist. Daniel smiled and eagerly fist bumped him and said, "Fire and…" and as if on cue, Sung finished with, "Ice!" As they let out a laugh.

Clara looked at Yuka smiling and said, "Boys, so silly!"

"I think it's cute," said Yuka as she scooped up the last bit of rice into her mouth.

"Hey Yuka," said Sung as he got her attention.

Yuka looked at him as he held the origami crane in front of him, "I'm going to bring this home with me and learn origami and make you something the next time we see each other."

Yuka clasped her hands in her lap and bowed as she said with a smile, "*Domo arigato.*"

That's when Clara and Daniel brought out their origami cranes and showed it to Yuka with pride as everyone laughed heartily.

"Hey Daniel," said Sung.

"What's up?" he responded.

"How does a buffalo fold origami?" asked Sung slyly.

Daniel thought about it and answered, "I give up, how?"

Sung looked at everyone who was in anticipation of the answer, "Behooves me!"

Everyone groaned, but soon burst into laughter.

"You better not let my Guardian Buffalo hear you say that!" Daniel pointed mockingly at Sung.

"Hey, what's said between the Azen Warriors, stays with the Azen Warriors. Besides, mad respect for your Guardian Buffalo. For all of our guardians."

They all looked at each other and nodded when their moment of silence was broken by another voice.

"Azen Warriors… I like the sound of that. It's shorter than the Warriors of Azen," said the Guardian Panda as he approached the meal table. "Azen Warriors, please finish up your meal, as it's time to go."

The Azen Warriors took their last bite and gulp of tea. They got up from the meal table and followed the Guardian Panda. Clara walked alongside him in silence. More than a week ago, she was aghast at meeting a talking panda and now, she couldn't think of pandas in any other way.

As they approached the Portal Circle, the warriors could see that the other guardian animals were already present, and a sense of sadness fell upon the group. They were asked to take off their shoes. They laughed but soon walked into the Portal Circle. They respectfully greeted each guardian.

The Guardian Crane stepped into the Portal Circle and made eye contact with all the warriors and spoke. "Warriors of Azen…" she stopped when the Guardian Panda coughed and signaled with his hand. The Guardian Crane looked curiously surprised and gestured to the Guardian Panda.

"I don't mean to interrupt, but I was just hearing the warriors calling themselves, 'Azen Warriors.' There's a brevity to it that I like," offered the Guardian Panda.

The Guardian Crane's beady eyes blinked a couple of times and uttered, "Azen Warriors, I'll try that. Azen Warriors, you all fought well yesterday, and you are now battle tested. There are still three Warlock battles to fight, but with each day, you'll get stronger and be even more ready. That we are sure of."

The Guardian Tiger stepped in as the Guardian Crane exited. "It will be some time before the next lunar eclipse, and in the past, we have kept previous warriors for all of that time. However, in our experience, we have found that the extended absences proved problematic. As the Portal Books allow passage between our world and yours, you may go home to your earthly lives. But there is one grave rule that you must abide by."

The pause was wrenching as he prowled on all fours, looking sternly in the eyes of each of the warriors. "You must not try to find each other in your world during this time of battle. For reasons we cannot explain, this is the one rule you cannot break. But what I can tell you is that the collective victories can only be achieved when it is experienced as a collective, on Azen. Is that clear?"

Clara looked about her as everyone else shared the same disappointed look among themselves. But she knew that she was in a realm bound by its own rules and nodded her head, as did everyone else.

"Just trust us on this one rule. Upon your return to Azen, more will be explained," said the Guardian Tiger. "And yes, it was an honor to fight alongside each and every one of you yesterday. You would have made previous warriors proud."

"Hua Mulan," Clara whispered underneath her breath as she grinned.

The Guardian Tiger exited as the Guardian Buffalo entered, with his horns returned to their original state.

"As you leave the realm of Azen," the Guardian Buffalo started. "Continue to manifest your Qi elements. You saw yesterday how a single battle can deplete your arsenal of Qi elements. You can manifest more Qi elements in your own world using your Portal Book."

"Way cool," said Daniel excitedly.

"Your power and your nurturing of it will only come if you embrace your heritage and find the power within. Some of us will have to work twice as hard," said the Guardian Buffalo as he eyed Daniel. He looked down and nodded his head and looked up as he raised his hand.

"Yes, Emperor Warrior Nguyen?" asked the Guardian Buffalo as he turned his massive body toward him.

"I just want to say, that this experience has taught me so much. I had trouble accepting being Vietnamese but now, now I know how valuable it is and how powerful it can be. I will work twice as hard to become the best Vietnamese possible," said Daniel humbly.

The Guardian Buffalo looked at Daniel sternly and said, "Emperor Warrior Nguyen, I am humbled by your work ethic. You will make your Vietnamese mother very proud of you."

The words fell on Daniel heavily as he absorbed them uncomfortably. "No one has ever said that to me," said Daniel as he choked back on those words. He wiped his eye and smiled, "Actually no, that's not true. There's one person who says that. My mother, my *mẹ*."

Clara and Yuka felt tears forming at the corner of their eyes. "Hey, you got us, your Azen Warriors," Sung reminded Daniel with a smile.

Daniel smiled, and a happy thought came to him. "I'm going to give my *mẹ* the biggest hug when I see her! And she's going to think it's all weird!" he exclaimed.

"That turned out to be more emotional than I thought," muttered gruffly the Guardian Buffalo, as he exited the Portal Circle while the Guardian Panda entered.

"Speaking of home, Azen Warriors," began the Guardian Panda. "A reminder that you can manifest the Qi elements with your Portal Book as you've done with your paired Portal Book in the Portal Circle. But you won't be able to invoke any of your powers. However, because your martial arts skills have been physically acquired, you will carry that training back to your world."

Everyone's eyes lit up upon hearing the news. "I will know Kung Fu back home?" Clara blurted out.

"Yes, you always had the opportunity to learn the martial arts of your heritage. Being here on Azen, that training was simply accelerated for you. But we must admonish you, you should take care with your newfound capabilities and not exploit them. Please only use your martial arts skills only for the most just and right causes."

"Very well then," continued the Guardian Panda. "Emperor Warrior Nguyen, you may go first."

Daniel looked at everyone with a grin and looked into the calm red eyes of his Guardian Buffalo. He humbly said *thank you* in Vietnamese, "*Cảm ơn bạn,*" to which the Guardian Buffalo said, "Until your return. *Cảm ơn bạn.*"

To everyone's surprise, Daniel vanished in a bright light after he wrote home in Vietnamese with his horned brush. "Awesome!" Sung exclaimed.

The Guardian Crane looked down at Yuka, whose eyes reflected sadness. "I will miss you," said Yuka, and the Guardian Crane said, "We will fly again soon," which brought a smile to her face. She brushed the Japanese character for home into her Portal Book with her red feather quill brush. The embers swirled out from the black characters and enveloped her in a bright golden light, then she was gone.

As the light subsided, Sung and Clara looked at each other. He smiled at her as the Guardian Tiger told him he was next. Sung looked up at the Guardian Tiger's steely blue eyes and said, "No one would believe me," to which the Guardian Tiger said, "And no one should."

With the Clawdium brush, he brushed out the Korean word for home, and Sung turned to Clara. "Keep up with those Korean dramas," he said.

"Oh, which one do you…" her voice trailed as Sung vanished before her eyes. She exhaled and turned to the Guardian Panda.

"I guess it's my turn," said Clara as she reached for the brush when the Guardian Panda's paw rested gently on top of it.

"Huh?" said Clara as she looked up.

"Not just yet, there's something we have for you," said the Guardian Panda. He handed her a flat box. It was covered in a green fabric and was ornately embroidered with a tiny golden latch at the front.

"For me?" asked Clara as she looked at it.

"Open it," he said.

Clara carefully flipped up the latch as it clicked in place and flipped open the box. Within it was red fabric nestling a green jade bracelet.

"Oh, it's beautiful!" said Clara as she gingerly picked it up. "It's just like the one my mother gave me. She won't be able to tell."

"Well, let's put it on and send you home," said the Guardian Panda as he took away the box.

Clara slid on the jade bracelet and with some might, she was able to pull it over her left thumb as it slid in place around her wrist. She admired it as it glistened in the sunlight before she walked back to the Portal Book.

"Okay, ready to go back home to New York City," said Clara.

"I will see you soon, Empress Warrior Wu," said the Guardian Panda.

"For Azen," said Clara as she beautifully brushed the Chinese character for home and placed the bamboo brush down.

Her eyes were mesmerized by the fiery embers emanating from the characters and as the warm golden light enveloped her, she heard the Guardian Panda say, "For Azen."

She felt like she was floating in a bath of warm light that cocooned her, and soon the light faded away and the scene before her started to come into focus. Moments later, she could feel herself sitting back in her chair. There was a subtle jolt as she felt herself appear in her room, at her desk, as the embers from the black inked character for *home* faded away from her Portal Book.

"Whoa," said Clara as she looked around. She was back in her room indeed.

She looked down and saw that she was all there, along with the clothing she had on when she was taken away. She shot a look to her left. No one was coming through the door, all was silent. She pushed back her chair, rushed to the nightstand by her bed, and picked up her phone. She poked at it to wake it and looked down in astonishment.

The phone's display showed the same day she first left for Azen. Her mouth fell open as she looked up and quickly looked down at the time: 5:35. Only 30 minutes had passed! Her astonishment was all over her face as she turned her head to see her stuffed panda looking up at her.

She put her phone down to pick up Bo Bo and said jovially, "I missed you! And guess what? I met your older brother!"

She held her stuffed panda close and hugged him. Then she looked at the door. Her last conversation with her mother came back into her head, and a sudden sense of shame came over her. After everything she'd just been through on Azen, she realized that telling her mother that she hated being Chinese was so wrong.

She put down her stuffed panda and approached her desk. Just as she was about to pick up the Portal Book, she stopped abruptly. She cautiously reached into her back jean pocket and pulled out the origami crane from Yuka. She brought it to her eyes and smiled. She gently unfurled its wings and balanced it on her desk and admired it. With a nod, she reached into her left jean pocket and pulled out her bamboo ribbon hair accessory, which she placed next to the *origami* crane. Then she collected her Portal Book and went to the door. The doorknob was cool as she paused and thought more about how to apologize to her mother.

A strange thought passed through her mind. *I am the Empress Warrior Wu, and I've just won a battle against thousands of Huo Dou fire demon dogs. And yet, here I am back home, living with my parents.*

The thought of her mother and father made her smile as she pictured their familiar faces. She turned the doorknob and looked out. All was quiet, but the scent of her mother's cooking wafted through the air as she tiptoed down the hallway. She peered from behind the kitchen opening and spied her mother prepping something by the sink. The faucet was on, and Clara gasped softly, flashing back once again to observing her mother at the Origins Pool from the vantage point of the faucet's water. Her mother's left hand reached for the faucet and turned it off.

Clara mustered the warrior's strength and softly strode into the kitchen. If her mother noticed, she didn't let on as she continued to cut up a carrot.

"Mom?" said Clara weakly.

Her mother continued cutting up the carrot and let out, "Yes?"

"Mom, I'm sorry for what I said before. I didn't mean it," said Clara with as much shame as possible.

Her mother stopped cutting and simply looked forward, "Maybe you are right, teaching you both Mandarin and Cantonese is too hard."

"No Mom, I'm wrong," said Clara as she rushed to the kitchen table. She spread out her Portal Book and opened to a blank page that already had a grid on it. "And I really want to learn Chinese, from you."

Her mother turned to her eager daughter and smiled as she put down the cleaver. She walked toward Clara as she untied the back of her apron. Clara smiled and sat down as her mother pulled up a chair next to her.

Her mother's eyes admired the beautiful pages of the Portal Book as she gently glided the fingertips of her left hand over the corner of the page. That's when Clara's eyes fell onto the green jade bracelet on her mother's left wrist, and she coyly looked up at her mother with curious awe. She shook off the thought and spread out the page.

"There's a lot I need you to teach me," said Clara enthusiastically.

"Where did all this energy come from?" asked her mother.

Clara looked up at her mother and admired her brown eyes staring back down at her. "Because mom, I'm proud to be Chinese."

THIRTY - EIGHT

The Guardian Panda stripped off a bamboo leaf and chewed slowly as he sat on a rock outside of the Portal Circle. He stopped chewing as his eyes rolled upward slightly and exclaimed, "I can smell you."

The white and black striped tiger peered over the boulder that he surmounted from behind and saw the white furry top of the panda's head. He muttered, "Old friend."

The Guardian Panda looked up and met the Guardian Tiger's blue eyes as his white and black fur, along with his whiskers, drooped downward. "Old friend indeed," responded the Guardian Panda.

In an instant, the Guardian Tiger leapt off the boulder, gracefully flew through the air and deftly landed a few feet away on all fours. He circled the grass a bit and soon settled onto his stomach and his thick white and black striped tail swayed back and forth.

The Guardian Panda pulled off another bamboo leaf and chewed.

"Impressive warriors this time," said the Guardian Tiger casually.

"They are very impressive," said the Guardian Panda.

The Guardian Tiger then said starkly, "Which one do you think it will be this time?"

A few moments passed before the Guardian Panda uttered, "I don't know."

THANK YOU

If you have come to the end of "Clara Wu and the Portal Book," which is Book One of the Clara Wu Book Series, I hope you enjoyed it and were inspired by Clara Wu, Sung Kim, Yuka Satoh and Daniel Nguyen!

I also hope you enjoyed all the amazing Asian inspired animal kingdoms on Azen along with the amazing Guardian Panda, White Tiger, Red Crown Crane and the Water Buffalo.

My goal is to create authentic Asian American stories with heroes so that Asian American readers can see themselves as the heroes. We've always been, we just need more writers to put them on paper.

Please tell your friends about this book and flip to the section where I give some tips on how to promote this book to better positive Asian Representation!

A big thank you to SantiSann who refreshed the cover art to Book One. Isn't it amazing? Check out SantiSann's work at:

Instagram: @santisann88

Another thank you goes out to Gloria Tsai for voicing the audio teaser for Book One which you may find on YouTube by searching for "Clara Wu." Check out her work at:

http://www.gloriatsai.com/voiceover.html

I also wanted to take a moment to thank my editor, Felicia Lee of Cambridge Editors, who has been my editor since my first book. Check out her profile at:

https://cambridgeeditors.com/editors/

Please check out my Web site at **www.vincentsstories.com** where you can check out my two other books, which are also available on Amazon:

The Purple Heart
The Tamago Stories

There are four more books in this exciting young adult Asian American fantasy series! Flip to the next page to see the title of book two!

BOOK TWO

CLARA WU

AND THE

JADE LABYRINTH

BY VINCENT YEE

AVAILABLE NOW!

ABOUT THE AUTHOR

Vincent Yee was born in Boston, Massachusetts. For most of his career, he has worked for several Fortune 100 companies in various managerial roles. At all other times, he has a vision…

"To write for better Asian Representation."

His first novel, "The Purple Heart," is a story about love and courage set during the Japanese American experience in WWII. His second book is a collection of 8 riveting contemporary Asian American short stories. His third book project, the Clara Wu Books, is an epic young adult Asian American fantasy series consisting of five books that will be all launched within one year. So far "Clara Wu and the Portal Book, Jade Labyrinth and Rescue," have been launched with two more in the series to come. Vincent Yee was a former National President for the National Association of Asian American Professionals (NAAAP). He also co-founded the ERG at his last employer and grew it to be one of the largest ERGs with over 450+ members within a few months. He's also been known to create artistic culinary dishes for friends. When he is not writing, he may be binging a K-Drama on Netflix. He now lives in Cambridge, Massachusetts.

HOW TO SUPPORT

Help spread the word on this young adult Asian American fantasy story:

1) **FACEBOOK**
   Go to facebook.com/clarawubooks and LIKE the page to stay up to date with updates and be invited to online events with other fans.
2) **INSTAGRAM**
   Go to Instagram and like @clarawubooks
3) **SELFIE or PICTURE**
   TAKE a selfie picture or a picture with your child, if you are comfortable with that and without exposing any identifying information, with the book or your e-reader.
   Please tag the Facebook Page clarawubooks and IG @clarawubooks and use the hashtags #clarawu #clarawubooks

   TAKE a staged picture of the book with your favorite mug or other fun item, and post it on your social media page and please tag the Facebook Page clarawubooks and IG @clarawubooks and use the hashtags #clarawu #clarawubooks
4) **WEB**
   Go to www.clarawubooks.com and add your email to the distribution list to find out the fun ways on how to engage with this series. You'll find my contact info here.
5) If your child goes to any Asian cultural school (e.g. Chinese, Korean, Japanese, Vietnamese, etc), please tell the other parents and students.
6) Does your child go to any martial arts school? Consider telling the parents and students at those schools. I will attend any event over Zoom.
7) If you belong to a book club, please consider recommending this book for your next read. I will attend your book club over Zoom.
8) **AMAZON/GOODREADS**
   If you loved this book, please write a review for each book in the Clara Wu Books on Amazon or Goodreads.
9) **EDUCATORS**
   Are you an elementary or high school teacher? This would be great for your students!
10) **LIBRARIES/BOOKSTORES**
    Are you a librarian or a bookstore owner? Please consider getting this book into your library system or store.
11) If you are part of any Asian American community organization, please consider reaching out to me to do a Meet the Author event, in person or over Zoom. Go to www.clarawubooks.com for more info.
12) If you are part of any Asian American corporate ERG /BRG/Affinity group, please consider reaching out to me to do a Meet the Author event, in person or over Zoom. Go to www.clarawubooks.com for more info.
13) If you know of any Asian American Influencers/Podcasters, please consider recommending this book to them.

14) If you would like to host a Meet the Author event over Zoom for your group of friends, your organization or your work AA group, I'll be there!

Let's **PROVE** that there is a market for positive and authentic Asian American stories especially ones that will give the next generation of Asian American readers, heroes that look like them.

DICTIONARY

Word	Language	Meaning
abeoji	Korean	father
Ao Dai	Vietnamese	A traditional Vietnamese dress that is a long gown worn with trousers.
baba	Cantonese – Chinese	Father informal, affectionate
ban chans	Korean	A collection of side dishes like kimchi, radish or cucumber usually served along with meals.
baos	Chinese	A Chinese white bun filled a variety of ingredients.
Bukdaemun	Korean	North Big Gate – One of the eight gates in Korea.
cảm ơn bạn	Vietnamese	thank you
chigae	Korean	Korean stew made from a variety of ingredients.
dahm	Korean	wall
dali	Korean	bridge
đẩy	Vietnamese	thrust
dò-jeh	Cantonese – Chinese	thank you
domo arigato	Japanese	*Thank you very much*
Dongdaemun	Korean	East Big Gate – One of the eight gates in Korea.
fang jian	Mandarin	release
eomma	Korean	Mother informal, affectionate
Galbi	Korean	grilled ribs (aka kalbi)
gam-sa-ham-ni-da	Korean	thank you
gong gyuck	Korean	attack
Hạ Long Bay	Vietnamese	Famous beautiful bay in Vietnam that is also a UNESCO World Heritage Site
Hangul	Korean	Writing system of the Korean language.
Huo Dou	Chinese	A large black dog that can emit flames from its mouth.
jinju	Korean	pearl
jo sun	Cantonese – Chinese	Good morning in Cantonese
joh-eun achim	Korean	*Good morning with beautiful sun*
jōshō suru	Japanese	ascend
kabe	Japanese	wall

Karate	Japanese	A Japanese martial art that means *empty hand.*
kata	Japanese	In Karate, a set pattern of movements that is practiced as part of training.
katana	Japanese	Usually refers to a long single edged sword usually used by the Samurai.
kimchi	Korean	A spicy fermented cabbage that is a delicacy in Korea.
kimono	Japanese	A beautiful and traditionally wrapped garment for Japanese women that may come in a variety of colors and patterns.
Kting voar	Vietnamese	Mystical horned creature that existed in Vietnam and Cambodia. Its true origin has never been determined though its unusual horns have left researchers puzzled about the creature.
Kung Fu	Chinese	A Chinese martial art with many styles.
makimono	Japanese	A Japanese roll of seaweed and sushi rice that may contain vegetables, fish or both.
mẹ	Vietnamese	mother
moushi wake arimasen deshita	Japanese	*No excuses can justify my actions and I apologize*
Namdaemun	Korean	South Big Gate – One of the eight gates in Korea.
ngọc trai	Vietnamese	pearl
nigiri	Japanese	Usually, a ball of sushi rice that is topped off with raw fish or other seafood.
ohayo gozaimasu	Japanese	good morning
origami	Japanese	The art of folding paper.
otosan	Japanese	father formal
pãru	Japanese	pearl
pho	Vietnamese	A Vietnamese soup noodle dish usually made from a slow cooked beef bone broth, with rice noodles and beef slices or brisket.
Seodaemun	Korean	West Big Gate – One of the eight gates in Korea.
seoping	Korean	surf
Seosomun	Korean	West Small Gate - – One of the eight gates in Korea.

shuriken	Japanese	Throwing star made popular in the era of Ninjas.
Soohorang	Korean	Tiger of Protection – *Soohoo* means protection and *rang* comes from Ho-rang-i for tiger. Known to be a sacred guardian animal in Korea.
Sungeuni mangeukhaeumnida	Korean	*Your grace is immeasurable*
Tae Kwan Do	Korean	A Korean martial art that is known for its powerful and dynamic kicks.
taegeuk	Korean	In Tae Kwan Do, a set pattern of movements that is practiced as part of training.
tatami	Japanese	A type of traditional Japanese flooring.
tei hum	Cantonese – Chinese	sinkhole
teng-bing	Cantonese – Chinese	wall
the-oung	Vietnamese	wall
thit bo voi bo	Vietnamese	well known beef dish
tō	Japanese	Japanese pagoda like tower structure.
tobu	Japanese	fly
Vovinam	Vietnamese	A Vietnamese martial art
yakitori	Japanese	skewered grilled meat
Yonggirang	Korean	Tiger of Courage – *Yong-gi* for courage and *rang* comes from Ho-rang-i for tiger. The Guardian Animal from the White Tiger Kingdom.
zao shang hao	Mandarin – Chinese	good morning in Mandarin
zhēnzhū	Mandarin – Chinese	pearl